The Boson's Chair

To Janet.
A short piece of history including East London!
Very best wishes.
Colin.
14.03.2018

Ladders In The Sky

Edited and Typeset by Colin Walker
Cover by Valerie Walker of Dennington
Photography by Camera Talks, London.
Drawings from the Admiralty Manual of Seamanship and
Ansell Jones (Specialists in Lifting and Marine Equipment)
Walsall, England.

Published and printed by:
The Leiston Press,
Unit 1, Master Lord Industrial Estate,
Leiston,
Suffolk, England.
IP16 4XS

Copyright: © Colin Walker 2001

All rights reserved. No part of this publication may be reproduced, stored in a retrieval system, or transmitted, in any form or by any means, without the prior consent of Colin Walker.

ISBN:0-9538308-2-9

Foreword

This novel is dedicated to my mother and my father and also to my brother who, like others and myself lived in the time just after the Second World War, before so many consumer 'essentials' became so readily available to the man and woman in the street. The Clean Air Act (1956), the Factories Act (1960), the Health and Safety at Work Act (1974) and other legislation affecting working place practices had not been enacted and working men and women did whatever they thought was realistic and appropriate under the circumstances. Times have changed since then and we have become a nation controlled by legislation, particularly at the work place. Much of this legislation has improved working conditions and the environment beyond all expectations. For example the Clean Air Act has prohibited certain emissions, including black smoke, from industrial and other chimneys and, within the last six years has compelled local authorities in the United Kingdom to spend on average over £500,000 at each crematorium to reduce emissions to meet the requirements of the Act.

The story that is about to unfold is a snapshot of how working class families lived, how some of their menfolk died, and when decisions on safe working practices were left more to the individual's understanding of 'safe' rather than to regulation by Acts of Parliament.

The character Joe Walkinshaw, one of the main characters in this book, is based on my father. I feel sure he would not have objected. Roger Bruce, under whose name this book is written, was my brother who tragically died from pneumonia at the age of two years and six months, just before penicillin became available through the National Health Service. His name lives on as author of this novel.

The real names of places and people who may have been associated with some of the events referred to in this book have not always been used because to have done so could cause embarrassment to those still living and, possibly to the families of those who have since died.

I hope you enjoy reading this story that relates to the grit, grime and, on many occasions, the fun and camaraderie associated with steeplejacking as it was almost half a century ago.

CONTENTS

		Page
1.	A Small Beginning	2
2.	Joe's Unexpected Baptism	11
3.	North by Northwest	22
4.	Company Capers	51
5.	Rose of Rockingham	58
6.	Chimneys	67
7.	Bobbyboy	93
8.	Bill Bennett	103
9.	The Fall Guy	110
10.	Snakes and Ladders	117
11.	A Burning Sensation	126
12.	The Convention	134
13.	A Not So Early Retirement	143
14.	When The Cat's Away	156
15.	The Gasworks	164
16.	Maid In Shenstone	171

CHAPTER 1

A SMALL BEGINNING

Figure of Eight Knot

Dennis Walkinshaw was eleven years of age when he climbed his first church spire. Dennis had been pressing his father, Joe, over many months for permission to go to work with him so that he could gain first hand experience of some of the things he had heard about from his father and other steeplejacks when they visited the family home in Barking. Joe had learned the many skills of a steeplejack from his own father and, over a number of years, had become one of the most knowledgeable and respected steeplejacks in the country.

Dennis' introduction to steeplejacking at such a tender age could be thought of as strange, possibly foolhardy, but he was a natural climber. Even at the age of eight he had regularly climbed out of his first floor bedroom window at the front of the house in Woodbridge Road, reached across to his parent's bedroom window using the sills as footholds, and climbed in through the fanlight. Neighbours regularly reported Dennis to his parents, so much so that he had had to change his habits. He climbed out of the bathroom window, stepped across from one windowsill to another and in through the fanlight of the adjacent toilet window at the back of the house.

This forced change to his climbing habits opened up a new route from the bathroom to Dennis' bedroom, for it was far too boring to walk along the corridor. He found that with a little ingenuity it was possible to stand on the tiled windowsill, reach round the open bathroom window and, holding fast to the frame, thrust his right leg out to find the flat roof of the garage with the toe of his shoe. Rocking his body to-and-frow, he could then launch himself across the gap to satisfy the challenge of getting onto the roof of the garage and to set up the first stage of a new route to his bedroom window.

From the garden, Dennis' sister Pamela witnessed the fourth of a row of successful launches across to the garage roof. A neighbour also saw Dennis climbing in through his bedroom window a short time afterwards and both reported these matters to Dennis' mother in next to no time at all. Dennis' bed was moved downstairs into the sitting room and he was not allowed to go upstairs without someone accompanying him.

Dennis felt very sore about being kept from his favourite past-time and was determined to get even with Pam and his other two sisters, Josie and Barbara, after they had received firm instructions from their mother to keep an eye on him and to let her know if he attempted to climb anywhere at all.

It was after listening to "The Man in Black" narrated by Valentine Dial on the radio one evening that Dennis hatched a plan to scare the living daylights out of his sisters. Knowing all three of them had changed into their night clothing and were preparing for bed on the landing at the top of the stairs, Dennis turned off the stairway light from the downstairs hallway and, with a torch in his hand, stole up the staircase in the darkness. He let out a ghostly moan as he reached the top of the stairs, then shone the torch from beneath his chin onto his face revealing an attempt at pulling his face into a grotesque mask.

The girls screamed as one. So much so that their mother, fearing the worst, ran from the kitchen to find out what had happened. The hall and stairway was in darkness, except for a small light seen coming from the top of the stairs. She quickly switched on the lights to reveal Dennis crouched on the stairs holding the torch. All three girls and their mother shouted and pointed towards Dennis. He began to have serious second thoughts about his own safety as he had also been listening to "The Man in Black" and his thoughts and fears overcame his boyish bravado. There must be bogeymen in front and behind him. After all the girls were pointing in one direction and his mother in another. Dennis joined in the screaming until he realised he was the only one remaining terrified and was the subject of hysterical laughter coming from his mother and sisters.

Joe, who had been working away for two weeks in the north of England, got to hear of his son's escapades on returning home.

"Beatrice, we shall have to do something with Dennis before he becomes a major problem," decided Joe who was looking for support from his wife. "The lad needs a challenge and he's not getting it here at Woodbridge Road during the weekends and school holidays. One of his latest escapades of falling off Michael Hagan's motorcycle that's kept in the garage after starting it and not being able to stop it is a good example of his boredom. If you agree I'll arrange to take him to work with me next Saturday when I start another job on a small church spire in Essex. Pulling on ropes and fetching and carrying will tire him out. He won't have the energy to even climb the stairs when he gets home and certainly not enough energy to upset the girls or climb out of the windows".

And so with his mother's agreement, Dennis had been granted his most sought after wish. That Saturday morning in late summer 1949, Dennis' mother arose early and prepared two sandwich packs instead of the usual one before she anxiously saw her husband and son off to work from the front door of the house. Joe would buy Dennis his first workman's railway ticket at Ilford Station.

The early morning air felt fresh and damp as they walked together matching strides with canvas haversacks, containing tools, sandwiches and flasks of tea, slung over their shoulders.

It was a short walk from the bus stop at Barking Broadway to Fanshaw Avenue where the trolley buses ran to Ilford. It seemed to Dennis that the whole population of Barking was hurrying to get to work, even at this time of the day, when Dennis thought most of them would still be in bed.

The trolley buses ran quite frequently, unless one of the trailing arms on top of a bus became detached from the electric power wires that hung from posts at the side of the road. Dennis had seen such an event on an earlier occasion when the trolley bus conductor had had to withdraw a long pole from under the bus and reach up with it to replace the trailing arm on the overhead wire. Today there was no such hold-up and they hadn't long to wait before a 'trolley' came along heading in the right direction. The rearward-facing seat at the very front of the lower deck was a novelty to a boy who had become accustomed to travelling by conventional bus. He decided that this would be where they would sit.

The electric motor clicked into life drawing its power from the overhead power lines as the trolley bus made its way quietly towards Ilford. Each time the driver increased speed or started after a stop the electric motor clicked its approval. Dennis noticed the driver had a small window open at hip level to his right hand side. As the trolley bus drew away from a bus stop the driver's right hand and part of his arm with a white band sewn onto its sleeve would appear outside the cab indicating to traffic following behind of his intention to move out into the centre if the roadway.

"Tickets please," called the conductor as he moved along the gangway and behind a standing passenger who was about to pull the cord to signal he wanted to get off at the next stop.

"You're up early young man. Going to work with your dad?"

"Yes, we're steeplejacks," replied Dennis to the embarrassment of his father and to the nodding approval of the conductor.

Through gaps between buildings, created by Hitler's bombs in the Second World War, Dennis could see the rays of the sun appearing over the eastern horizon. The short trolley bus journey was soon over and at Ilford two steam trains waited at their respective platforms below the railway station's ticket office. White steam hissed quietly from their boilers and floated lazily upwards into the morning air. The smell of coal smoke was everywhere as Joe and Dennis crossed the wooden boards outside the ticket office and went down the steps that led to one of the platforms where a train was waiting. Dennis felt a sense of urgency. It was as if they had to catch this train, because there may not be another. After all, he was going to work for the first time.

The door slammed shut behind them after they got into the carriage immediately behind the locomotive. Dennis could hear the thump of other carriage doors closing along the length of the train as Joe and he sought seats by the window so that they could look out to see where they were going. Joe pulled on the leather strap to close the window in the door to keep the steam and smoke from the locomotive out of the carriage, as a shrill whistle from the guard on the platform gave the engine driver his cue to urge the train forward. They were on their way.

Passengers, who had not found a seat, held onto the luggage racks above their heads in front of Dennis as the engine laboured and gathered speed. When the train stopped at stations some of the passengers got off and others got on, pushing by their fellow travellers in the process. It was all very new to

Dennis.

The train journey ended at Chelmsford where, Joe told Dennis, they were to get onto a bus at the local bus station. Dennis had been used to seeing and travelling on tall, red, double-decked, London Transport buses in the east end and it was a surprise to him to see the much lower, green double-decked Eastern National buses arriving and leaving the bus station.

Ken Missen, an experienced steeplejack's mate who regularly worked with Joe, was standing under a canopy outside the bus station with his bag of tools at his side when they arrived. Ken was a short, wiry man with mouse coloured curly hair cut short in the no nonsense fashion of the day. He was dressed in a yellowing green two-piece work suit. A grubby ex–army small pack slung over Ken's shoulders contained his vitals for the day. It was apparent when he smiled that his nicotine-stained teeth were in dire need of attention. A fact he tried to hide with a hand when he observed Dennis looking attentively at him.

A small black dog wandered along the footpath sniffing at the corner of the door to the waiting room behind where Ken was standing. The dog found little interest in the scent left behind by some other animal and moved across to Ken's bag of tools, cocked its leg over it and peed. Ken felt something unusual was happening when his foot became warm and wet and looked down in time to see the dog finishing its natural activity for this time of the morning.

"Good dog. Good little dog," called Ken after the mongrel now making its way from the bus station along Duke Street. "Come to Kenny. I'll strangle you, if I can catch you."

The dog wasn't to be caught. It increased its pace from a wander to a trot as it looked over its shoulder at Ken as he ran after it.

"That bloody dog pissed on my bag and in my shoe," snarled Ken. "I'll stink for the rest of the day."

"Come on Ken," called Joe as he chuckled and gestured towards the waiting bus. "Leave the dog alone or we'll miss the bus. You can catch the dog tomorrow morning. The bus won't wait."

The bus conductor was standing by the stairs when they got on the bus. Dennis dodged past him and up the stairs to the top deck, noting that the man was not wearing a uniform as he would have expected. The London Transport drivers and conductors did, so why not these men?

He spotted a vacant seat near to the very front of the bus that would give him a good view of the road ahead. To get to his preferred seat by the window nearest the kerb meant walking along a low gangway on the right hand side of the bus and, after almost bending double to avoid hitting his head on the roof, stepping up onto a platform on which the seat was bolted. He shuffled sideways towards the side window, holding onto the back of the seat in front of him to keep his balance before sitting down. Joe and Ken followed in crumpled postures and placed their haversacks on the floor, lodging them safely between their feet.

"Fag?" invited Joe to Ken as he reached into his jacket pocket and then undid a slim packet of five Woodbine cigarettes.

As Joe took two cigarettes from the packet of Woodbines, Dennis noted how Joe's thumbs were flexibly jointed where they joined his hands. He looked down at his own hands to see whether he had inherited the same unusual features as those of his father, but he had not.

"Yes, I'll join you with a woody Woodbine", replied Ken. "Haven't had a smoke since half past six this morning. I need a fag to steady my nerves after what that dog did to my bag at the bus station."

Both men placed a cigarette between their lips. Ken rummaged through his trousers' pockets to find a box of Swan Vestas matches. He reached over to light Joe's cigarette from a red tipped match that had just spat into life after being struck on the edge of its box.

Dennis inhaled the acrid smoke from the match. He liked to do this whenever he had the opportunity. He never knew why! He watched as the tips of the cigarettes glowed when both men drew in the smoke and, after a short pause during which time traces of smoke secretly crept from out of their nostrils, exhaled smoke through pursed lips. Dennis was fascinated to see how the blue cigarette smoke spiralled into the air and dispersed throughout the top deck of the bus. It seemed almost everyone seated there received the benefit, or otherwise, from the smoke of the woody Woodbines.

As the bus made its way along the road towards Braintree,

Dennis could see the old houses and buildings in the villages and hamlets untouched by the events of the preceding war years. Some houses seemed so close to the side of the road that he could easily have touched them if the windows of the bus had been open.

From the bottom of the stairway the bus conductor called out that they were approaching Great Saling. It was time for them to collect their haversacks, stub out their fags under foot and make their way down the stairs to get off.

"Thanks mate," Joe called out to the conductor whom he had met on previous journeys to Bredfield church. "We'll no doubt see you on the return journey this evening."

The bus conductor raised one arm in farewell to them from the platform of the bus, his aluminium ticket dispenser hanging in front of him gleaming in the morning sunlight as the bus pulled away from the bus stop.

"Probably. I'm on this run for the rest of the day. Don't forget to call into the Queen's Head for lunch. The landlord's my brother-in-law. He does a good steak and kidney pie. You tell him I told you so."

Joe, Ken and Dennis walked one behind the other along the main road until they reached a country lane leading off to the village of Bredfield. Ken, without any warning, broke into a short trot and then leapt over a ditch to disappear behind a hedgerow. Dennis wondered where Ken had gone, but soon realised there was good reason for his disappearance.

Within a moment or two the sound of long grass rubbing against the spokes of bicycle wheels was heard and Ken reappeared between a gap in the hedge with two ex-army bicycles. This was to be the means by which they were to complete the final part of their journey to Bredfield church.

Because there were only two bikes, Dennis had to sit on the crossbar of Joe's bicycle for the three miles journey to the village. The pain caused by the crossbar on that journey and the return bicycle ride later that evening would be imprinted in his memory for many years to come!

On arrival at Bredfield church, Dennis noticed it had a square, flint faced tower topped by a parapet wall. A small oak shingled spire, with a gilded cockerel weathervane, rose from behind the wall pointing into the sky. The steeplejacks were to erect a wooden pole scaffold around the spire so that Joe and Ken could repair the weathervane and renew the timbers of the spire that had been damaged by death-watch beetle and dry rot. Even in 1949 it was no longer usual to use wooden poles for scaffolding as steel and aluminium tubes were stronger and easier to put up. But, it was not for Dennis to wonder why. He would learn how to 'square tie' fourteen-foot poles at ninety-degree angles to one another and to 'splice' other poles, end to end, to extend them in either vertical or horizontal directions.

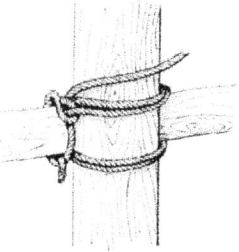

Wooden Scaffold Pole With 'Square Tie'

The peace and quietness of a rural churchyard in the morning is something to be enjoyed. Dennis found it to be so different from the urban life he knew. In the years ahead he would look forward to arriving at new work locations to start another job. New situations meant new challenges and he would do his best to master them, where he could.

Dennis' role, as a boy, was to pull on the hauling lines when equipment was needed to be raised aloft and to fetch and carry the small things that others had forgotten or needed at short notice. From time to time he would be given the opportunity to climb ladders and scaffolding, but only when Joe approved and was present during the climb. It was on one of those occasions at Bredfield that the heavens opened and the rain came down like stair rods.

Thunderclouds rolled around the sky and from the scaffolding at the top of the spire flashes of lightning could be seen. The lightning flashed across the sky from one cloud to another or forked directly to earth in a magnificent display of power. In either instance the crashing or rumbling of thunder followed the display in the sky. Dennis became very concerned that the spire would be struck. This concern was probably due to him being shown his father's burned and buckled cigarette case on another occasion after it had been struck by lightning whilst in his breast pocket when working on another steeple.

The work was hard and by the end of the day Dennis was pleased when Joe decided to call a halt to their labours. After all they still had the joy of the bicycle ride to the main road to contend with and Dennis' backside was still sore from that morning's journey when he had had to sit on the bicycle's crossbar! But when he got home what stories he would have to tell his mother. Particularly how Ken had been so rudely treated by the dog at the bus station that morning.

Dennis would spend more time with his father during school holidays and at weekends working on church spires, brick and steel chimneys and even a wooden electricity pylon in the middle of a field. He learned how to tie a variety of knots, splice ropes and wire cables, whip the ends of ropes and lashings and safely tie a boson's chair to a riding line. As importantly, he would learn to become self-reliant under difficult circumstances and to have trust in his mates, and they in him. The lifestyle of a steeplejack was to suit Dennis for a number of years, but then he knew little about other occupations and nothing about the professions.

Having grown up with steeplejacks, Dennis had got to know a number of them very well. He had a glass of ginger beer with them when they called into country pubs on those occasions he 'worked' with them and already imagining himself to be a full member of the steeplejack fraternity.

Dennis' chance to become a full-time steeplejack's mate would occur in 1954, after he left school at fifteen years of age. The events that follow in this novel are based on true-life experiences before legislation and modifications to social behaviour changed the way steeplejacks travelled the country and carried out their work.

CHAPTER 2

JOE'S UNEXPECTED BAPTISM

Double Sheeved Rope Block

Dennis had left grammar school a rangy six footer, earlier than recommended by his headmaster, to embark on a career as a steeplejack. School and cushy numbers in offices were not for him, he wanted to work with his hands and travel the country just like his father did. He had been accepted as a learner steeplejack with the Firm and it was agreed he should receive two shillings and four pence an hour over a forty-four hour week.

His first week's take-home pay looked like a king's ransom when it arrived by registered post at his home one Saturday morning. The large white registered letter in which Joe's and Dennis' wage envelopes were sealed had a thin blue band around it and was made of a woven material. Dennis' mother had had to sign for the letter when the postman called to make the delivery and it lay on the mantleshelf unopened until Joe and Dennis returned from work later that day.

Dennis thumbed the short ends of the pound notes that revealed themselves through a cut-off corner of the brown envelope in which they were sealed and counted them and the coins that could be seen through the round perforations in the envelope's side. It would be difficult to spend all of the money on himself, particularly as he would probably receive similar sums each week now he was in regular employment.

But the realities of life had to be faced.

"Now that you're working Dennis you will have to pay for your keep," explained his mother.

"And also buy some tools and kit yourself out with some decent clothes," said his father.

Little by little the sum of the weekly wage eroded before his eyes. There would not be much left after deductions for domestic purposes by all accounts.

One cold February morning, Dennis and Ken arrived at St. Margaret's Church at Five Ashes in Essex to start work on the wooden church spire. Dennis' father, Joe, planned to join them later on in the day after a meeting with the board of directors of Steeplejacks International, the company they were employed by. "The Firm", as the company was referred to whenever it was spoken of, was in the process of reorganisation after a difficult year's trading and the recruitment of an additional director who had injected more money into the business. But Dennis and Ken had little interest in the financial side of business and cared even less about meetings of boards of directors or even the directors themselves.

"Where do flies go in the winter?" Ken asked Dennis as they prepared to strip the curled oak shingles from the spire.

"Haven't got a clue." Dennis replied.

"Well, you'll soon find out my lad. Remember to keep your mouth closed when we start stripping the shingles off!"

Ken's advice was to be worth remembering.

British Road Services, the nationalised road transport organisation, had delivered their ladders, ropes and other equipment to the church earlier in the week. It hadn't taken the steeplejacks long the previous day to erect the ladders up the side of the tower and to the top of the spire. Their boson's chairs and riding lines hung from a steel hawser tied around the top of the spire ready for them to start the day's work.

"We'll crack on and surprise Joe when he comes back this afternoon. We might be able to get most of the shingles off the lower part of the spire by then if all goes well," said Ken.

The moss covered oak shingles had been on the spire for the past sixty years. Some of them had been blown off by the wind and others had curled up like dry sandwiches during the years they had been nailed there.

"I'll be surprised if the wooden boarding is as sound as the vicar hopes it'll be. But then we'll find out for sure once the shingles are off," suggested Ken as they made their way into the

Flying Scaffold St. Gile's Church, Camberwell, London

bell ringers' chamber to change into their blue boilersuits.

Having changed, they were walking to the back of the tower in readiness to climb the ladders when they heard a vehicle coming along the road towards the church. It was rare to hear the sound of an engine and at this early hour as Five Ashes was normally a quiet, sleepy place with only occasional through traffic. A battered grey Land Rover squealed to a stop by the church gates. Ken, being inquisitive, walked back towards the bell ringers' chamber and rounded the corner of the tower to see who might be calling.

While he was gone Dennis continued with the usual early morning routine and removed a scaffold board from the bottom ladder he had placed there the previous evening, a precaution that was always taken to stop local children from climbing the ladders when the steeplejacks were not around. He untied the boson's chairs and riding lines from the sides of the ladders and placed the scaffold board on the ground. Ken had not returned by this time and Dennis became curious to find out why.

Rounding the corner of the tower, Dennis saw a portly man in his late forties, wearing a cloth cap and Wellington boots, get out of the Land Rover and begin to walk along the gravel path leading to the church. The man met Ken about half way along the path where they shook hands. Dennis couldn't hear what was being said, but he noticed the man take off his cap and gesture with it towards the spire and then to a gravestone in the cemetery before returning to the Land Rover and driving away. Ken, having seen to the departure of their visitor, turned and walked towards Dennis, both hands in the air, thumbs up.

"He's a local farmer," Ken explained. "He wants to climb to the top of the spire to see if there's an oak shingle nailed there with his father's signature on the back of it. It seems that when the spire was last repaired local people paid a shilling to sign the back of a shingle before it was fixed to the spire and the money collected was put towards the cost of repairs. If we can find his father's signature on the back of one of them, it should be somewhere among the last of the courses at the top of the spire, he'll give us a fiver. I've told him to come back in half an hour or so when we'll be ready for him. I've also told him he'll have to change out of his wellies before climbing our ladders."

Within the half an hour the Land Rover returned and soon the portly man was at the bottom of the ladders calling up to Ken who had been busy tightening the rope lashings holding the ladders to the spire.

"We don't want him getting the jitters because the ladders are loose," Ken decided. "We could lose the five quid."

Another man, who later introduced himself as the portly man's son, joined his father and stood back from the ladders with a camera, ready to record the climb to the top of the steeple.

Ken climbed down to meet them.

From the boson's chair hanging half way down the spire Dennis had a good view of what was happening on the ground. He could see and hear the portly man draw a deep breath before placing his foot on the first rung of the ladders. Showing obvious signs of determination, the novice climber grasped hold of the sides the first ladder with both hands and began to climb up. Ken followed close behind.

As the leading climber reached the top of the tower Dennis could hear him breathing heavily. Ken was also aware of this and called a temporary halt by suggesting a break as 'there was no hurry'.

After a short pause both men began climbing again. The higher the portly man climbed, the more short of breath he became and the closer his belly got to the rungs of the ladders until the front of his jacket was rubbing against them. He was no longer climbing the ladders in a natural way, but was stepping stiffly up one rung at a time, placing both feet on a rung, pausing, then stepping up again. As the portly climber drew nearer to where Dennis waited in his chair, his hands and arms shook noticeably as he reached up to clench the sides of the ladders. Dennis decided to slide down the riding line to come alongside the inexperienced climber to give him as much encouragement as he could. Each time a step up the ladder was taken, Dennis pulled himself up to be beside the shaking man who, during pauses for breath, introduced himself as Charles.

The light-hearted conversation between all three men during the climb up the spire tried to disguise the difficulties Charles was having. But he was determined to reach the top, although by his own admittance, the experience was far more difficult than he first thought it would be. Ken and Dennis were also determined to make sure he climbed safely to the top of the spire and down again. After all, there was a fiver at stake!

Charles had climbed almost to the top before he realised the outline of the spire in front of him had changed to become pencil thin. There was hardly anything of substance to be seen immediately ahead of the ladder and nothing to either side or behind him. Distant fields and trees had replaced the apparent safety of the oak shingles he had seen framed by the rungs of the ladder as he had inched upwards.

"Whoa!" bellowed Charles in a way that indicated either triumph or plain basic fear. He realised he was not as fit as he had hoped; his knees and feet were trembling after the effort of climbing and were demanding a rest and, even more hopefully, an end to their torment. Dennis looped a rope lashing round Charles' waist and tied him to the ladder he was desperately clinging to. Ken pulled the second boson's chair towards Charles and persuaded him to step through its ropes and sit down.

Charles snorted mists of expired breath into the cold atmosphere whilst grimly holding onto the rungs of the ladder as he followed the instructions given him. It seemed to take an eternity but he managed to lower himself into the chair, thrusting his legs out like oars towards the ladder and holding firmly onto the riding line in front of him. He became aware that his fingers were numb with cold, his arms ached and the sweat on his forehead was forming into icy globules, but he dare not let go of the riding line he was hugging onto for fear of falling backwards out of the chair.

Charles began feeling more relaxed once he became more used to his new position in the world below the weather vane and looked beyond the spire and over the countryside to identify some of the landmarks he knew so well.

An anxious call came from the ground enquired, "Are you alright Dad?"

"Of course I'm bloody alright," was Charles' shouted reply. "Just like climbing up a bloody haystack. I can see for bloody miles up here." He turned to Ken and in a low voice complained, "That boy never understands when I'm enjoying myself."

"Now, you sit there guv and enjoy the view," said Ken. "Dennis will take off the last three courses of old shingles and we'll see whether your old man's signature is on the back of one of them."

Dennis, now hanging in his boson's chair on the opposite side of the spire from where Charles was seated, carefully stripped away the top courses of shingles with a wrecking bar and examined the backs of all of them. But no signatures were to be found. The rain and damp weather must have erased the signatures over the years, as the undersides of the shingles were very wet and twisted.

Rather than put Charles through the trauma of climbing down the ladders after his rigorous climb and disappointment at not finding his father's signature, Ken persuaded him to remain in the boson's chair whilst they lowered him to the ground.

"You should enjoy this," Ken said convincingly. "Keep seated, hold onto the rope in front of you and walk your legs down the rungs of the ladders. We'll do the rest."

Ken climbed swiftly down the ladders, swaying from side to side as he went. Once on the ground he took hold of the free end of Charles' riding line and pulled it taught. This was Dennis' cue to slacken off the rope lashing holding Charles to the ladder and to repeat the instructions to "keep hold of the rope and don't let go." Dennis gripped the up and down ropes of Charles' riding line together with one hand as he undid the boson's chair stop-knot before Ken began lowering Charles to the ground.

"What's he doing now?" enquired the son who had come up close to where Ken was standing and showing signs of concern for his father's safety. "He's always up to some mischief. He's as eccentric as his ancestors have been for centuries."

"His family roots go back some time then," suggested Ken.

"Oh yes. He's the Earl of Five Ashes when he's not at home."

"I didn't know that. We'd better lower his Lordship down gently then. We mustn't allow him to graze his noble knees," replied Ken with a wicked grin on his face.

Ken twisted the riding line round his leg and stood on the free end where it lay on the ground. He signalled to Dennis that he, Ken, and he alone was in control of the Earl's future in this world.

Charles came down as gracefully as an earl should. He got his **feet stuck** between the rungs of the ladders on a couple of **occasions** but was able to free them and arrived safely beside Ken in a very excited state.

"Did you see me come down in the bloody boson's chair?" he shouted to his relieved son who was standing back taking photographs. "Bloody exhilarating. I haven't had so much excitement for years. Not since I was button boy at Shotley as a lad in the Royal Navy."

"Here my man!" he called to Ken as he disentangled himself from the ropes and freed himself from the chair. " Take this ten quid. I know we didn't find my father's signature but I've enjoyed myself so much it's been worth every penny."

"Thank you, my Lord," said a relieved Ken. "The next time we're in the Bricklayer's Arms, we'll drink to your health."

Both father and son turned and walked back along the gravel path laughing and talking about the earl's experiences that morning. Dennis saw them from his seat in the sky get into the Land Rover and drive off to return to their farm and everyday duties.

Almost half the morning had been taken up by the visit and Ken knew they must get on with stripping the shingles off the spire. A small wrecking bar did the job very well. Between the shingles and the boards lay thousands of mummified bodies of dead flies that had crawled under the twisted oak shingles to take shelter from the weather. Among the husks, a few live flies crept hopelessly away to find safety. As the wind blew, the husks wafted in all directions, including into any open mouth or up a nostril.

"I told you that stripping shingles off a spire is a filthy job," said Ken as he sat in his chair ready to start work. "Watch out for these hand made iron nails as well. They break off just above the boards and they'll scrape or jab into you given half a chance. Don't forget to wear your gloves for a cut hand will almost certainly become infected."

Joe arrived earlier than expected that afternoon. Half the spire was bare to the boards now that the oak shingles had been removed. By the end of the day the three of them would have completed the job.

The exposed boarding and timbers of the spire could now receive a coat of wood preservative and treatment for woodworm infestation. A job they would tackle the next day.

But before then, during the afternoon's tea break, Joe went through some of the events of his meeting with the directors. It was clear that the meeting had been a very difficult one.

"We have to make the business more profitable," he said. "And included in this is the suspension of our bonus scheme until things pick up. Dennis, your hourly rate has been reduced to one and eight pence an hour as the senior director cannot believe you have to climb with us to do your job. He expects you to be given ground duties until you're older!"

This revelation was a blow to Dennis' morale. He withdrew into a dark cloud of disbelief. He had given up his schooling for the chance of adventure and was now grounded without any say in the matter.

The following day Dennis travelled with Joe to Five Ashes in Joe's hand-painted blue Ford twelve-hundredweight van. Ken was already on site when they arrived and had the tea brewing in a large metal teapot in the bell ringers' chamber. A small amount of snow had fallen overnight and the ladders, ropes and boson's chairs were coated with a thin layer of ice. When untied the ropes felt cold, hard and stiff to the touch. According to the weather forecast a thaw should set in later that morning and they looked forward to this, even though it would result in icy water running under their sleeves and up their arms as they pulled on the hauling and riding lines. Within an hour or two their fingers would be numb from the cold and the toughest of hands would be sore from handling the wet hemp ropes. A return to the bell ringers' chamber for a break and a hot cup of tea at that time would be very welcome.

The rector arrived at the church mid-way through the morning to enquire how they were getting on. Seeing that the old shingles had been removed and the boarding on the spire was exposed he was prompted to tell Joe that a number of metal drums of wood preservative had been found at a second church in his parish. If suitable, he proposed, the preservative could be collected and used on the Five Ashes church spire as it would save the expense of buying new supplies.

Joe agreed and it was not long before Dennis and he got into the Ford van to follow the rector in his Morris 8 to St. Edmund's church at Brandish, some three miles away. While they were collecting the drums Ken was left to carry the new bundles of cedar shingles from their storage area by the front gate of the church to the back of the tower.

On arrival at St. Edmund's church, the rector took Joe and Dennis inside to show them where the drums were. He lifted one end of a long length of red carpet that ran along the centre isle covering a metal floor grating and pointed down to where the drums lay.

"I hope you will find the contents of the drums suitable," he said. "They've been there for some time, in fact since we had the builders in here to repair death-watch beetle damage about six years ago."

Joe eased three of the floor gratings out of their frames and lifted them to one side. Two feet below, in a floor well, he could see four five-gallon drums lying on their sides. In the poor light it was not possible to read the lettering stamped on them and Joe kneeled down to get a better view. He still couldn't read what was printed in their sides and, with one hand on the floor, vaulted the short distance into the floor well to get closer.

The empty church echoed to a sharp crack as Joe's feet went through an inch of ice floating on top of very cold water. Except for the slopping of water on the walls of the floor well and the rubbing of broken ice on the sides of the drums a pensive silence ensued. Dennis, unable to contain his composure, wept with laughter at the sight of Joe kneeling motionless in the freezing water, soaked up to his waist.

The rector, standing in the aisle and now a genuine disbeliever, also stood very still. He was unable to utter a word for some time and this was very prudent under the circumstances.

"You bleeding well knew there was frozen water in here. Didn't you?" cursed the shivering Joe to a rector who was looking down at him through fixed eyes.

The rector muttered something that could not be heard, cleared his throat; then seized on an apology.

"I'm terribly sorry Joe," he said. "I honestly didn't know there was water in there. You must be dreadfully wet and cold. Why not come along to the rectory to dry and warm yourself. My wife will sort you out a change of clothing."

"Well now that I'm bloody well down here I may as well get these sodding drums out," said Joe, now standing in ice and water up to the top of his legs. "Thanks for the offer rector, but I'll need more than a change of clothing after this."

Joe grasped the half-empty drums and heaved them in a

determined fashion, upwards, in Dennis' direction.

"You can stop laughing Dennis and get these into the van," he said in an authoritatively parental voice.

Dennis took the first of the wet drums from him, rolled it out of the church and rumbled it along the gravel path to the van still choking with laughter. He thought it best not to return too quickly. At least, not until he had regained control of himself.

Joe was not a happy man when he climbed out of the pit and stood dripping in the aisle after his unexpected baptism. By the time Dennis had the floor grills back in place and the carpet down Joe's overalls were stiffening as the water froze in them.

The rector stood on one foot and then the other before apologising once more to Joe. Dennis rolled the last of the drums out of the church and realising the fragility of the situation, looked up as he passed by the rector.

"It's one of those things that happens," he said. "Dad's soaking was not your fault. It could have happened to anyone, anywhere."

Dennis realised immediately he had not helped the situation at all. He had to try even harder from thereon to keep Joe from making any unnecessarily loud comments.

"Not your fault at all old boy," said Joe in a restrained but pointed way as they made their way towards the van. Joe was never one to be in a hurry. On this occasion, in an attempt to keep his wet clothes from his nether parts, he 'waddled' like a cowboy on the way to a rodeo.

"Let's get home before I bleeding well freeze to death!" he said.

As Joe started the van's engine Dennis received instructions to, "get the blow lamp going in the back and warm this bloody place up." They needed warmth inside the van and, as the van had no heater, the only way this could be provided was from a blow lamp kept in the back specially for the purpose. This day would also be one of those few occasions when Joe intentionally swore in Dennis' presence! Like the rector, Dennis felt silence was the best option for the time being.

They drove from Brandish to Five Ashes to let Ken know there had been a change of plan for the day. Besides, the weather was so bad it would be better if work was abandoned for reasons of safety. All three would take the remainder of the day off and hope for better weather conditions the next day.

The heat from the blow lamp helped to bring the temperature up a degree or two, but did little to stop Joe's trouser legs from freezing as a cold draught blew unhindered through the floor of the van by the foot pedals. By the time Joe and Dennis arrived home, Joe was complaining that 'he couldn't feel his bleeding legs.' He was however, and to his credit, beginning to see the funny side of things once again. Dennis felt he could laugh aloud once more as he explained Joe's predicament to his mother.

Once in front of a warm coal fire and in fresh clothes, Joe was almost back to his old self once again.

The rector must have been a very busy man for he didn't visit St. Margaret's church for a day or two after Joe's baptism. When he did pay a visit Dennis was still grounded and he noticed the rector had a half-smile on his face that he had not seen there before. However, the rector was a man of the cloth who had no need to mention certain events of the past. Not on that occasion anyway.

CHAPTER 3

NORTH BY NORTHWEST

Thimble For Eye of Wire Rope

The weather in the north west of England is renowned for its unpredictability and, of course, bad weather has an adverse affect on the work of steeplejacks who are likely to bear the full force of nature when working on tall structures.

Dennis' strength of character and physical fitness were tested to the full after the completion of the Five Ashes job when he and Joe were despatched to a remote village close to the Lake District to repair another shingled church spire. Being a young man of sixteen years everything was an adventure. Dennis had no responsibilities or worries and he was earning reasonable wages. Working away from home would also attract expenses for lodgings and travel and the icing on the cake was that his confinement to working on the ground had been withdrawn when the impracticability of the directive became obvious as steeplejacks normally worked in teams of two or three.

Dennis and Joe travelled from Essex to Cartmel in Lancashire in the Ford van. Dennis had not travelled so far north before and was looking forward to seeing where the permafrost began. He began keeping records of the journey and in his log recorded that the journey took two days to complete at an average on the road speed of 28 miles per hour. The weather was foul. On his Ever Ready portable radio the BBC's Home Service reported heavy mist and fog and icy road conditions on the A6 Trunk Road, particularly through Matlock in Derbyshire. This journey was bound to be different from any other Dennis had experienced before.

Since buying the van, Joe had made noticeable improvements to the interior comforts for the passengers. Originally Ford had only provided the driver with a seat. With approval from Beatrice an armchair from the sitting room had been placed in the back of the van to give Dennis more comfortable travelling conditions. He had used the armchair for a couple of months and was pleased with it, although it tended to slide about or even tip over when the van went over a bumpy road or took a sharp corner too quickly.

Joe must have had a special affinity for chairs in the back of vans, for four years later, when he and Beatrice went on a camping holiday with the rest of the family near to Tenby, he took his armchair with him in his new Ford van. The armchair was placed in the tent at night to make room for him and Beatrice to sleep in the van, for she didn't like the idea of lying on the grass. This arrangement was fine until, one night, a courting couple attempted a "knee trembler" using the side of the van for a prop! During breakfast the next morning Beatrice explained how she thumped loudly on the inside of the van to dampen their ardour.

For the long journey north Joe had installed even more luxurious seating for Dennis. He now had a genuine Ford passenger seat bolted to the floor beside the driver. This had been bought from a scrap yard in east London for a fair price. There were few other passenger comforts. It was unheard of to have a 'wish list' that included an internal heater. They would have to make do with the paraffin blow lamp to keep them warm during the journey. The blow lamp was to be placed in the middle of a coil of rope in the back of the van where Dennis could keep an eye on it to make sure that it didn't fall over. He was to listen for any hissing noise that would indicate pressure was running low and the paraffin needed to be topped up.

As importantly, after each refill, the blow lamp's prickers had to be used to clear the jet to ensure that the lamp did not become a flame-thrower after it was lit. If they should come across very cold weather, a paraffin fuelled Primus stove was held in reserve.

Dennis and Joe stayed overnight just north of Matlock on the A6 trunk road at a roadside café that also did bed and breakfast. The sleeping quarters, located above the café and overlooking the lorry park, were very basic. An unheated communal bedroom, its floor covered by brown linoleum, slept eight men. Each lumpy bed separated from the next by a grubby yellow curtain hung from a rail suspended from the ceiling. There was no other furniture or even a mat in the room, only beds with their pitiful bedclothes and one pillow per bed.

Dennis found it was possible to see out through the frost covered windows if he took the trouble to huff on the windowpane for a few minutes and then rub the pane with his hand. There wasn't much to see and he decided to leave the primitive surroundings of the bedroom to find the dining room.

After a large dinner of piping hot roast beef and Yorkshire pudding followed by apple pie and custard, Joe and Dennis took a walk through the shadows of the icy, puddle strewn lorry park and along the unlit road to stretch their legs. The lorry park was full of unattended lorries, most of them in the livery of 'BRS', their drivers either being in the café reading a newspaper, listening to music on the jukebox or asleep on their beds. When they returned to their dormitory to 'turn in' Dennis didn't change into pyjamas. The only place to hang his outer clothes in the damp room lit only by the floodlights from the lorry park was from the curtain rail.

He decided to sleep with all of his outdoor clothes on, having listened to the tales told to him by seasoned travellers of wallets being stolen whilst their owners slept; or even worse!

As a light sleeper, Dennis was pleased to get up the next morning. Throughout the night he had heard men coughing, talking loudly and tripping over an oddment of things on the floor as they came in and out of the dormitory. The flushing of the toilet on so many occasions had almost driven Dennis to exasperation. He thought Joe and he would be making an early start if they arose at six thirty, but his sleep was disturbed much earlier than this by café staff rousing sleeping drivers from four o'clock in the morning. After the third disturbance waking a driver Dennis checked his watch to find it was five thirty.

Having dozed off again, Dennis was awakened by the smell and sound of bacon sizzling in the kitchen downstairs. He found the awakening of his senses more inviting than the hard, lumpy bed he was lying in. He got up, moved the curtain around his bed to one side and; found himself in an empty room. All the drivers had left their beds and were either on the road or in the café having breakfast.

Dennis found Joe seated at a table in the dining room smoking a rolled cigarette and drinking tea.

"I wondered how much longer you would stay in bed," he said. "I was pleased to get up as the bed was so cold and hard. I've told the proprietor how cold I found the bed, just as of a dead man had lain in it for a couple of days. He told me how strange that was because a driver had died in my bed only last week."

The hairs on Dennis' neck stood up and a cold shiver went down his back.

"Anyway, now you're here we can order breakfast," suggested Joe.

The trucker's breakfast was as huge as it was wholesome. With bellies full they went out into the lorry park to find the van covered by half an inch of snow. After clearing the windscreen and starting the unwilling engine with the starting handle they set off again, northwards, the blow lamp roaring furiously in the back to get the 'bleeding place warmed up'.

The van's engine had built up to normal working temperature and was sounding much healthier when Dennis recalled sitting in the dining room of the café the previous evening. A young lady, he believed her to be the daughter of the owner, had come into the room to get some crockery out of the dresser. He had discretely watched her, like any true-blooded 16 year-old male would, as she crouched down, her shapely bottom contouring her jeans in an impressive way, to find the things she wanted from the dresser. His interest had been sharpened when he noticed she was wearing a long hunting knife in a scabbard attached to a belt around her waist. There had been a clear warning not to tamper with the goods if ever he had seen one.

The weather became milder as the van approached the west coast of Lancashire and to the north of Manchester although the skies never cleared of rain clouds. They drove through a couple of heavy downpours when the van's vacuum driven windscreen wipers had great difficulty keeping up with the torrent of water. Even though the vacuum cylinders hissed in defiance it was an uneven match for them and from time to time they gave up the ghost and stopped, particularly when the van's engine laboured heavily going uphill nearing the Lake District.

Joe and Dennis arrived at Cartmel in mid-afternoon to look for the local builder who should have arranged accommodation for them. They found Sam in his joinery workshop close by, pencil behind one ear, cloth cap at a jaunty angle and carpenter's apron about his middle. All was in hand, for the landlord of the Royal Eagle Public House in the centre of the village had agreed to put them up.

"You'll find the accommodation at the pub to your liking no doubt," suggested the builder. "Don't take too much notice of what the landlord's wife has to say. She doesn't mean any harm. She just likes to wear the trousers in that establishment and she doesn't have much competition from her husband."

"Fore-warned is fore-armed," acknowledged Joe with a knowing nod in Sam's direction.

The Royal Eagle.
Dick, the landlord of the Royal Eagle, was busy off-loading barrels of beer from a brewer's dray when Joe and Dennis pulled up outside the pub. He looked, and was, a hen-pecked, balding man in his fifties. He left the driver to finish lowering the barrels into the beer cellar in front of the pub once he recognised he had customers who had come to stay. He went behind the bar to rummage among some papers lying close to the telephone.

"You must be Mr. Walkinshaw and this must be your son," he mused. "Welcome to The Royal Eagle. We're quiet at this time of the year so you shouldn't be disturbed at night. There's no racing on at the racecourse."

The Royal Eagle was a small pub with one bar room leading off the main doorway from the square. At the end nearest to the bar was a glowing coal fire. It all looked very bright and attractive with quartered, highly polished copper-hooped beer barrels forming the front of the bar standing out as an unusual feature. Lists of fixtures for dart matches hung on the bar room wall together with old pencilled sketches of the pub going back almost to the dark ages. Cribbage seemed also to be one of the main past-times for visitors to the pub and sets of dominoes lay on tables in shadowy corners ready for use.

The landlord's wife, Madge, must have been fitted with radar for she was soon beside the new residents as they stood in front of the bar with their suitcases. She was a bespectacled, big busted, blond haired woman in her mid-forties. Although she was beginning to put on more weight than she might have liked, Madge still retained most of the attributes of a younger woman.

It was obvious she wanted to impress members of the opposite sex and had no difficulty in introducing herself. She suggested to Joe that Dennis might like to view the rooms she had prepared, they were up a narrow stairway leading off the bar room. Bustling from room to room with Joe and Dennis in tow she was, as Sam had warned, a very dominant and self-opinionated woman. There was no doubt she had an eye for Joe, although he probably wasn't aware of it at the time.

Dennis wrestled Madge's attention away from Joe and spoke about the roads being very icy on the way up from Essex. This had been the case until they reached Manchester where the temperature had changed for the better and they had had to drive through heavy rain.

Madge seized the right to be the centre of conversation again. "We Lancashire girls have a saying. Manchester rain wets your knickers. I can vouch for it as I've been out in the rain in Manchester when it's rained so hard that it bounced off the pavement and up under my skirt. High enough to wet my pants."

Dennis wondered how Scotsmen might have got on in similar circumstances.

The single bed and a small wardrobe in Dennis' bedroom were adequate for him and his belongings. They stood on polished oak floorboards that sloped gently towards the window at the front of the pub. But strangely, he found later when he opened the latch to the bedroom door, it always swung fully open towards the window and an uncanny force took over and drew him towards the window that was always open at knee height. He thought it would be so very easy to fall out of the window onto the pavement below and he had better keep his wits about him.

In the latter part of their first day at Cartmel, Joe and Dennis took advantage of a lull in the bad weather to drive out to the job at Great Baylham church. Its stone tower with an oak shingled spire perched on top behind its parapet wall stood on a hill overlooking a valley and was totally isolated from the village. As they approached a great, swooping mass of black jackdaws circled the spire, the product of their calling to one another making a tremendous noise. Dennis, looking through his binoculars, could see the birds' point of interest some way up the spire. A jackdaw was trapped some forty feet above the tower with one of its legs wedged between two wooden boards that had been exposed after shingles had been blown off by the wind.

Dennis handed the binoculars to Joe for him to pass an opinion.

"Looks as though we've come at the right time," sighed Joe. "International Bird Rescue is our second name. We'd better get busy straight away."

What appeared to be a fairly simple task when viewed through binoculars from the ground, proved not to be the case in practice.

It was fortunate that the climbing gear had been delivered to the church before they arrived. Sam, the local builder had been present when the ropes and ladders had been dropped off by a British Railways lorry a week or so before their arrival and everything was stacked tidily against the wall of the tower and covered by a tarpaulin.

Joe found the large, rusted key to the door of the spiral staircase in the porch of the church and after opening the heavy oak door began making his way up the stairway with a long length of rope, long enough to haul the ladders to the top of the tower, over his shoulders. He didn't get very far because the stairway was blocked about twenty feet up by a barrier of straw, bracken and bird lime brought in over the years by jackdaws. Before anyone could pass, it would be necessary to clear the stairway of the filthy mess.

The only way to deal with the problem was to force a way through the gigantic birds' nest and kick the tangle down the stairway. Dennis could hear Joe's oaths echoing out from the doorway at the bottom of the stairs as he kicked and trod the tangled mass downwards. It was Dennis' job to clear the bracken away after Joe trod it down by pulling the material away from the tower as it appeared, snapping and cracking, from above the doorway.

From the commentary he was giving, Joe appeared to be making good progress when, mid way up the staircase, he shouted, "No wonder the bells have been silent for years. The jackdaws have also taken over the bell chamber."

A mattress of jackdaw bedding material, and their droppings, stood over four feet high against the wooden bell frames. Clearing up this mess would have to wait for another day as they had more urgent work to do on the spire above.

Joe was relieved when he finally cleared a pathway up the staircase and he could get out of the doorway leading to the bottom of the spire and the parapet wall at the top of the tower. He threw the end of the rope over the wall and it went singing down to where Dennis was standing on the ground.

"Send up three fifteen feet ladders," Joe shouted. "Three long wire hawsers and a few rope lashings. That's all we'll need."

Dennis tied each ladder and the wire hawsers to the rope in turn and watched them ratchet upwards, swaying from side to side, as Joe pulled them up by hand.

"Come up and join me," shouted Joe to Dennis as he pulled the last of the ladders over the parapet wall. "You may as well do the laddering from here."

Dennis hadn't expected to be given such an opportunity for some time and was soon rattling up the spiral staircase with the rope lashings in one hand like a hind being chased by a pack of wolves. Three ladders, he rehearsed, were all that was needed to reach the stricken bird from the top of the tower and each ladder had to be lifted by hand and placed in sockets at the top of the lower one, then tied to a wire hawser placed around the spire.

His first laddering job partially completed Dennis was able to reach out to the trapped jackdaw from the top of the third ladder, but he was concerned it would take fright and break its leg. From his perch on the last rung of the top ladder, Dennis looked across to the bird that cowed back and stared at him through sharp, beady eyes. Although not happy at being where it was, it looked well fed and must have received food from other jackdaws during the time it had been trapped.

Dennis began to cut through the boarding with his pocket knife to allow the jackdaw to pull its leg free. The jackdaw knew before Dennis had an inkling of his own when the moment had come to fly free, for with a flutter of wings and a scramble of skinny legs it took to the air, headed away and swooped towards a group of trees on the horizon. The freed jackdaw was soon lost among others in the flock that rose squawking, almost as one, from the branches of trees after watching events from a safe distance.

Joe and Dennis heard later from villagers that the jackdaws had been wheeling noisily around the spire for some days before their arrival. The birds had no doubt learned a lesson or two, for during the time work was in progress on the spire they never returned to the churchyard.

During one of the many nights Dennis lay awake in his bedroom at the Royal Eagle listening to the howl of the wind outside, he heard the latch to his bedroom door open and the sound of bare feet padding about his darkened room. After some thought and hope he was wrong in his assessment of the situation, he leapt out of his bed and switched on the light. But, although the door had swung open, no one was there.

He sat on his bed wondering what the noise might have been. He looked around the room and after a while thought he could see the oak floorboards moving very slightly up and down. He came to the conclusion that the floorboards had dried out over the years and the iron nails used to fix them to the joists no longer held them firmly in place.

"Elementary my dear Walkinshaw," Dennis mused to himself. "The wind blowing under the joists is making the boards move up and down and it sounds like someone is walking around in bare feet. Believe that if you will. The door couldn't have been closed properly before I got into bed and the wind must have opened it."

Having convinced himself all was well, Dennis returned to his bed but his night's sleep would be interrupted again within the hour. A tremendous crash on the roof above him and the sound of masonry rolling down the slate roof suggested that the chimney pots had blown down. The suddenness of the noise startled him from his bed once more.

Dennis moved quickly across to the window and looked out into the village square to see where the rubble had landed as the Ford van was parked close by. Voices coming from below indicated others were already surveying the damage and, "as long as no water came into his room through the ceiling, he should not concern himself." With this assurance, Dennis went back to bed again.

The next morning, at breakfast, everyone was black-eyed through loss of sleep. Joe looked nervous as he received his plate of eggs, bacon and black pudding from Madge. Dennis thought this very strange and made a mental note to ask Joe later on if he was feeling ill.

After breakfast Joe and Dennis gathered their working clothes from the cupboard next to the kitchen range, where they had been drying, and prepared to make their way to Great Baylham to begin the day's work. Their preparations were interrupted when Dennis heard Joe being called into the kitchen by Madge.

"Seeing that you are such a tall man Joe, could you reach up and get me those pans from the top shelf?"

As Joe reached up, Madge moved closer to him, holding out her arms as if to hug him, but restrained herself at the last moment. She took the pans as they were handed to her, giggled girlishly and turned away when she saw Dennis looking on.

Dennis felt it best if he went about his own business and made his way out into the square to start the van's engine with the starting handle and clear the ice off the windscreen. Within a short while Joe joined him and, grim faced, got into the driver's seat.

Regularly, at around seven forty-five each morning, a Ribble Valley coach came into the village square as part of its regular run to and from Grange Over Sands. The driver courteously cut the engine to avoid making too much noise so early in the morning and coasted the last thirty yards before stopping outside the Royal Eagle. Unfortunately on this morning, neither Joe nor Dennis were at their best. Dennis had not cleared the van's rear windows and Joe, without second thoughts, reversed the van into the side of the coach that had quietly parked behind it.

The jolt as the van came to a halt brought them to their senses.

Joe, looking from the driver's now open door swore. "Where the bleeding hell did that come from? I'm bloody sure it wasn't there when I got into the driver's seat. Didn't you see it Dennis?"

They got out to inspect the damage expecting to find the back of the van and the side of the bus dented at least. But by luck, the van had hit the coach's rear wheel and there was hardly any damage to be seen.

"I get a feeling it's going to be one of those mornings," grumbled Joe as he moved the van forward and then reversed around the coach. "Better get away from here before any more bleeding damage is done."

"Aren't you feeling very well today?" Dennis asked him. "You seemed a bit strained at the breakfast table."

"I don't feel one hundred percent," replied Joe grudgingly. "But then neither would you if you had had the same experience as I did in the middle of the night."

"I heard the chimney pot fall down," remarked Dennis.

"I don't mean that," interrupted Joe. "There's more to it. I haven't told you much about the way men and women behave towards each other, but Madge, clothed only in a short night-dress, paid me a visit in the early hours. She wanted to know whether I had everything I needed for the night. It was only the chimney pot hitting the roof that saved me from a fate far worse than death."

Dennis began to wonder whether the opening of his door and the sound of bare feet in his bedroom could now be put down to the floorboards moving in the wind. Madge might have mistaken his room for Joe's. The more he thought about what could have been, the more his imagination ran wild!

"We'd better start looking for other digs," decided Joe after a moment or two. "There must be bed and breakfast accommodation around here where we can get a good night's undisturbed sleep."

Due to the extremely poor weather and to Dennis' relative inexperience, Joe thought it best to call for additional assistance in the form of another steeplejack from London. Once the shingles had been stripped from the spire the rain got through the boarding and there was the possibility that internal damage could be caused. They had tied tarpaulin sheets over the stripped areas of the spire, but they were soon torn away and into shreds by the high winds.

The Third Man.

Joe collected David Morton from Grange Over Sands Railway Station a week or so after the start of work at Great Baylham. A Scotsman of stocky stature with a ginger beard, David was his own man. He enjoyed his beer and liked gambling. His charm with the ladies was legendary.

Dennis had met David some months before at Lee in south London before being grounded by the Firm when he had helped with the lifting of new stonework up to the scaffolding around the church spire. David had demonstrated his strength and complete lack of fear on that occasion when he flew himself like a flag from a scaffold pole above the streets of London. Legs and arms apart in the configuration of the Scottish flag, his hands gripping tightly onto an upright scaffold pole at the very top of the spire.

Not content with this, when it was time for tea, David was first down to the mess hut to put the kettle on, one hundred and sixty feet below, having slid down the hauling line attached to the flying scaffold like a monkey down a vine from a tall tree.

David could sleep anywhere, and was known to have done so – particularly in GPO telephone boxes. If he found a box to be dirty, he would telephone the exchange the next morning to tell them about it and ask for a reduction for his night's accommodation. But generally he was not fussy and was prepared to put up with almost anything, providing it was cheap or, better still, free.

Following a recommendation from Sam, the builder, David found lodgings with a married couple just outside Cartmel. Each morning Joe and Dennis collected him from his digs and, after finishing work for the day, dropped him off there in the evening. These arrangements suited David extremely well because he could spend his free time as it suited him, for his interests were limited to drinking in the local pubs in Cartmel and Grange and chatting up the local talent.

Very quickly he became friendly with a local girl he met in the Royal Eagle after paying a call on Joe and Dennis one evening. Shortly afterwards he changed digs.

Unknown to the couple he was staying with, David invited his new lady friend to spend time with him at his lodgings and had taken her to his room.

As he later explained to Joe, "Och, it was oonly ter be an evening of musical entertainment listening to Jimmy Shand's band. But my landlord had keen ears and was naturally suspicious when he heard unusual noises coming from my room above the kitchen. It was not long before he was knocking on my door to accuse me of having someone in there!"

He continued after winking in Dennis' direction. "Not me sir," I replied in my broadest Scots accent, as it sometimes frightens folk when I take this line and they tend to leave me in peace. I've been listening to Jimmy Shand and his band and prancing to his music. I invited him to come in and look for himself."

David's offer had been taken up, but the landlord was not able to find anyone else in the room.

"I must admit I was nervous when he hesitated before leaving, for I could see his eyes taking in everything in my room. But he settled for a fixed stare at the floor. Before he left, and after apologising to me for being so suspicious, he told me he had been through a similar experience last summer when there had been a non-paying guest in the room and he had asked her to leave straight away with her partner."

Known only to David, the latest non-paying guest was hiding behind two pairs of his overalls in the bedroom wardrobe.

Having seen off the suspicious man, David unlocked the wardrobe to free his lady friend from her hiding place. It was then that he saw a pair of ladies high-heeled shoes lying on the floor by his bed.

The unexpected caller had done nothing to enhance the idea of a romantic evening the two had planned. The young lady was insistent on leaving without further ado, for to be found there would be disastrous. The village gossips would have a field day.

"I turned up the volume on the radio," David continued. "Opened the bedroom door and went down the stairs to the kitchen to apologise for the noise I had made. It was part of a plan to divert the attention of my landlord and his wife with some tall story while my friend made her escape through the front door."

David was convinced his plan had worked, for both the landlord and his wife appeared to accept his version of events without any doubts for he shared the remainder of the evening with them. The story he told them about repairing his sister's shoes in his spare time seemed to go down well and his willingness to mend the wife's shoes was gratefully accepted.

The next morning, however, just after breakfast, David was requested to find alternative accommodation and to settle his account forthwith. Overnight, other factors had overturned the attempted deceit. Including a telephone call from a neighbour who thought she had seen her grand daughter leaving the house the previous evening.

The weather remained atrocious for the full six weeks of the work on Great Baylham church. Cold, penetrating, incessant rain and high winds made the work extremely arduous. For the first two weeks the men were never dry and always cold. Most of the work was done from boson's chairs attached to the top of the spire and, on occasions, the winds were so strong that the men were blown away from the spire like rags on the end of a cord. It became necessary to tie their chairs to a steel hawser placed around the spire to keep them in positions from where they could work.

On those occasions when the weather was too bad for even the most hardy to work on the spire, they took shelter at the top of the spiral staircase. Sitting on the stone steps huddled around a Primus stove they made tea and shared the packed lunches prepared by the landlord of the Royal Eagle.

Dennis was having difficulty getting his shoes on each morning as the chilblains on his feet were red and sore and not getting any better. He felt that the cold stone floors, the lack of warmth and the poor drying facilities for their clothes made the problem worse. As Joe had suggested, when the opportunity came along to move into better digs, they should seize upon it without delay.

Baylham House.

The rector heard that the facilities at the Royal Eagle were not to the liking of 'his men' and made enquiries to see whether any of the local people in Great Baylham could put them up. Joe and Dennis were pleased when the rector met them in the churchyard one morning to let them know bed and breakfast might be available at Baylham House, just a short distance from the church. They decided to check this out straight away.

An elderly lady and her middle-aged daughter lived in the large manor house that had been owned by their family for many years. A son of the older of the two women ran his tailoring business from there and had his cutting room in the basement. He was a solitary man who was seldom to be seen, choosing to spend his time elsewhere.

The two ladies were pleased to see the men when they arrived at their door and invited them in. After half an hour, during which time Joe and Dennis had tea with them in the sitting room and talked about themselves, it was agreed that they could stay at Baylham House as paying guests. Nora, the daughter, showed them to a first floor bedroom that Joe and Dennis would share.

It was a large room with a tall ceiling. From the sash windows overlooking the front garden, it was possible to see the entrance gates and the sweeping gravel driveway that forked to the left and behind the house and to the right to the front door of the house. Dennis felt that this was surely the way lords, gentlemen and ladies of the manor lived. He felt he could get used to living here. The ladies must have been expecting them to stay for the room was spotless and fully prepared for two men. Home comforts included hot water bottles in knitted covers hanging from the bottom rail of a mahogany bed and flannelette sheets covering a thick, feather mattress. Standing against the wall, reaching almost to the ceiling, were two large mahogany wardrobes with brass handles and a mirror, both ready to receive their clothes.

More than satisfied, Joe and Dennis returned to the sitting room with its inviting fire to confirm they were pleased with the arrangements. Mrs. Preston, Nora's mother, was delighted they had accepted for she felt the house was much too large for just her daughter and herself. It would be nice to have company once again. As they left to return to the church, Nora told them they could also use the sitting room in the evening, as if they were at home in Essex.

That evening Joe made their best excuses to Dick, the landlord of the Royal Eagle, before they packed their cases ready to move out the following morning. Madge was most upset when she heard of their decision to leave. She couldn't understand why they had decided to go. After all, as she said to Joe at the time "I could give you everything you need while you are away from home."

Dennis could only imagine how it would feel to be warm and dry again. He knew his chilblains would soon get better.

Alex, the tailor, had a young daughter, Debbie, a tall brunette who was a year younger than Dennis. She was in the fifth form of her high school at Ulverston. Debbie had a great interest in the piano, probably because she had been encouraged and tutored by her Aunt Nora from the time she was a young child. Alex and Debbie lived in a bungalow within the grounds of Baylham House with Debbie's mother, Iris. Debbie's mother, like her husband, was rarely to be seen for she worked away from home in the Lake District as an hotel receptionist.

Debbie and Dennis became friends and met from time to time at Baylham House when Debbie attended for her music lessons. With prior approval from Nora, Dennis took Debbie to the cinema at Ulverston on a couple of occasions on the Ribble Valley bus. However, it was made clear to him that he would never be permitted to call on Debbie at the bungalow when her parents were not there. And that meant never in the eyes of Nora, albeit that such words did not have the same meaning for the two young people concerned.

Dennis had never suffered from constipation before taking up lodgings with Nora and her mother. His problem was mainly due to the bathroom being located at the end of a long corridor and his cowardice.

When the electricity supply was installed at Baylham House, the electricians fixed only one light in the middle of the long, dark corridor that led to the bathroom on the first floor. A switch at each end of the corridor could turn the light on or off. Four doors led off the corridor to one side and on the other, about a third of the way along, a window positioned at head height, overlooked the courtyard at the back of the house. Dennis wondered where the doors led to and who (or what) was in those rooms. To an impressionable young man there were a number of horrors that could take place in the short time it took to sprint along the corridor to and from the bathroom.

The corridor was so dimly lit even in daylight hours that the light needed to be switched on to see the way. Dennis was scared that someone would switch off the light whilst he was between light switches. Just as worrying was the possibility that someone might open one of the doors as he went by and hoick him into a room. He was just a lad. He might be over six feet tall, but the possibilities were scary. He found it even more scary when he was alone in the bathroom and remained there for the absolute minimum of time, especially when his trousers were unbelted and hanging about his ankles. He developed the signs and symptoms of a man with Parkinson's disease, trembling uncontrollably on those occasions he was unable to avoid a visit to the bathroom.

There must have been psychic reasons for feeling the way he did, and it was not long before he witnessed something very strange indeed.

Late one evening, whilst he was in his bedroom at Baylham House, he heard the sound of horses' hooves and that of a carriage travelling along the gravel driveway from the road. He looked out of one of the window overlooking the front garden but couldn't see anything in the winter's darkness. He could, however, follow the sounds of the hooves and wheels making their way round to the courtyard at the back of the house.

He was curious to know who was arriving, as the ladies had not told him they were expecting visitors. On such occasions Joe and Dennis had been asked to be discreet and remain in their room until the visitors had gone. The ladies didn't want the whole village to know they had taken in boarders.

Mastering his dubious courage, Dennis knew he could see over the courtyard from the window in the corridor. From there, he would be able to see who was arriving in such grand style.

He sprinted on his toes, surprisingly not concerned with switching on the light, along the unlit corridor to look out of the window into the night. He could just see the figure of an elderly woman in a long black dress getting out of the coach aided by a coachman. She stood by the door of the coach in the glimmer of its oil lamps for a minute or two brushing the creases from her dress with her white-gloved hands. She moved serenely towards the house raising her skirts just sufficiently to stop them touching the ground. Her movements were so very refined Dennis couldn't see any movement of her legs or feet. It was as though she was floating over the ground.

He was startled when the lights in the corridor came on. Nora stood there looking in his direction, surprised to see him by the window.

"I thought you would be greeting your guests in the courtyard," Dennis blurted out. "I heard the sound of horses and a carriage coming in. They've stopped in the courtyard. Didn't you hear them?"

Dennis beckoned to Nora to join him and look through the

window to confirm what he had seen. But when they both looked down into the courtyard it was in complete darkness without anything to be seen.

Nora smiled. "And did you see anyone get out of the carriage?" she enquired.

"I thought I saw a lady dressed in a long black dress" said Dennis in a doubting voice. "She walked towards the house, but I lost her in the darkness."

"Did she seem to glide over the ground as if she was on casters?"

"Well, to come to think of it," Dennis replied more hopefully. "Yes, that's just how it seemed."

"Why don't you come down to the sitting room, Dennis," suggested Nora. "I'd like you to speak with my mother."

Dennis took up Nora's offer and went downstairs with her. He noticed on the way that there were two red carpeted staircases. Each staircase led to a different part of the house, although a gallery connected them on the first floor. Nora saw him looking towards the second staircase as they came down the wider of the two into the hall. She overcame Dennis' curiosity by telling him that many years before they bought the house a previous owner had ridden a white horse up one staircase and down the other for a bet.

"We haven't done that yet," she reassured him.

But where was the elderly lady in the long black dress? Dennis hadn't heard her enter the house or the coach leave the courtyard. He was very confused.

Nora took him into the sitting room. Her mother was sitting by the fireside in a comfortable, off-white, armchair working on a floral tapestry. Dennis was invited to sit down on a chair beside her, still wondering where their guest was.

"Mother, Dennis has something to tell you. He's just seen Aunt Ethel."

"Oh, she's not come back again," replied Nora's mother in amazement. "She's been away for such a long time. I thought we had lost her for good. Where was she young Dennis?"

Dennis repeated what he had seen and wondered where Aunt Ethel might be now. He began to realise that the lady he had seen looked very much like Nora's mother. He was even more puzzled.

Nora's mother pondered a while. "Well dear, she's probably in one of the bedrooms upstairs. Ethel was my mother's sister. She's been dead for a number of years of course, but she returns from time to time to visit us in her coach. I keep her rooms as they were when she was alive. I never know when she plans to come here until she does." Reassuringly she went on. "I'll go to her room in a minute or so to make sure she's settled in."

"Is her room one of those off the corridor leading to the bathroom?" Dennis enquired with keen interest.

"Yes dear, she has two of those rooms. There's an interconnecting door between them," Nora's mother replied.

"Oh my God. What have we become involved in now?" wondered Dennis as the truth of the matter became clearer in his mind. "How am I going to live with this?"

Although his most recent experience had cured him of his constipation, Dennis knew this would not last and he would have further difficulties in the days ahead. Unless that was, he saw Aunt Ethel again for she wouldn't stay in her room all of the time. Would she?

The matter was not raised again. Dennis never mentioned his conversation with Nora and her mother to anyone. Neither did he speak to anyone about the things he had seen in the courtyard or the sounds he had heard for many years after his stay at Baylham House.

Tuppence.

During other dark evenings Dennis enjoyed reading in front of the open fire in the sitting room. Nora and he exchanged stories about their lives and experiences, she had much to tell that interested him. Being an excellent pianist she had met well-known and interesting people at some of the best music schools. One of her stories about her childhood, mostly spent in the village, held great poignancy.

Nora and her three brothers had been invited to tea with a married couple in the village. The couple regularly attended the local church and had become friendly with the children and their parents. After tea, it was decided they would all play a game of cards seated around the dining room table. During the game some of the cards dropped onto the floor. Nora had climbed down from her chair to retrieve them. Whilst gathering the cards, she found two pennies on the floor under the table and secretly placed them in her pocket. Tuppence was a lot of money to a child in those days.

A day or two later Nora's mother found the two pennies in Nora's pocket and, of course, wanted to know how she had come by them. Nora explained how she had found the money under the neighbour's table while they were playing cards and thought she would like to keep it.

Nora was scolded and made to take the coins back and to apologise for taking something that did not belong to her.

In the fullness of time, Nora's mother made a point of speaking with friends in the village about her daughter finding the money and how she had insisted Nora return it. She was taken aback when she was told that the couple concerned were well known for placing money under the table when they invited groups of children for tea. It was also arranged for the cards to be dropped on the floor and a child encouraged to collect them. This was done to check on the honesty of the children. It was a talking point in the village that Nora had failed the honesty test by picking up the two pennies and placing them in her pocket.

"It was such a long time ago," remarked Norah with a sigh. "But I still wonder why people were like that in those days. I hope it doesn't happen now for it caused such bitterness for so many years."

An Error of Judgement.

As the oak shingles were stripped from the spire, the wind swept them away to where it could and scattered them over the churchyard like confetti. Old shingles make very good kindling wood and anyone who burned wood in their grate at home was welcome to collect a load. In many instances the iron nails remained pierced through the shingles as they fell to the ground and made deadly traps for the unwary, for the nails could easily pierce the sole of a shoe and cause a nasty wound. It became one of Dennis' regular chores to collect fallen shingles and stack them in tidy piles against the churchyard wall.

Many of the old shingles never fell to the ground but fluttered into the gully between the bottom of the spire and the stone parapet wall of the tower. They had to be regularly collected so that a walkway could be maintained around the tower to get to a second set of ladders that had been erected up the opposite face of the spire. Whilst Joe was re-aligning the boson's chairs, David came to the conclusion that the most effective way to solve the problem of clutter was to package some of the fallen shingles in a tarpaulin and then push them over the side of the tower. The packaging would 'stop the wind from blowing them hither and thither' he claimed.

The wind had seemingly blown itself out when Dennis placed the tarpaulin over the flat roof of the spiral staircase. But knowing how changeable the weather had been, the respite could only last for a short time. David shovelled heaps of wet, moss covered shingles onto the tarpaulin until it would hold no more. Dennis then pulled the edges of the bundle together with long rope lashings.

Standing on the flat roof, Dennis felt a breeze around his ears and realised the wind was about to pick up again. He knew it would be more difficult to use a rope to lower the bundle to the ground, but instinct told him that would be the safest way now that the wind was becoming stronger.

Looking down from the top of the tower, he felt very uneasy as the roof of the church lay just a little off beam to where he stood. Any squall could blow the bundle onto it and cause untold damage. He chose the cowards way out and suggested that, "If David wanted the bundle pushed off the tower, then he should push it". Besides, the wind was almost blowing his underwear off by then.

David saw the comment as a challenge to his masculine virility. He climbed onto the roof of the spiral staircase, almost brushing Dennis to one side, placed his foot under the tarpaulin, shoved hard and, sure enough, the bundle of shingles disappeared over the side. Regretfully, the inevitable happened. A squall caught the bundle and took it off course. Viewed from above its descent seemed to take an eternity but, as sure as God made little apples, it flew like a deflating balloon towards the tiled roof below.

With disbelief, contact with the roof was seen through three pairs of eyes. The sound of broken, sliding tiles echoed everywhere, until an 'end of the world' silence descended on Great Baylham.

"Och mun. Whaterwee doo noo?" asked David, as all three stared over the tower at the carnage below.

Joe and Dennis were already scrambling for the door of the spiral staircase. A ground level damage assessment was called for without delay.

Luckily, the noise heard from above sounded far worse than the actual damage to the tiles on the roof. No structural damage had been done. Lady Fortune was surely looking on them that day, for they found a number of spare tiles stored in the eaves of the church porch and, within no time at all, David and Joe had ladders on the roof and repairs were completed in record time. No one would ever be the wiser.

Afterthoughts.

Following completion of the work at Great Baylham, Nora wrote to Joe to let him know that a group of local schoolchildren had been taken to the top of the church tower to look at the reshingled spire. The schoolmistress who accompanied them was a keen mathematician for she made arrangements for the children to take measurements of the angles that had been cut when new cedar shingles were fixed to the spire. The children's measurements confirmed the angles to be within one degree of total accuracy. Pretty good work under the circumstances.

Beatrice was the first to read the letter when it arrived at home and there were scenes when Joe returned that evening. Although not questioned at the time, Dennis felt his mother's eyes searching for answers to questions that were never raised.

Amberley.

The church authorities must have checked the children's homework and recognised the results of their calculations for they urgently requested the Firm to inspect a church steeple at Amberley close to Ullswater. Rainwater was streaming into the tower through the joints between the stones of the spire.

David had returned to London to start work on another job. Dennis was not to hear from him again, although tales abounded about his escapades. One tale, related by Ken Missen, allegedly happened in west London.

David had gone "up west" to see a show at the Piccadilly Theatre. After the show he called at a bar in Soho for a drink and, knowing David, probably to find female company. He struck up a friendship with an attractive looking young lady who, after sharing a few drinks with him, invited him back to her flat that was conveniently close by.

Unfortunately for David it was not to be his night. The seductively low lights and soft music concealed the fact that he had chosen the wrong bar and the wrong 'girl' in his search for pleasures of the flesh. Settled comfortably on the sofa, David was wooed tenderly and felt the time had come to grasp his opportunity to passionately kiss and fondle his willing partner.

A roar as loud as that heard at Hampden Park on a Saturday afternoon confirmed David had found two under-developed bollocks and a small penis nestled beneath the 'lady's' short skirt!

Dennis was appalled to hear of such goings on.

"You're no more appalled than David was me boy," said Ken as he went on with the story. "I'm told David was never the same man again. He had lost his claim that he could never be fooled by a queer."

Amberley is a very pleasant town, particularly in mid-summer when the sun is shining. But this was mid-winter and it was raining. The spire was built directly onto a stone tower and there was no way up to the outside of it, except directly from the ground. Joe and Dennis would have to erect their ladders straight up the wall of the tower.

Scaling the tower was routine work, suitable for a steeple-jack's mate like Dennis to do following his experience at Great Baylham. However, his skills were put to the test when he reached the top of the tower and found that the spire overhung by more than he had estimated. To get past the overhang, a ladder had to be spliced to the one below it, then angled outwards and tied to two dogs (steel spikes) hammered into the wall of the tower. Climbing up the overhanging ladder was difficult at first as Dennis' feet tended to slip off the rungs but, after some practice, he managed to keep his body tight into the ladder, arms and hands low, to offset the effects of gravity that was trying to pull him off. Once past the overhang, laddering became more comfortable again and Dennis could take time to look over the countryside and the town and enjoy the spectacular scenery around the church.

He tied a set of riding tackle from a chain around the top of the spire so that an inspection of the stonework could start and began looking for reasons why the rainwater was getting in.

They had brought their equipment from Great Baylham but

Ladders being erected up the church tower

knew that the riding line would not be long enough to loop completely from the ground to the top of the spire and down again. The length of riding line available was half as long as it should have been and just long enough to loop between the top and bottom of the spire. Although the use of short ropes was not considered good working practice, it was decided to use what they had under the circumstances, but as a safety measure Joe tied a large figure of eight knot to the free end of the line as a stopper and a warning to them not to drop down any further should either of them get too near the end of the rope when sitting in the boson's chair.

When it was Dennis' turn to inspect one of the faces of the spire, the closer he got to the end of his line, the more cautious he became. It was not a healthy feeling to have when the end of the riding line dangled just below his knees and he was still a hundred feet above the ground, even if the rope had a figure of eight knot tied at the end of it.

Joe's verbal report to the church's architect left a degree of uncertainty in her mind as the initial inspection could not determine why the spire should be leaking to the extent it was. A site visit by one of the architects was thought to be the best way forward.

The next morning a very small, round lady, dressed in a tweed trouser suit, introduced herself as the architect responsible for recommending repairs to the spire. She held a camera in one hand and her handbag in the other. Gwendolyn McIntyre wanted to look at the problem first hand, if this could be arranged.

Joe was surprised when she said she intended to climb the ladders to the top of the spire.

"We'll have to put a harness on you Gwendolyn," he warned in a paternalistic fashion. "And a rope."

She was not put off by his apparent uncertainty about her capabilities.

Joe put her camera into the haversack he had slung over his shoulder and suggested Dennis should look after the lady's handbag during the climb. One end of the hauling line was then tied round Gwendolyn's waist 'as a safety measure'.

"If you're ready Gwendolyn. You go first. I'll be behind you. There's no hurry. If you feel you want a rest or want to stop, let me know. When you rest, tuck you leg over a rung of the ladder like this." Joe demonstrated the procedure after climbing a short way up the first ladder. "The rope is only tied round your waist as a precaution. Dennis will keep the rope taught all of the way up."

Gwendolyn and Joe steadily climbed the first ladder with Dennis holding onto the rope once he had hidden the handbag behind a bush near to the wall of the tower.

After they had climbed two ladders Gwendolyn took her first rest. A second rest was taken after the third ladder. It was then that Joe noticed Gwendolyn begin to falter. Dennis also felt the weight of the rope getting lighter in his hands.

When the climbers reached the three-quarters point up the tower, the 'feel' of the rope suggested that the downside weight would soon be close to the weight of Gwendolyn. Another ten feet or so and she could start to dangle like a puppet on a string. Dennis called to Joe to warn him of this.

At about the same time Gwendolyn must have become aware that her feet were getting lighter on the rungs of the ladders because she called a justifiable halt to the climb at that stage.

"We're coming down now, Dennis. We've seen all we need to. Slacken off the rope," Joe shouted.

Flush faced and smiling, Gwendolyn stood on firm ground again. "Thank you for letting me climb your ladders," she said. "If you would just take photographs for me and send them to my office, that will be fine. I've seen all I need to for today. We'll be in touch with you."

She collected her handbag and strode off on short, dumpy legs through the churchyard to her office.

Joe and Dennis took down the riding and hauling lines but left the ladders in position in case they were required to return to finish the job. Within a couple of months of the architect's visit, the Firm received instructions to repoint the stonework of the spire. The two of them were earmarked for the job.

When Beatrice got to hear that her husband and son were to return to the Lake District to work on another church, she was insistent that they found new digs and should not return to Baylham House. "I'm not sure what has gone on before," she remarked in a questioning voice when they were both present. "But it's wise not to re-open old wounds."

The weather was glorious for the full five weeks Joe and Dennis were there.

Brian Wardle called to see them while they were working at Amberley. He was the firm's new business manager who travelled the country looking for new contracts. Brian had held this position for a couple of months since returning to work following a road traffic accident in which his young son had been killed after he had fallen out of the back of the van Brian was driving. Brian had broken both of his legs in the accident after he lost control of the vehicle when he realised what had happened. The fractures had been so bad that the surgeons had completely removed his kneecaps, leaving him partially crippled and unable to walk very far or to climb ladders.

Dennis heard someone calling from below whilst working about a third of the way down the spire. He could see a vague figure that was not recognisable from such a distance as his eyesight was not as good as it might have been. The time was getting close when he should have to wear spectacles permanently. He knew Joe would not easily accept this and had been putting off the day when the inevitable would be necessary. Joe's attitude when it was recognised Dennis needed spectacles to read the blackboard at school was still fresh in Dennis' mind when Joe had asked him if he *really* needed to wear glasses. In Joe's opinion, as was the case at that time in other quarters, 'only sissies wore glasses.'

"I believe that's Brian Wardle down there," said Joe as he propelled himself towards the ladders in his boson's chair, polished shoes scuffing over the stones of the spire. "I'll go down to see what he wants."

Dennis continued chipping out loose mastick from the joints in the stonework and repointed the joints with fresh mortar. In many places the mastick had already fallen out and had left cavities through which rainwater penetrated. The heat of the sun reflected off the grey stone spire with the power of an electric fire. Dennis was enjoying the weather stripped to the waist and was as brown as a berry.

From inside the tower the clock struck twelve. Dennis had finished using the mortar in the bucket attached to his boson's chair and was beginning to feel hungry. He was also thinking about a very attractive young assistant in the baker's shop just down the road from the church. The women working there had been encouraging him to invite her out. It was time for him to go below to buy his quota of cakes for the day.

On reaching the ground Dennis could see Brian and Joe sitting on a low wall in the shade of a tree alongside the footpath that traversed the perimeter of the churchyard. They were deep in conversation. Dennis had met Brian in the latter stages of the War when Brian was still in the Royal Artillery. He had regularly stayed with them when he was on leave. As Dennis approached, Brian looked up and winked an eye at him. Dennis just caught the end of the conversation.

"Well I couldn't hang around any longer as I would have attracted attention. It was one of those times when cars drove into the garage for petrol, one after the other. I knew that I had struck it lucky because, after I chatted her up, she kept smiling in my direction."

"Another gigolo," Dennis thought. "Must go with the job!"

"We may as well break for lunch," interrupted Joe in an effort to change the subject.

At Brian's invitation all three got into his luxurious Austin Westminster car to head for the nearest pub. A pint and a ploughman's lunch would go down very nicely they agreed, and they could go over old times and talk about the Firm's plans for the future.

From the conversation over lunch, it seemed that the directors wanted Dennis to transfer to the south of England branch. This was due to increased work in that area and, as it was put, to give Dennis the opportunity for promotion. It was quite clear Joe was opposed to this. There were too many advantages in Dennis working with him for these to be lost.

Dennis thought through the idea of working with Brian as his manager, but came to the same conclusion that any advantages of working independently from Joe were outweighed by the many disadvantages. Realisation began to set in that he may have become wholly dependent on his father. Joe always paid when they ate in a café, paid the accommodation bills, completed the timesheets and made most of the decisions. Joe also decided, in rare instances, when and where they should go for entertainment in the evenings and at weekends when they were away from home.

On the other hand, Dennis realised that Joe could be protecting him. Over recent months Dennis had had some doubts about his own suitability to continue working as a steeplejack. There had been two or three occasions when he felt that he would rather be doing something different with his time, not struggling with the elements and risking life and limb. Scaling the overhang of the spire at the top of the tower at Amberley church was a good example. That had worried him. Had his legs trembled through fear or fatigue, as Charles' had at Five Ashes church, when he was having problems with the overhanging ladder?

Another question concerned him, one that he alone could not answer. Was it becoming noticeable that he didn't have the 'bottle' for the job?

"Another half pint Dennis," enquired Brian, breaking into his thoughts.

"Oh, no thanks Brian," Dennis replied. "Better keep a clear head."

Dennis returned to his thoughts as Brian and Joe continued with their conversation about the present state of the Firm's business.

Many steeplejacks drank like fish. If they could, they would be in a pub as soon as it opened and stay there until it closed. Maybe that's how they managed to remain steeplejacks for so many years. 'El Blotto' was possibly the answer. But no, that was not for Dennis. He had seen the ugly results of heavy drinking in other people. One day he would make the change that took him away from steeplejacking. What that change would be, he didn't know. But he would make the change.

It was time to return to Amberley church. They thanked the landlord, said they would be back some time, then got in Brian's car for the return journey.

Brian dropped Joe and Dennis off at the gates to the church, said his goodbyes and sped off down the road.

"He'll never change," said Joe. "Women and fast cars will be his final downfall!"

On the way back from the pub Dennis remembered he had not collected his cheesecakes. Before returning to work, he walked back along the road to the baker's shop to see what fare was left for him to choose from. A number of customers were already in the shop when he went in and it was clear that some of them were visitors to the town who were on holiday in the Lake District.

"Hello young man. What can we do for you today?" asked one of the assistants from behind the counter. "It must be very hot up there swinging from the spire."

The visitors turned to look in Dennis' direction. An overweight lady, wearing a broad brimmed hat took up the conversation in a Yorkshire accent. "Ooh. Is that you up there on the steeple? I don't know how you do it. I can't stand on a chair without feeling dizzy."

Dennis felt a female hand grip hold of his arm.

"He's tall, dark and handsome. He's the man of my dreams I've been looking for."

The overweight lady stroked his arm and continued in an alluring voice, "Nice arms. Strong muscles. Ooh."

Amid a chorus of laughter from the group, Dennis placed both hands on the overweight lady's shoulders and gave her a kiss on the cheek. The kiss must have been appreciated, as she paid for his cheesecakes when at last he managed to place his order.

Although Dennis looked for her, the young lady he had intended to befriend was not in the shop. Whenever he called in for his cakes during the weeks he was at Amberley he looked to see if she was there. But it was not to be. He could only assume she had left to find another job as the women never mentioned her to him again.

"Well, that was a turn up for the book," said Joe as Dennis met him at the hut containing their tools and equipment after he returned from the bakers. "It seems work is in short supply again. Brian is travelling the country looking for new business. If things don't pick up, we may be laid off."

This was not to be the case. Brian was making a job for himself. He knew he needed to make an impression with the directors to protect his new position within the company.

CHAPTER 4

COMPANY CAPERS

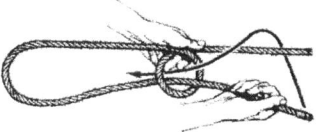

Bowline

Before the Firm moved its stores to south London, they were sited in part of a yard leased from Coles the Builders close to the Mile End underground station in the east end of London. Whenever Dennis visited the Mile End yard to collect or return equipment, he was reminded of the journeys he had made to Mile End as a boy when attending the Coopers' Company School in Tredegar Square, the school being a short distance from the station. Coopers' sister school, the Coborn High School for Girls, was within walking distance and almost opposite the Bow Road underground station.

Dennis had been a member of both schools' Highland dancing team. The girls from the Coborn school joined the boys for Scottish dancing evenings on open days. All of the dancers were kitted out in full regalia and wore the kilt with as much pride as any Scotsman or Scotswoman on Burns Night. The small ginger haired Scottish schoolmaster who taught them the Dashing White Sergeant and the Eightsome Reel spent a great deal of his time teaching them the steps and made sure everyone kept in time to the stirring Highland music he played on his violin.

"Memories," thought Dennis as he walked from the railway station. "I wonder where the schoolmaster and others in the Highland dancing team are now?"

Inside the gates to Cole's yard, on the left-hand side, were three offices. Mr. Coles and his wife worked in the larger of them, a young, pale-skinned buxom secretary in the second and an overweight middle-aged quantity surveyor nicknamed 'Fatguts' by the yardmen in the third. Where the offices finished, wooden huts containing builders' equipment and second-hand building materials continued to the end of the unmade road where the railway line ran by. The last three huts belonged to the Firm and were stocked with steeplejacks' equipment and copper lightning conductor materials.

The Firm's storeman, Fred Hulbutt was a retired steeplejack. Fred, a true Londoner, was a conscientious man who insisted on 'the job being done proper.' He looked well-worn and close to his seventieth birthday, but the men who had known Fred for many years contended he had always looked that old. His weather beaten, wrinkled face supported a large splodge of a nose that had the contours similar to those of the cratered face of the moon.

The relationship between Mr. Coles and the Firm's staff left a great deal to be desired. There was always an atmosphere, particularly when copper lightning conductor materials went missing from the stores. Strangely, this seemed to happen over weekends when the lightning conductor stores were locked and unattended.

Although Dennis was not a frequent visitor to the yard, when he did visit Brian Wardle was generally there or would arrive soon afterwards. This seemed odd as he thought Brian was supposed to be travelling the country looking for work on behalf of the Firm. On one occasion, as Dennis was drawing his list of stores items from Fred, there was a tremendous curfuffle by the builder's offices. Fred and Dennis hurried out into the yard to see the buxom secretary, dressed in a tight white sweater and short black skirt, outside her office exercising her lungs, screaming and hitting out at an apologetic quantity surveyor. Fatguts was in deep trouble and doing his best to avoid being permanently disfigured.

"He touched me," wailed the secretary to Mrs. Coles, who had come out of her office to see what the fuss was about. "He put his hand under my skirt and touched the inside of my leg. I can't bear him touching me."

Mrs. Coles put her arm round the shoulders of the distressed girl, shouted a double obscenity at Fatguts, then ushered the sobbing young woman into Mr. Cole's office. Fatguts returned to his office red-faced and denying all of the allegations made against him to anyone prepared to listen. There were not, however, many sympathetic to his cause.

"E's a dirty ol bugger," Fred said to Dennis as they walked

back into the store room. "Mind you she's flaunted it and 'as given it to ovvers in work time."

"Oh!" said Dennis, surprised at Fred's frankness. "Who's involved?"

"There's one," said Fred pointing towards the gate as Brian Wardle drove into the yard to head in their direction. "I'll tell yer more some ovver time."

Brian parked his Austin Westminster outside the stores and went in.

"Been some trouble darn the yard between the secretary and Fat Guts," explained Fred. "Don't know if yer interested?"

"Why, should I be? What's happened?"

"Might pay yer to find out," said Fred.

Brian hesitated a while to think the situation through, then left the store to walk the short distance back down the unmade road to the builder's offices. Fred and Dennis watched him go into Mr. Coles' office, wondering whether Fatguts would be called to account within the next few minutes.

"Nar, as I was saying," said Fred. "This'll brighten yer day and, at the same time, furver yer edication, but yer not to say I told yer."

Fred went on to tell Dennis how he routinely locked up the stores at one o'clock each afternoon, usually for an hour, when he went along the Mile End Road to a café for his lunch.

After locking up and almost reaching the café on one of those occasions, he realised he had left his pipe behind and had returned to collect it.

"I was only gawn about ten minutes," he said. "When I gits back, I farnd the door to the stores was undone. I remembers locking it 'cause I 'ad the key to the padlock wiv me in me pocket. I was careful and crept in, quiet like. Tried me office door wivout making a sarnd. Couldn't undo it 'cause there was somefing in the way. There was giggling noises and I 'eard Brian's voice. Couldn't 'ear fully what he said although there was mention about 'er furry fanny."

Fred went on to explain how he went round the back of the hut to look in through the window.

"Fell over evry bloody fing in me haste. There on the other side of the winder they were, 'er wiv 'er skirts up round 'er waist, spread over me table and 'im, wiv nar trousers on, stuck across her. I watched 'em fer a while, just to be sure of what I was seeing, then tapped loudly on the winder and buggered orf back to the café. They never knewed who it was watching them."

Fred enjoyed telling Dennis the tale and finished with a coarse laugh.

"Do you mean Brian and the secretary?" Dennis asked.

"That's wot I means," said Fred with a smirk. "I'd know those bums anywhere!"

It took a little while for the things that Fred had told Dennis to sink in.

"You say, no one else knows about this."

"Well, I cud 'ave mentioned it to Fatguts in passing. Come to fink of it, I did."

After a pause Fred continued, 'Ere! 'e's probably tried it on terday. Didn't get far though from accounts."

"How do you think Brian and the secretary got into the hut?" Dennis asked.

Fred pondered. "Nar idea. When I gits back from the café, the place is all locked up agin."

"Let's take a look at the padlocks and all of the keys you have," Dennis suggested.

Fred produced three keys, each labelled to show which padlock they belonged to, and the padlock for the rope stores hut.

"Nar, this blue 'un belongs to the lightning conductor store, the red to the rope store, where we is now, and the green 'un to the ladder store," he explained. "I'll show yer where the padlocks are fitted."

They went out into the roadway with the keys and the padlock in Fred's hands. Fred went to the lightning conductor store first, fumbling for the right key on the way. He placed the red labelled key into the lock and undid it.

"This place worries me," he said as they peered in. "I lose stuff out of 'ere regular. Don't know where it goes."

"Just a minute Fred. You've opened the padlock with the red key." Dennis reached for the padlock that was now in Fred's hand.

"So I 'ave mate," he said, surprised with his failure to use the right key. "Nar that's strange, ain't it? Never fought about it before, must have done it many times."

After unlocking and relocking the padlock to the lightning

conductor store, it was found that any of the keys fitted all three padlocks. Looking closer, it also became obvious that all three keys had the same identification number stamped on them.

"Supposing we take a walk down the road and try the padlocks to Mr. Coles' stores," Dennis suggested.

"OK mate, let's do that." Fred seemed pleased that someone was taking an interest in the loss of gear he had regularly brought to the attention of senior managers.

"I'll turn and stand in front of you, as if chatting, so that those in the builder's offices can't see what we're up to, if you'll try your keys in the padlocks as we pass by."

Fred's keenness to become involved in something underhanded shone out of his face. As he opened and closed each padlock he became more and more excited, until he exploded, "The farts! I kin open all of their padlocks wiv me keys. They must be able to open mine wiv theirs."

It was true, any padlock key could open any storeroom door.

Fred and Dennis turned to go back to Fred's office. Fred was fuming. Retracing their steps they heard the sound of the door to the builder's office close a short distance from them. Looking back they saw Brian Wardle, head down, walking with pronounced difficulty in their direction.

Dennis began to press Fred for more information about Brian before he had the chance to join them.

"I thought Brian was our new business manager. Doesn't he travel the country looking for new work?"

"'E's a crafty wagon of monkeys if yers ask me," volunteered Fred. "Wouldn't surprise me if 'e don't arrange 'is contracts over the phone, then books 'is travel and expenses wivout 'aving to go nowhere."

Brian caught them up as they reached the doorway to the rope store as one of the three green ex-army lorries owned by Coles passed along the roadway.

"Bit of a carry on down there!" he reported. "Thought World War Three had begun." He went into Fred's office and sat down at the table. "What are you two up to then. Nothing better to do than walk up and down the road?"

Dennis felt he had been accused of wasting time and looked across at Fred to see how he was reacting to the accusation. It was noticeable that Fred's face was very red and he was becoming very agitated.

"Yer git out of my chair!" he shouted. "Yer might have used me table to fornicate on in the past, but nar it's out in the open I'll 'ave nar more of it."

Brian looked very surprised that this elderly cockney sparrow could turn so nasty. Automatically he stood up and moved away from the chair, holding onto the table for support.

"Come on Fred. Don't be like that. We've known each other for a long time."

Dennis felt that he had done more than enough damage for one day.

"I'll be going then Fred, unless you want me to stay. I've got all of the gear I came for."

"That's all right mate," Fred replied in a voice beginning to sound more like that normally owned by him. "I'll take care of fings from 'ere on."

When Dennis met up with Joe later that day he told him the full story of the turmoil at the Mile End yard.

"That's one of the reasons I don't want you working with the others," Joe quietly explained. "They'd give you the wrong ideas. You may like to know that Brian is well known for his womanising. He, and others, can tell a tale or two and I know he's had some narrow squeaks with angry men. There's more than one husband who would like to get their hands on Brian."

When Dennis next visited Fred at the yard he was a much happier man. He had a "proper" desk, albeit a second hand one, a telephone, an electric heater in his office and the padlocks to the stores had been changed.

"Ain't lost nuffink recent," he told Dennis. "Let's go for a cupper darn the road. It's on me, lad. I'll lock the shop up."

This was something previously unheard of. Fred buying tea for someone.

In the café, Fred was more forthcoming. "Yer did me a good turn," he said in an almost embarrassed voice. "I've 'ad nightmares about that store, but nar one listened. Aving Brian over a barrel, so to speak, I got them fings I've wanted fer some time. Better watch me step from 'ere on though."

Knowing that Fred was a close friend of his father's, Dennis mentioned to Fred that he had discussed the problems at Mile End with him.

Steeplejack's training session

"Yer dad and I goes back a long way," he said. "Fings 'ave changed round 'ere and they're not all fer the good. I'll tell yer two funny stories though, but 'agin, don't tell anyone I told yer."

Dennis agreed *never* to reveal the identity of the storyteller.

"Well, yer remember the green lorry that came along the roadway in the yard when Fatguts were in trouble? That's just one of three Coles 'ave. All three 'ave the same registration number and they look alike. But there's only one tax disk and motor insurance and they're kept in the office in case any of the lorries gets stopped by the coppers. It's 'appened once already when old Coles 'ad to race orf with the disk and insurance after the driver got on the blower to tell 'im the coppers wanted to see them. I don't know 'ow 'e gets away wiv it."

Fred paused to draw on his pipe and then noisily sipped a mouthful of tea from his cup.

"Nar as I was saying." Fred hunched himself over the tea-stained table, elbows on its edge, nobbly hands supporting his unshaven chin. "Those lorries reminded me of somefing else. After Brian came out of the army, 'e got a job as an 'andyman in a big 'ouse near Epping. The 'ouse was on the main road opposite a bus stop. As yer know, Brian 'as always liked a bit of crumpet on the side and 'e found a bit in the 'ouse. She was the cleaner there. They used to meet in an upstairs room at the front of the 'ouse in the evening when the governor took a nap. Got up to all sorts of mischief, they did in that room. That's until they saw the queue at the bus stop git longer each evening as the nights draws in and the street lights outside the 'ouse comes on that much earlier. They never did pull them curtains in the front of the 'ouse till then!"

Fred enjoyed telling the tale. For he laughed as Dennis had never seen him laugh before. He only became conscious of his open mouth when he coughed and dislodged his dentures.

CHAPTER 5

ROCKINGHAM CATHEDRAL

Rope Whipping

Following a short break at home following their experiences in the Lake District, Joe and Dennis received instructions from the Firm to report to the architect's office at Rockingham Cathedral in Kent on Monday morning. They were to be employed on 'day' work that meant the Firm would be paid according to the number of hours they spent working on the job. The on-site architect would be responsible for clocking them in and out each day between Monday and Friday.

Dennis was to discover that the architect, a tall, pompous man in his early forties would be difficult to get on with. He seemed a desolate character who sat in his office in the courtyard leading to the cathedral apparently without a friend in the world. On the occasions Dennis called on him to collect and return the key of the tower, he barely spoke a word. Very soon the architect earned the nickname of 'Arc the Herald' for on those rare occasions he found time to speak with Joe, he always bore tidings of little joy.

Early one morning, a week or so after work had started on the lead spire of the cathedral, Dennis found Arc the Herald in pain, crouched on the floor in his office, barely able to move. Arc had severe back pains and had great difficulty moving.

"I've got a slipped disk," he explained to Dennis. "It doesn't trouble me for a while then, for some unknown reason, my back packs in. If I can get to my chair I'll be alright in an hour or so."

Dennis very carefully helped him into a near upright position until they were able to stagger across the room to Arc's desk where he eased himself gingerly onto his chair and, after a few exercises to help straighten his back, said he was more comfortable.

Dennis left Arc sifting through his papers, thinking that he may have broken through one of the class barriers that seemed to permeate the cloisters of the cathedral. Although Dennis may have convinced the architect on this occasion that he could be considered a reasonable member of society, this was not the case with some of the cathedral's vergers who, Dennis believed, thought Joe and he to be common workmen who should keep to their station in life.

It was rare to find churches with toilet facilities. In fact so rare, that the two toilets beneath the spiral staircase leading to the top of the tower were the first church toilets Dennis had come across in his short career. They were tucked away in a not too obvious a place and not for the use of members of the public. One of the two suites had a pink toilet pan, a pink hand basin and a mirror on the wall and was reserved for people in high places.

Before climbing the spiral staircase, Dennis had made it a practice to use the toilet in the pink suite as it was better equipped than the white one next to it. On one occasion when he emerged from the pink suite a man in a black gown cautioned him.

"You shouldn't use that toilet lad."

"Well, which one should I use then?" Dennis enquired.

"When you need to, you can use the white suite which is in the next cubicle to the one you've just used," he explained. "The toilet with the pink suite is reserved for clergy."

"What makes me so different that I'm banned from using the pink toilet?" Dennis asked cheekily, becoming pink with embarrassment.

"You're not clergy," the man in the black gown explained.

His opinion and attitude made little difference to Dennis as he made the point of using the pink suite on every occasion he felt it desirable to do so.

A day or so later, Dennis followed his usual routine before climbing the stairs and opened the door to the pink suite anticipating it to be empty. But to his surprise, there in all his glory sat the man in the black gown, trousers around his ankles, reading the Daily Express.

"Do pardon me," Dennis apologised as he hurriedly closed the door to cover his embarrassment. "I was looking for the bishop."

The weight of the lead sheets covering the cathedral's spire and their continual expansion and contraction with the change in temperature had caused the sheets to slip and split in a number of places. Arc the Herald had decided that gunmetal clips should be fitted over the lead rolls joining the sheets together on the spire and that the brackets should be bolted to the spire. It had also been discovered that the wooden timbers forming the frame of the spire had dried out and their doweled joints had begun to separate. To strengthen the joints zinc coated metal brackets were to be bolted in place to stop them from weakening further.

It was mid December, winter had set in again and brought with it close to arctic conditions. Joe and Dennis had erected a scaffold up the lee face of the spire from the top of the tower and they took it in turns to work outside on the scaffold or from a boson's chair to share the rigours of the north-easterly wind that blew straight off the river. It was essential to wear windproof clothing, hoods and gloves at all times. The slightest touch of a hand on a scaffold tube or on the lead of the spire meant a cold burn. Worse still, if one's hand remained in contact with a metal surface for more than a second it froze to it. There was no alternative when this happened but to pull the hand away, knowing that the top layer of flesh would be painfully stripped off and left behind on the metal.

It was cosy inside the spire in comparison with the conditions outside. Joe got Dennis to build a small workshop just inside the door of the spire that led out to the stone parapet wall. The workshop was used for drilling holes in the cast gunmetal brackets and to resharpen drills when they became blunt. A platform, similar to a tree house, but made up of scaffolding and scaffold boards, was also built high in the rafters of the spire from where its interior could be illuminated by floodlights. The platform became a canteen where Joe and Dennis took their breaks, drank hot tea and warmed themselves with the heat from a Primus stove. It was all so reminiscent of the days spent at Great Baylham.

Rose and Ivy

It was not long before they found a very good café within walking distance in the High Street. Joe and Dennis went there for lunch whenever they could and often stayed longer than first intended. Although mostly warm and comfortable inside, it paid to choose a table well away from the entrance as the door was opened and closed constantly as customers came in or went out accompanied by gusts of cold air that ruffled the pink plastic table top covers.

Rose, the owner of the café, was a full bodied, granite-faced woman in her fifties. "A tough old bird," thought Dennis when he got on the wrong side of her, as happened from time to time. She brooked no nonsense from anyone. It was either, 'take it as it is' or, 'leave it and get out!' Joe admitted to 'having taken it as it was' on most occasions and to being very wary of her.

The food prepared by Ivy the cook was exceptionally good and there was always plenty on the plate when it arrived straight from the kitchen. Dennis caught the occasional glimpse of the ever-busy Ivy through the doorway to the kitchen as the door regularly opened one way and then the other. She bustled about keeping her assistants on their toes. Dennis' regular choice of meal was mashed potatoes, Brussels sprouts and a pork chop. He was always ready to eat his meal and rarely left anything on the plate.

Working his way through the University of Life, Dennis was learning fast. It was apparent that, in general, women didn't have the same sense of humour as men. There had been times when it was best not to make too light of an embarrassing situation in their company. Such was the case on one particular day when the meal was not up to the usual high standard.

The steamy Brussels sprouts on Dennis' plate smelled good. He halved the first one with his knife, speared it with his fork and ate it hungrily with mashed potato. He then chose a cut of pork chop, heaped more mashed potato onto it and sought the remaining half of the sprout. He was about to combine the sprout with the assortment on his fork when he noticed the remains of a slug, cooked medium rare, lying in state within it.

"Oh sod," he said quietly, stomach heaving. "I must have eaten the other part of it. I thought it tasted a bit salty."

Joe, ever prepared to take on the cause of the underdog, took the matter in hand.

"We'll send the meal back to the kitchen with a befitting sign for Ivy to see. I've seen this done before and you'll get a fresh dinner out of this. You wait and see."

Joe put his hand into his pocket and pulled out a box of matches. Taking two of them he made them into the form of a cross, covered the slug with potato and pushed the cross into it.

"A fitting burial," he said as he lifted the plate off the table and called across to the counter to where Rose was busy accepting payment from another customer.

"Rose. Would you return this plate to Ivy with our compliments please?"

Dennis cringed for he felt this was not a good time to upset Ivy, but then there's never good a time to upset a cook in a café, if you place any value on your life.

"Why, is anything wrong?" Rose asked in an authoritative way.

Joe half smiled. "Please, just take the plate to Ivy with our compliments," he insisted.

Rose came over to the table, took the plate from him, huffily turned and whisked off into the kitchen.

Joe and Dennis waited in anticipation of an apology from the kitchen. It never came. However, within seconds a chorus of voices was heard that got louder as it closed in on their table. Ivy was surrounded by a cloak of steam as she came through the kitchen doorway. The cloak followed her every movement as she headed in their direction. Danger was threatening for Rose was in hot pursuit. Neither woman was in an apologetic mood. Joe and Dennis were the ones in dire trouble.

"What's the meaning of this?" cried Ivy, wringing her pinny in her hot hands. "Are you suggesting that I run a dirty kitchen? How dare you! I think you're disgusting. Get out of here you rude men and don't come back again."

It hadn't worked. Dennis looked at the angry woman's raw hands wringing at the pinny and thought how lucky it was her hands were not round their necks. It seemed he wasn't about to get another meal.

Joe was taken aback by the ferocity of Ivy's attack and by the backing given to her by Rose. He immediately apologised for his error of judgement. He had never intended to be offensive.

Joe and Dennis left the café with their tails between their legs and decided to call into a grocery shop along the ice covered High Street on the way back to the cathedral to buy a snack to see them through the afternoon. They took their pork pies and cakes back to the safety of their camp high in the rafters of the spire. Dennis put the kettle on the Primus stove, waited for it to boil and relaxed with his feet in front of the stove, watching the steam rising from the leather soles of his shoes.

"Even Rose and Ivy can't get to us here," said Joe in a subdued tone. "I never expected them to take the joke so personally."

Both had learned a salutary lesson. But it was easy to laugh at such a narrow escape from where they were now!

That afternoon Dennis would learn another, much harder, lesson that would be a constant reminder to him for the rest of his life. Not to take unnecessary risks.

Lights Out

To get to the internal boarding of the spire to tighten the nuts holding the gunmetal brackets in place involved tying a scaling ladder to the rafters of the spire from the central upright post (or king post). The structural timbers of the spire look very much like the frame of an umbrella, the rafters being the umbrella's spokes. Although the inside of the spire was floodlit, timbers immediately in front of the floodlamp cast dark shadows and it was also difficult to see anything above where the lamp was tied to the king post.

Twenty feet down from the top of the spire the rafters had a very short span and Dennis found a scaling ladder was too long to be used from that point upwards. There was a choice of getting a shorter ladder or making do by sitting astride each of the sets of four rafters in turn and crawling up to where the holes were being drilled in the boarding. For convenience, he chose the latter method.

Reaching the points where the drill holes came through the boarding became routinely simple and, after some practice, Dennis found he could walk up the rafters instead of crawling up them. What he hadn't allowed for was an unseen change in the construction of the spire over the top of one of the rafters.

Dennis thought something had struck him a terrible blow to his head before a black cloud descended on him.

He must have lain on the ladder beneath the rafter he had been working from for some minutes before Joe found him. Dennis had fallen ten feet onto the rafter below. By chance he had left a ladder tied to this rafter after finishing work there an hour or so beforehand. The outstretched ladder had broken his fall that would otherwise have only ended when he fell onto the cathedral's bells far below in the tower.

Dennis' head hurt as it had never done before. His body felt as if it had been trampled on by a heard of elephants. He felt sick and worried about how he was going to get down from his precarious perch. Even though Joe was pulling him a short distance towards the platform that was their camp, what would happen once he got there? He knew he would still have to climb down the ladders and then the spiral staircase to reach the ground.

Reaching the safety of the camp for the second time that day, Dennis took stock. He felt with his tongue for a front tooth that was no longer there and tasted the blood coming from a cut inside his mouth. He pushed on his bruised lower chest to check if he had broken a rib, but he was breathing without any sharp pains so that must be a good sign in itself.

"Can't think what happened," he said apologetically to Joe as he raised himself into a sitting position. "For a moment I thought Ivy had caught up with me!"

"I can," said Joe looking up to where Dennis had been before he had fallen. "See that overhanging beam. You can see it from where you are now but, as you climb higher, it's hidden in shadow. You hit your head on that beam and knocked yourself out."

"It's surprising what a cup of strong Typhoo tea will do to bring a man round to himself again," said Joe as he brewed up while Dennis recovered his thoughts seated on the platform. They sat together for a full half-hour to give Dennis time to recover, realising how lucky he was to be alive.

When Dennis felt fit enough they climbed down the ladders and wound their way down the spiral staircase, from where it was only a short walk to the van. It was time to go home and to make arrangements for Dennis to visit a dentist.

But that would only happen after Joe had unknowingly driven backwards into a window cleaner's ladder placed behind the parked van in the cathedral's courtyard, and completing an exchange of views with the window cleaner whilst the unfortunate man scurried frantically down his ladder to safety.

The Sailor
One morning, running close to their scheduled start time, the

Ford van was moving slowly in heavy traffic along Rockingham High Street. Dennis glanced up at the round-faced clock that overhung the pavement on the off-side of the road. The clock showed it was five to eight.

"We'll probably be late this morning," he said to Joe who was showing signs of boredom with the lack of progress.

"Why, what time is it?"

"It's about five to eight by that clock," Dennis replied indicating towards the opposite pavement.

Involuntarily Joe glanced over his right shoulder and through the van's side window to check for himself. At that moment the traffic chose to come to a standstill. They had been following a motor scooter ridden by a sailor, but as the traffic had come to a halt the sailor was sitting stationary on his machine, left foot on the road, in the queue of traffic immediately in front of them. It was obvious to Dennis the van was not slowing down.

"Look out ahead!" he shouted.

But, it was too late. The van hit the scooter from behind, the engine spluttering to a halt as Joe belatedly hit the brakes.

The sailor rolled back over the scooter's seat in slow time. His round sailor's hat went high in the air. It hovered for a split second, then joined its owner lying in a heap on the road.

"What the flaming hell are you doing?" bellowed a strong Welsh voice from below the van's radiator.

The window on the passenger's side of the van darkened as the navy blue tunic of a policeman blocked Dennis' view. The policeman's silver buttons looked very bright at this time of the morning as Dennis stared through the window at them.

"What yer mean?" enquired Joe, who was now out of the van standing beside the prone sailor.

The Welsh voice was adamant. "You ran into the back of my scooter."

"You suddenly slammed your brakes on. Didn't give me a chance," replied Joe.

Dennis decided to keep a low profile from the safety of the passenger seat inside the van.

The policeman stood and viewed the scene before him, listening to the intense conversation between Joe and the sailor. He seemed to recognise the man in sailor's uniform and began to examine the scooter for lighting defects and looked for its road fund licence.

"Why not get the scooter off the road to let the traffic pass sir," the policeman suggested to the now standing sailor. Whilst the sailor struggled to comply, Joe was receiving more advice from the constable.

"I know him sir. He and his mates have been giving us a hard time here in Rockingham. These Chatham tars are a troublesome bunch. No doubt you're a busy man. I suggest you go about your business. I'll deal with the matter."

Joe didn't need any encouragement, besides they were late and must be getting along.

On the way to the top

CHAPTER 6

CHIMNEYS

Ends of Wire Hawser and Joining Shackle

Soon after work was finished on Rockingham cathedral's spire and just before Dennis' seventeenth birthday, the trio of Joe, Ken and Dennis found themselves involved on the industrial side of steeplejacking. For the next few months they would be busy taking down and repairing tall chimneys. The first was at a brewery near Maidstone in Kent.

The brickwork at the top of the two hundred feet tall circular chimney had cracked with the heat generated by the boilers and was noticeably breaking up. The Firm had been called in to take down the top forty feet of the chimney and then rebuild it to a higher specification.

Access to the chimney was restricted by its position at the centre of the brewery, the adjacent boiler house and bottling plant. The most practical way to get to the chimney was found to be from the boiler house yard. From there it was possible to climb up to the flat roof over the bottle store and place ladders and scaffold boards as walkways and bridges over pitched roofs and across walls of adjoining buildings. All of the ladders and ropes needed to scale the chimney would have to be carried over this obstacle course before a flying scaffold could be constructed at the top of the chimney.

To compound the difficulties the brewery could not close down its production for any length of time, therefore the boilers would remain fired up for all of the time work was underway on the chimney, except for two days over one weekend.

In the week leading up to the two-day close down, the flying scaffold was to be put in place around the top forty feet of the chimney. Four sections of flanged, steel chimney liner had already been delivered to the site. These liners, ten feet long and five feet in diameter, would be bolted together once inside the brick chimney to channel the smoke and heat away as work progressed on the scaffold.

Dennis found that erecting a flying-scaffold at the top of an industrial chimney required initiative and a great deal of original thought. Joe had decided to cut four holes through the side of the chimney, each pair of holes to be level and opposite the other pair at the point where the scaffold would begin one hundred and sixty feet above the ground. Long steel scaffold poles were then to be inserted into these holes and pushed through the chimney and out the other side. The two steel poles would form the base on which the internal chimney liners would sit. They would also provide the starting point for the external flying-scaffold.

Before any of this work could begin, ladders would have to be erected up the side of the chimney and riding tackle in the form of boson's chairs, rope blocks and ropes fixed at the top of the chimney. A long chain was then to be fed behind the ladders and shackled to a steel chimney band, taken to the top of the chimney and pushed across to its other side with block and tackle attached. It was Dennis' job to assist Ken with this work whilst Joe prepared other equipment on the ground.

Ken and Dennis made a number of trips over the obstacle course to carry the four hundred feet of coiled rope, rope blocks, chain, rope lashings, ladders and scaffold boards to where the chimney thrust its bulk through the roof of the brewery. As they recovered their breath after the last sortie, Ken told Dennis a tale that had been a legend in steeplejack circles for many years. It involved the flying of a kite over the top of a chimney with a light string attached to its tail.

"They do tell me," said Ken in a knowing way. "Having flown the kite directly over the chimney, the old boys would allow it to fly on until the string tied to its tail was on the other side of the chimney. The kite would then be pulled down to the ground and removed from its string. After that they would join a stronger length of string to the first and pull it back over the top of the chimney to the ground on other side. The process of adding even stronger lengths of string and then rope continued until it was possible for them to pull a rope block and hauling line to the top of the chimney. They say it saved a lot of the work we are about to start now."

Dennis was not sure whether Ken was telling the truth or just pulling his leg. It was later when he reached the top of this juggernaut, after Ken had finished putting up the ladders, that he saw the impracticality of the idea, for there were many cracks in the brickwork where string (or rope) could become snagged. Also, as he looked over the top of the chimney and down inside its abyss, he lost his eyebrows and eyelashes to the searing heat that issued from the black hole that threatened to consume him. The heat would not have done the string, or the kite, any good at all. Someone might have flown a kite over a chimney at some time, but they wouldn't have had much success with this one.

Once Ken had the ladders in place up the side of the chimney and a riding line with boson's chair hooked over a rung of the top ladder, he signalled for Dennis to join him. A chimney was a different kettle of fish to climb in comparison to a church spire. The ladders went directly upwards without any deviations. Looking between rungs of the ladders on the way up revealed nothing but row upon row of dirty bricks that formed the outer circle of the chimney.

Looking down, after climbing for a while, Dennis noticed there were four smaller chimneys in the brewery close to the one he was climbing. He peered down into their black throats as a dentist might into a patient's mouth. Their steamy-grey breath rose menacingly up towards him and brought with it the smell of hops brewing below.

Dennis reached Ken on the last ladder but one from the top. Ken had pulled a long loop in the riding line attached to the boson's chair and was busy tying the chair to the ladder about twenty feet down from the top where the rope went through its block.

Making his way to the top of the ladder once again, Ken shouted for Dennis to follow him.

"I hope the bleeding wind doesn't change. If it keeps like this it'll be alright. I don't fancy getting even one lung full of the stuff that's coming out of this old girl".

Fortune was with them for the wind blew from behind their backs and kept the smoke at bay, although an occasional back-draught made sure they didn't become too complacent.

Dennis was surprised by the intensity of the heat coming out of the chimney and learned not to become too inquisitive after looking into the depths of the monster. For that was when his eyebrows and eyelashes were "fizzed" off by the heat leaving them blackened at their roots.

"Pass me the end of the chain Dennis," shouted Ken when they were both on the top ladder. "The one you tied onto the hauling line. Shackle the lower end of it to the lug of the last chimney band. I'll then pull the chain up behind the ladder and tie it off there. After I've done that hand me the rope block on the riding line and then one of the scaffold boards."

Dennis followed the instructions. He knew Ken would need help at the very top of the last ladder to push the scaffold board across the top of the chimney. He was also to hand Ken another board so that the free end of the chain with the riding gear attached to it could be pushed across to the other side of its gaping mouth.

The brickwork was fourteen inches thick at the top of the chimney and there was an empty hole in the middle of it, seven feet wide. It was a struggle to get the tackle across the yawning gap but with perseverance and a few kind words from Ken the end of the chain holding the 'moused' swan-necked block and riding line finally dropped down below the rim on the far side of the chimney and out of sight.

"Moused Hook"

Ken securely tightened the chain to the chimney band, for later he or someone else would climb into the boson's chair from the ladder below and swing round to the back of the chimney. An experience never to be forgotten when attempted for the first time and a true confirmation of one man's faith in another to 'get the job right first time'; for it was never possible to see where the rope block had finally located itself at the back of the chimney. After take-off from the safety of the ladders the first ride in a newly positioned boson's chair always tightened the chain it hung on. This gave the double 'thrill' of swinging out and around the chimney whilst at the same time experiencing the boson's chair dropping a few inches that seemed to be a few feet.

It was time for lunch when Ken and Dennis finished setting up the gear. Joe called to them from the roof below to join him. They secured the scaffold boards to a chimney band before racing down the ladders, two rungs at a time to meet up with him. There was a café a few hundred yards along the road from the brewery and together the three of them made their way to this working man's Mecca.

Bert, an harassed, thin, balding man in his late forties was the joint owner of the café. He served at the counter whilst his wife and business partner, Penny, did the cooking in the kitchen helped by two young girls in their early twenties. When Bert was elsewhere, to the delight of his customers, the girls served at the counter.

One of them, Jill, a tall, well-spoken girl with mousy hair, was as thin as a rake. She lived with her parents on the far side of town. Most of the men who came into the café had a soft spot for Jill. They treated her well and would not hear an unkind word about her. The other girl, June, was a lively, extremely attractive and curvaceous brunette who 'lived in' over the café. The men found June to be lustfully different.

Dennis also found June to be very attractive and wondered why she was working in such a lowly place. With her good looks she could certainly have done better for herself, but perhaps her upbringing had a bearing on where she fitted in society. He thought of ways to speak with her when Bert was not posted as sentry on the counter, but then others would be in earshot.

Working with Joe was also a handicap for having his father close by most of the time didn't give many opportunities to develop close friendships. June was older than he by at least five years – an age gap that appeared to be too wide to bridge. More to the point, Dennis didn't know how to go about impressing her. Perhaps she would think he was just a kid and embarrassingly dismiss his advances out of hand.

He was unaware at the time, but all of Dennis' inhibitions in this direction would be overcome within the next week after meeting up with Bob Massey.

"Three cups of tea and six rounds of buttered toast please governor."

"With sugar?"

"Yes please, two in each. Do you have any cheesecakes?"

"Yes, fresh in this morning."

"Fine. I'll have three of those as well."

The tea was poured from a large aluminium teapot into three cups that formed part of a larger group of about twenty sitting on a wide aluminium tray on the counter. Dennis noted that Bert was adept at pouring the tea from the spout without interruption when passing from one cup to another. Surprisingly, there was little spillage.

"Used to work for British Railways," said Bert as he swept the teapot along the row of cups. "That's where I get my skills from."

He was joking of course. Bert's origins were linked to the Royal Marine Commandos. It was his proud boast that he was one of the first to land in Normandy prior to 'D' Day.

Bert scraped around the glass sugar bowl with a spoon that was tied to the counter with a length of string and ladled the spoon's encrusted contents into the cups. "Two in each you said?"

"Yes, that's right!"

"OK. I'll call you when your toast is ready. Do you want to take your cheesecakes with you now?"

"Yes. I'll take them but eat them later."

The order having been placed, Joe paid and then sought out three seats where they might settle for half an hour or so. It was warm in the café and so different to being outside in the wind and rain showers of an early spring.

Within five minutes the order was ready. Dennis was summoned by Bert in military style to the counter to collect three plates loaded with hot, thick sliced buttered toast. He made his way to the counter his eyes settling on June's shapely figure as she worked in the kitchen.

"Here you are son," Bert's voice interrupted Dennis' admiring glances. "Take these over to your table for me will you?"

Dennis, brought back to reality, realised Bert must have read his inner thoughts and had deliberately broken into them.

Returning to their table with the third plate of toast after his rebuff, Dennis noticed two men had come into the café. They made towards the counter.

"Morning, you old bugger. How's that wife of yours? Bet she 's been watering the milk down again." Both men roared with laughter.

Bert ignored them contemptuously. The door to the kitchen flew open and Bert's wife appeared, hot and flustered.

"Hello Bob. Nice to see you again. Have a good weekend?"

"Not so bad. Bobbyboy was home. He's been working on the Battersea Power Station for the last month and it was nice for the family to be together again."

Dennis had expected Bob to be on the receiving end of Penny's quick tongue, but it was just the opposite. She appeared to think the world of him.

Joe caught the sound of Bob's voice.

"Bob Massey! What are you doing here?"

Bob and his mate turned to look in the direction of Joe's table.

"Hello Joe. I might say the same to you. It's been a while since we last met. We're taking down the electricity board's chimney just across the road. This will be our second week here."

After the pleasantries had been completed, another table was pulled alongside where Joe and Ken were seated so that Bob and his mate, Paul, could join the group.

From the conversation that followed it was clear that Joe and Bob had known each other for a number of years. There was friendly rivalry between them as Bob and Paul worked for another steeplejacking company that was in competition with the Firm.

Bob went on to explain that they had just returned from a weekend at home. He and Paul were lodging with Bert and Penny in a spare room over the café.

"Comfortable digs," confirmed Bob in a low voice. "Home comforts too once Bert goes down to the pub for the evening. Penny's a 'goer'. She likes it regular and long."

Dennis thought he knew what Bob was talking about, but couldn't bring himself to believe his ears.

Bob's eyes sparkled as he spoke in a pointed way and in Dennis' direction.

"I've got plans this week to extend my interests. June's taken my fancy. She's next on the cards for me!"

Dennis was appalled. How could an old man of forty have such ideas? He realised how jealous he was of Bob's experiences and hoped Bob would not be successful with his plan of seduction that week. Time would prove Dennis to be wrong.

After their meeting with Bob and Paul in Bert's café, they went back to the brewery to restart work, Dennis carrying his cheesecakes in a paper bag. Far too much time had been spent in the smoke filled dining room, now they were hard pressed to complete all of the things Joe had planned for them to do that day. It was essential they cut the four holes in the side of the chimney and slide the two horizontal scaffold poles through them. A powered hammer would make the work that much easier as the brickwork was thought to be over two feet thick at the cutting points.

Ken had been present at the time of delivery of their equipment at the brewery a few days earlier and had checked to ensure everything that had been ordered from the Yard had been delivered. The Yard had moved from Mile End to some infilled railway arches in south London. Fred was still the storeman, his years of experience in the business had made him a very reliable man who could be counted upon to ensure that the stores order was complete, provided he had heard his instructions properly. With the passage of time Fred had become slightly deaf. His loss of hearing had created a problem with one delivery in the past. This was when he was asked to take a gallon tin of bitumastic paint to a London church at North Acton. His subsequent telephone call to the office from Northampton explaining he could not find the church became remembered as a typical Fred gaff.

Fred was renowned for not being the most hygienic of men and for not being the best dressed. A one-inch paintbrush and a bar of Sunlight soap had always formed part of his shaving equipment when he travelled the country. A visit to Fred's terraced house in Streatham was always memorable for the first time visitor. Fred kept chickens. Each chicken had its own name and was part of Fred's family, even to the point of sharing the sitting room with him and his wife. When anyone visited, he would find a seat for them by brushing one of the chickens off a chair. He was always pleased to see you, as he had few visitors.

Ken knew where to find the power hammer amongst their other equipment and went with Dennis to a locked storeroom near to the bottling plant Having found the tool, he tied a rope lashing to the hammer and slung it over his shoulders. Dennis in the meantime fished out a long length of electric cable that would connect the hammer to the electricity supply, slung it over his shoulders in imitation of his friend and made his way with Ken up to the flat roof and over the obstacle course once again.

By the time they reached the chimney Joe was well above them preparing to get into the boson's chair. After releasing the knot tying the boson's chair to the ladder, he launched himself into space and round to the far side of the chimney, flying wide as he would have done if he had been on a fairground ride.

"Now there's trust," thought Dennis. For he would have had some concern about relying upon others in a similar situation. But unknown to him, and only revealed later, Joe had double-checked the fixing of the tackle at the top of the chimney before he took the flyer.

Ken climbed up the ladders with the power hammer connected to the cable after giving Dennis an idea where to find the outlet for the electricity plug and left him to make his way across to the roof to the bottling plant.

Having fed the electric cable through a skylight, Dennis made his way across the obstacle course and down into the brewery to make the connection to the power supply. He found the electricity socket, pushed the plug into it and was rewarded by the almost instant sound of the power hammer cutting into the brickwork confirming all was in hand at the top of the chimney. Satisfied with the result Dennis returned to the delivery yard. In so doing he became aware of two giggling girls following him into the yard, one pushing the other in turn and then both holding onto one another for encouragement.

Before Dennis had any chance to say hello, a loud brown voice from the boiler house bellowed out, "You two. Clear off and leave the lad alone. He's busy and hasn't got time to loaf with you."

The girls turned tail and fled in the direction they had come.

Dennis wasn't sure that he liked being chaperoned by the boilerman. A chance to at least speak with the girls would have made his day.

It was a surprise when Bob and Paul called in at the brewery the next morning in borrowed clothes and shoes to tell Joe that the previous evening Bert had been most unreasonable and there had been an upset at their lodgings. They had had to leave their room over the café and spend the night sleeping rough in the bottom of the chimney they were taking down. It must have been a long night for they had no bedding and few personal possessions. However, they were not too downhearted about it.

"He chucked us out leaving us wearing just our vests," huffed Paul. "We didn't even have time to put our pants and shoes on before we were through the front door and it was slammed shut behind us. We had to run for it across the road and climb over the wall of the generating station without our trousers on. I'll tell you getting over an eight foot wall is not the easiest thing to do with your privates dangling. But we didn't take umbrage for later we fixed Bert's car for him. Pissed in his petrol tank and took out all its glass, with a brick."

The full meaning of what had happened began to become clear later in the day when it was discovered that Bert had been tipped off about the lecherous goings on in the flat when he was not there. Bert had returned home from the pub earlier than usual and had found Bob and Paul in the wrong beds. Bob was in bed with June and Paul with Penny. There was a terrible fight that eventually led to Bob and Paul being thrown out of the flat without ceremony.

After giving the matter careful thought, Bob and Paul decided to return home for a long weekend's break to put a few miles between them and Bert for a while and to replace their lost clothing. Next week they would have to look for new digs.

It was said that Bert had threatened to get even with Bob and Paul at whatever costs, for he prized his car above all else and had a long unsatisfied lust for the curvaceous June. A threat that anyone who knew Bert should not have taken lightly.

Joe decided that Dennis and he should travel to and from the brewery each day from Ilford. Although the journey took two and a half hours each way using the Blackwall tunnel, this was preferable to staying away from home. The Ford van had become very temperamental. Each morning it was the Dickens of a job to start. The electric starter turned the engine over but the engine wouldn't fire. Using the starting handle gave no better results. It made the engine huff and puff through its valves until the engine protested violently by kicking back and spinning the starting handle in the opposite direction. Joe and Dennis tried a number of recommended solutions to overcome this regular and frustrating problem.

Every morning, all four spark plugs were taken out of the engine, cleaned, then heated in the oven in the kitchen. While the plugs were 'cooking, Dennis called on Sid, the next door neighbour who had recently broken his leg in a motorcycle accident, for him to fearlessly crank the engine using the starting handle. A simple task carefully avoided by Joe and Dennis after both had almost broken an arm in attempting to stir the engine into life.

Sid was unaware of the of the engine's sadistic traits. He was so keen to impress for he was courting Dennis' eldest sister, Josie. Ignorance being bliss, Sid always succeeded in getting the engine to start and was praised every time, then helped back to bed to wait for the ambulancemen to call to take him to hospital for his physiotherapy.

Dennis' calculations showed that the van was doing thirty miles to the gallon of petrol and about the same to the pint of oil. He avoided looking back through the rear windows as the van went along after seeing the trail of oily black smoke coming from the exhaust pipe and the smoke's inclination to follow them, suspended just above the road surface, wherever they went.

Ken, on the other hand, travelled by train from Brixton every day. They met up in Bert's café each morning at seven thirty where they discussed the day's plan of activities over a cup of tea before going on site ready to start work at eight o'clock.

By Thursday the flying scaffold was in place and they were ready to lift the steel chimney liners onto the flat roof above the delivery yard. Shearlegs, similar to the ones used by the Royal Navy at the Royal Tournament's field gun race, ropes and blocks had to be set up on the roof for this purpose. Once in place the lifting gear would be used to haul a heavy hand winch onto the flat roof. The winch, when everything was ready, would hoist the steel sections to the top of the chimney.

Tied on the flying scaffold at the top of the chimney, a long wire rope was pulled out at a forty-five degrees angle and fixed to a steel girder on one of the buildings in the delivery yard. The wire rope was to act as a guide for the steel chimney liners to follow on their way up to the top of the chimney.

Dennis was not sure how they were to ease steel sections over the top of the scaffold and down inside the chimney. One of his grandfather's favourite quotations came to mind when he thought about the work ahead. "There are two ways of doing things in this world my boy. There's the 'easy way' and there's the 'hard way'. The 'easy way' is hard, but the 'hard way' is bloody hard." He hoped things would go the easy way but, if they didn't, he felt Joe had done these sorts of things many times before and could be relied upon to see the tricky operation through.

The brewery's manager had agreed to close the boilers down the next day, a Friday, for two days. As soon as possible they would open the steel inspection doors to the flues to allow cool air to be drawn through the chimney. Joe had planned the work schedule to take into account that the flues from the three coal-fired boilers should have cooled sufficiently by early Sunday morning to enable them to get inside the chimney to carry out an inspection and to insert the chimney liners from the scaffold.

The preparatory work having been completed, it was agreed that the steeplejacks should let the natural elements do their work and they should enjoy the rest of Friday and all of Saturday at home.

On Sunday morning Ken was found to be in Bert's café when Joe and Dennis arrived at seven thirty that morning. Never one to be late, Ken had been there since seven o'clock. From the conversation Dennis overheard between Ken and Joe when he went up to the counter to place his order Dennis suspected trouble was brewing.

Being a Sunday morning, the café was less busy than usual. There was no sign of Bert's wife or Joan, although June could be seen to be busy in the kitchen, but she unusually quiet and a little tearful. From the snatches of conversation Dennis heard Ken confirm the rumours of the previous week about Bob and Paul's indiscretions.

Bert had obviously made a point of speaking with Ken that morning for Ken told Joe that Bert had been very upset when he described what he had seen in the flat on his return from the pub the previous week. Bert and his wife had not been getting on too well since his demob from the Royal Marines, as the business took up most of their time leaving both of them tired and irritated with each other. Penny had decided the previous evening to leave him and go to live with her sister in Eltham. She had told Bert he wasn't the man she married. She wanted more excitement in her life. It didn't include working seven days a week in a café.

However, Bert was pleased to tell Ken that June had agreed to continue to work at the café and to live in the flat above. She had been, and still was, doing an excellent job and had almost taken over where Penny had left off.

Ken finished his update of the Bert and Penny saga as Dennis delivered the tea and toast to the table. Although it was not recognised for its meaning at the time, after a while, Bert shook off his melancholy and came over to join them at their table. He was keen to learn about the technical side of steeplejacking, particularly the type of scaling equipment used and the construction of industrial chimneys.

At eight o'clock, as agreed, Joe reported to the brewery's engineer for the inspection of the chimney flues.

"Dennis, you may as well come along with me. You are about to experience something that not many others will have the opportunity to do in their lifetime. You're coming inside an industrial chimney. You'll not forget this day."

Dennis had not been inside an industrial chimney before, but he felt it was going to be a hot, exhausting experience. As very young children, his sisters and he had taken hot bricks wrapped in towels to bed with them on cold nights. The warmth given off by the bricks made the bed very cosy and the bricks still felt warm in the morning. The bricks in the chimney would probably be similarly warm when they went inside.

Ken was detailed by Joe to complete the final preparations for raising the steel chimney liners to the top of the flying scaffold. Having finished that job he was to return to the boiler house to wait for Joe and Dennis at the door to the flue. Ken was to be their 'safety' man.

In the boiler house Joe and Dennis stripped off their outer clothing and put on boilersuits. Joe produced four tea towels from his haversack. Dennis had thought he had seen Joe rummaging through his mother's kitchen drawers before they left the house that morning, and now knew why.

"Tie the towel around your neck Dennis; under your boilersuit. Then tuck the legs of your boilersuit into your socks. Make sure the laces of your shoes are not too tight because your feet will get hot and swollen. Put cotton wool in your ears, place this other tea towel over your head and make sure it covers your ears. Pull your beret down as far as it will come over the tea towel to keep it in place."

Joe then handed Dennis a pair of grey asbestos gloves, a respirator to wear over his nose and mouth, a pair of goggles and an inspection lamp with a long, white electric lead to light their way.

The brewery's engineer had left the boiler room by then. It seemed he had no intention of being part of the group that went into the chimney as Joe and Dennis could be relied upon to undertake the inspection on his behalf.

The light from the lamp lit up the blackness ahead of them as Joe and Dennis climbed into the brick chimney flue through the doorway leading from the boiler house. It was hotter than Dennis had imagined. He shone the light around in wonderment and was surprised to see through his goggles how clean the flue appeared. He had previously had visions of wading through a sea of soot to reach the shaft of the chimney.

Moving onwards and inwards towards the centre it became even hotter. The vastness of the three flues, each having a coal-fired boiler at their origin, was unbelievable. Where all three joined could have been mistaken for the vaults of a cathedral.

"The bricklayers who built these flues must have known what they were doing," shouted Dennis, his voice muffled by his respirator. There was no response from Joe. He knew his words had not been heard but still felt obliged to continue to say something in his excitement. The heat inside the flues, the effort required to breathe through the respirators and the cotton wool in their ears made it impossible to talk to one another.

Small pieces of mortar and brick dust flew around them in a vortex 'tinging' against the lenses of their goggles as the particles flew by, drawn upwards by the draught created by the tall chimney. The further Joe and Dennis ventured inwards examining the flue lining the clearer it became that the brickwork was in good order and not in need of repair.

The hot brick surface they had been walking on began to feel softer with each step. A small cloud of black dust, kicked up by their feet, soon developed into a miniature tornado. It swirled past them, heading inwards and then upwards towards the white speck that was the outlet at the top of the chimney. The black cloud grew in size and density. By the time they reached the circular shape of the bottom of the chimney they were pushing through coarse, very hot and knee-deep soot. Each step disturbed more soot until they found themselves in the middle of a black, raging blizzard. It was impossible to see further than the end of one's hand. It was not pleasant. It was time to return to whence they came.

Joe tapped Dennis on the shoulder and gestured an about turn. Without a second's thought, Dennis turned and followed him back along the flues leading to the boiler house and fresh air, the length of white electric lead indicating the way.

Ken met them as they clambered through the doorway into the boiler house. Without any delay Dennis' hand automatically reached for the respirator covering his face. Almost with the same movement his goggles came off and fell to the floor. Gasping, he realised what luxury it was to breathe in fresh air again. It was then he felt his feet to be unbearably hot. Soot had filled his shoes. It was between his toes, up his nose, down his neck, in his pants and in his ears. Wherever soot could find a hiding place, it had. He felt like a boiled lobster. The difference was that he was still alive! What the hell if the tops of his ears had almost been burned off and the collar of his boilersuit was smouldering. He was out of that infernal black hole.

Dennis reached down to take off his shoes as his feet felt as though they had been through Bert's toaster in the café down the road. He quickly shed his outer garments, shook them and placed them on a wooden fence separating coal storage areas in the boiler house. Joe was engaged in a similar exercise, his white teeth showing out of a blackened face as he smiled in relief.

Stripped down to the waist with only their underpants on they washed their arms, legs, faces and upper bodies with water from a nearby water hose. It was here that Dennis met the boilerman who had shooed the bottle store girls away.

The boilerman wasn't as unpleasant as Dennis first thought he could have been. Coming out of the heat inside the flues he recognised that the men could probably do with a drink and offered to make tea, an offer that would never have been refused under any circumstances.

They sat in a circle, Ernie the boilerman, Ken, Joe and Dennis, drinking tea poured into large mugs and exchanged gossip until Joe and Dennis had cooled down and recovered from their ordeal.

"I don't suppose you have a coal fire in your house," suggested Ken to Ernie as he sat on a pile of Welsh steam coal sipping at his tea.

"No I don't now," Ernie replied. "But I had one when I lived in Romford. I was a fireman with British Railways working the steam locomotives on the London to Norwich run. Never went short of coal in my house," he claimed. "We had a good fiddle going on the footplate when we took freight from Stratford to the east coast. We had it off to a fine art in the end, until I became too greedy. We would choose a large piece of coal from the tender and place it on the footplate close to the doorway. As our loco went along an embankment that led down to a road close to where I lived, I would push the coal through the footplate doorway and it would roll down the embankment to stop close to where I could pick it up after my shift had finished."

It was Ernie's turn to sip his tea. He took a deep breath and continued.

"On one occasion as we passed the spot where I usually dumped the coal, I found that the piece I had chosen was too big to be pushed through the doorway and it got stuck. I was desperate to free it and began to kick at it in annoyance. When I did manage to break it loose we were well past the dropping off point and along by the marshalling yards at Romford. The lump of coal left the footplate at a pace and I could see it was heading for a guards van parked up for the night. It smashed to smithereens against the side of it. Later I found out that one of our guards had been sleeping inside the van, taking an unofficial break. The noise must have been startling for he thought he had been involved in a train smash."

Ernie laughed infectiously at the tale he had told many people before and soon he had all in his company joining in.

Suitably refreshed and brought back to normality, Joe and Dennis put on their usual working clothes then went in search of the brewery's engineer. They found him in his office working through a backlog of correspondence.

Joe reported that the boiler flues appeared to be in good condition. However, before work could start inside the chimney someone would need to clear the soot from the flues. Joe wanted to know when the contractors would be there to do this.

The engineer confirmed that a firm of chimney sweeps had been contracted to undertake the work. They should have been on site at nine o'clock, but that was an hour ago.

It was ten thirty when the chimneysweeps arrived. Dennis was in the delivery yard when they drove into the brewery in a grey Ford van similar to their own. The driver, who appeared to be in charge, left the van and went into the boiler house. His mate went over to Dennis, probably because Dennis appeared to be of a kindred spirit and as black as the ace of spades, even though Dennis had 'washed'.

Dennis told him of his experience inside the chimney flues whereby the chimneysweep's mate left to join his partner in the boiler house.

Some ten minutes later both chimneysweeps reappeared in the yard, but by this time Dennis was busy on the flat roof helping Ken tie the first section of chimney liner to the winch wire. They dragged half a dozen sacks of soot from the back of their van and proceeded to empty these against a wall in the yard. The empty sacks were returned to the van; the doors were closed and they drove away.

Dennis brought these strange goings-on to Joe's attention and Joe reported them to the engineer. Failure to clear the soot from the bottom of the chimney meant that within the hour Ken would be in the middle of a soot storm as he sat inside the chimney on his boson's chair.

Joe chained the riding tackle to the upper part of the scaffold and lowered the swan-necked block and riding line with the boson's chair attached inside the chimney. He wanted the chair to be positioned just right so that Ken could swing his legs over the rim and slide into the seat.

Ken was dressed in a similar fashion to that Joe and Dennis had been before they had gone inside the chimney flues. His appearance in goggles, respirator and woolly hat pulled down over his ears, although practical, looked most odd. He grasped the chain above the swan-necked block, eased himself over the top of the chimney, his feet searching for the safety of the boson's chair, then slid his body down so that his legs went between the ropes that were holding the chair to the riding line.

Dennis passed the satchel of tools over the rim of the chimney to him.

"Lower the end of the riding line into the chimney Dennis," he shouted. "Let the rope down gently, we don't want any soot storms."

Dennis lowered the end of the rope until only the last few feet attached to the boson's chair was left in his hands. Although Ken took the remaining length of rope from him to avoid any disturbance in the bowels of the chimney, the first faint signs of a soot cloud was seen to be rising from inside the chimney.

As Ken lowered himself further into the chimney his foot caught on a loose brick. It broke away to fall inside.

"Wait for it!" he shouted, his voice muffled by the respirator he was wearing.

There was a dull 'throomp' from below as the brick went into the heap of hot soot resting at the bottom. There was a short period of quietness and expectation before a great maelstrom of hot, blinding black soot raced up and out of the chimney soaring high into the sky. The soot storm blasted past Ken seated helplessly inside the chimney for a few minutes, before it petered out and normality resumed once again.

Relieved he could see and breathe again, Ken peered through his goggles to carefully check the internal brickwork for other loose material that could fall on him as he slid down the rope in his chair. Finding none, he loosened off his stop-lashing and lowered himself down the inner wall of the chimney to the point where the first chimney liner was to be sited on top of the scaffold poles, forty feet below.

Satisfied that the platform for the internal chimney was sound, Ken hauled himself up to the top of the stack, the sheaf in the swan-necked block turning, squealing and then stopping as he heaved kimself upwards and then paused, between lifts.

"It's still bloody hot in there," he gasped as he wrenched off his respirator and goggles after scrambling over the rim of the chimney and onto the scaffold. "When the soot storm hit me from below I wondered whether I was going to survive. Couldn't see, couldn't breathe, couldn't shout. It was a bloody nightmare."

Ken soon recovered, took off the surplus clothing he was wearing and began preparing for the next stage – landing the first chimney liner on the scaffold.

Being the youngest, Dennis was selected to be winchman. Tim, a short wiry labourer employed by the brewery who was known to be keen on horse racing, was also to give a hand. It was unusual for Tim not to have the Daily Mirror, turned to the racing page, tucked in his coat pocket. But it was Sunday and there was no racing on today. A bonus, because Tim was known to wander off when it took his fancy to place a bet or to collect his occasional winnings from the local bookies.

The steel chimney liner lay on the flat roof tied to the end of the winch cable ready for lift-off. It had two forward gears, one gear for slow movement and the second for even slower movement of the load. It also had a reverse gear that would be used when lowering the load onto the scaffold and then down into the mouth of the chimney. Dennis had been well briefed by Joe in advance. "Listen to my instructions," he had told him. "Take your time and take it easy."

Turning the winch handle round and round to raise the load off the flat roof seemed to take an eternity. The guide wire sagged, then became taught with the weight of the chimney liner. But at last it lifted off the roof, swung free and rocked gently beneath the cable like a rocket steadying for blast-off. The winch rope had taken the strain and the load was seen to be moving over the roofs towards its destination. The horizontal position of the chimney liner soon became a vertical one as the drum on the winch took on more lays of cable. After three or four pauses to ease their aching limbs, Tim and Dennis heard a sharp "Wo!" from above. The chimney liner had arrived safely alongside the scaffold.

Joe and Ken could be seen from the flat roof manhandling the liner over the scaffold rails. First releasing it from the guide wire and then rolling it round the scaffold uprights in preparation to lower it into the chimney.

Three arm movements downward followed by a shouted "down" signalled to the winchmen to begin lowering. The lowering operation went well with few hiccups. Except for the occasional binding of the liner against the internal wall of the chimney from where it was prized free with a long scaffold pole, it was a text book example as to how the job should be done. There were times when clouds of black soot welled up from within chimney as loosened masonry fell into its belly, but these were bearable, minor problems of little significance.

Once the liner was seated on its platform Ken was soon in his boson's chair again and descending inside wearing his fancy dress, for the rim of the liner needed to be sealed against the inner wall of the brick chimney.

Mission accomplished, Ken pulled himself up again and reached over the top of the chimney for the second time. He heaved himself onto the scaffold and suggested it was time for lunch. The uplifting of the other three sections of chimney liner could follow after a well-deserved break in Bert's café.

Bert was not impressed by their appearance when they arrived. He ushered them to a table in a corner away from the counter.

"Let me know what you want and I'll bring it to you," he said in lowered tones.

He didn't want to lose their trade, but on the other hand he thought, "these dirty looking ruffians didn't encourage business."

Joe, Ken, Tim and Dennis had a very successful afternoon. Other people might be relaxing, walking the dog in the country, or visiting friends and relatives. "We," as Tim put it. "Were stuffing a chimney with a steel tube."

By five o'clock the weekend's work had been completed. There was just the chore of cleaning up as far as this was possible with the rudimentary cleaning gear they had at their disposal and then report to the brewery's engineer so that he could restart his boilers. No one would know until Monday morning that the bottling plant would be put out of action for a whole day because of the soot that had settled on every horizontal surface within fifty yards of the open doors to the flues whilst the boilers were closed down.

At around ten o'clock on Monday morning Bob and Paul called in again at the brewery. They were short of railway sleepers for the 'chute' they were remaking inside the Electricity Board's chimney just along the road. In passing, Bob was pleased to announce that they had found other digs but, for obvious reasons, they would not be using Bert's café. There was another café on the main road a little further along that was just as convenient for them. They invited Joe, Ken and Dennis to visit them that afternoon to see how they were getting on with the demolition of their chimney.

After lunch, on the way back from Bert's café, Joe decided they had time to call in to look at the Electricity Board's chimney. Bob and Paul had almost finished remaking the chute that had become dislodged and damaged by the constant rain of bricks and rubble hurled from above. The chute was made up of heavy railway sleepers covered by a thick steel sheet. It lay on a huge pile of rubble inside the remains of the octagonal, red brick chimney and sloped down and outwards, through a large hole at the bottom of the chimney, into the yard. Tons of brick rubble littered the yard area, waiting to be loaded and taken away by lorry.

Dennis noticed that when the chimney was built, steel "U" shaped brackets had been bricked into the inside of the chimney's walls, all of the way to the top, as an internal ladder. The steeplejack's scaling ladders had been put up on the outside and led to the top of the chimney that was now half its original height. A length of rope and a rope block hung from the top of the ladders, he supposed they were there for lowering ladders when they were not required as the chimney's height got lower.

The Electricity Board's chimney was originally taller than the one at the brewery. It could not be 'felled' as buildings, still in use, stood in the way of such an enterprise. It had to be taken down piece by piece and the bricks dropped inside. The trick was not to clutter up the hole at the bottom. As the bricks fell, they should land on the steel plated 'chute' and be propelled out of the hole, away from the chimney and into the yard.

Suitably impressed, Joe, Ken and Dennis returned to their own chimney that was not to suffer the same fate as that of its neighbour.

The sound of hammers and chisels echoed around the brewery

as Joe and Ken hacked away at the brickwork at the top of the chimney, gradually revealing its new inner steel lining. As great chunks of masonry were loosened, it was carefully placed in a large wicker basket and sent zooming down a guide wire to Dennis in the yard below who was using an 'endless rope' to control the rate of descent of the basket. Joe had made the endless rope by splicing two very long ropes together to form a loop that ran through two rope blocks from the ground to the top of the scaffold and back again. Dennis had been shown how to grasp an old sack around the rope and to squeeze it tightly as it ran through the sack held in the palms of his hands. The harder he grasped the rope, the slower the load should travel towards him along the guide wire.

Joe had reminded him, "If you allow the load to *get away from you*, the hand pressure you will need to bring it back under control again will make the rope burn the sack and, if you aren't careful, your hands as well. So be warned."

Dennis soon found how easy it was for Joe's words to come true for not only did the sack burn, it burst into flames on one occasion causing him to lose control of the descending basket. It crashed into the girder to which the guide wire was tied and spilled the brick rubble over the yard. This experience was one too many and he made sure it was not repeated by paying greater attention to what he was doing. As a heavily laden basket came down the guide wire an empty one went aloft, the empty basket swinging freely as it passed above the full one half-way up the chimney.

The chisels used to cut away the brickwork became blunt after a while and needed to be re-sharpened. Dennis found when talking with Ernie the boilerman that the brewery employed its own blacksmith in a traditional forge across the cobbled street that separated the brewery onto two sites.

The forge was set back from the cobbled street in a yard behind the stables and cart shed and Dennis was intrigued by the old-fashioned machinery installed there. He could see how the canvas belts looped around a rotating shaft fixed to the roof trusses drove the machines and what a simple matter it was to slip a belt from one pulley to another when the blacksmith wanted to use a different machine. He welcomed the break from work when he was sent to get the chisels sharpened for he could stop to make a fuss of the shire horses and admire the hand painted carts kept in the shed in such pristine condition.

Bill Tillett, the blacksmith, was a man of few words. Strong as an ox, he could move steel fabrications around as if they were toys. He was also the brewery's farrier who shoed the shires that pulled the beautifully kept dray carts. Bill was always a busy man. "Leave them over there me boy and come back this afternoon," was one of his favourite expressions when Dennis called in to deliver more blunted chisels. This Dennis would do, but returned as early as he could so that he could watch the blacksmith heat the chisels in the furnace, hammer them into shape on his anvil and, when they were red hot, dip them into the water bath to cool them. Each chisel would hiss as it entered the water until its fiery glow changed to the bluish-grey of cold steel.

"You can take that one out now. Handle it carefully. It might still be hot!"

Once the chisels had been *drawn* they were taken across to the grinding wheel for sharpening to the delight of the small sparks that flew off in all directions as a keen edge was applied to each chisel. Placing the finished articles in a sack Dennis was ushered out of the forge as Bill had other work to do.

Although Dennis had been doing remarkably well in controlling the descending baskets and his arms were becoming as strong as Popeye's, he couldn't pull enough full baskets of new radiused bricks up to the scaffold as quickly as Joe and Ken wanted them for bricklaying. It was decided they should hire a petrol-engined winch to 'help Dennis out'. Dennis was very pleased with this decision, as he had been going home in the evening completely exhausted.

The petrol winch, although it took the effort out of hauling materials up the guide wire, was a beast to operate. The clutch was either in or out – there was no steady engagement of the motor. The basket either remained stationary or raced up the wire almost out of control until the hand throttle was released when the basket would come to a dead stop, swinging alarmingly above him.

Except for three consecutive days during the period of the contract, the weather stayed fair for the time of the year. On the second of those three days, as Joe, Ken and Dennis were taking shelter from the rain in the boiler house they heard the sound of an ambulance passing by the entrance to the brewery, its bell ringing furiously. The bell stopped ringing two or three hundred yards up the road from where they were and apparently close to the old generating station's half-demolished chimney. The abruptness of the silence brought cold shivers down the backs of those present in the boiler house and it suggested something serious had happened.

"I'll just pop up the road to see what's going on," said Ken as the sound of fire engines was heard clanging towards where the ambulance had stopped.

"I think we should all go," said Joe. "It could be Bob or Paul."

All three hurried through the rain along the cobbled street to the old generating station. An ambulance, two fire engines and a police car had arrived ahead of them. A thin crowd was beginning to form, among them were people Dennis had seen in the café, including Jill, June and Bert.

Checking with the fire officer in charge, Joe learned that two steeplejacks were probably trapped under brick rubble, inside the chimney. Other workmen had reported a thunderous noise and then dust coming out of the hole in the bottom of the chimney and there being no sign of the men who had been working inside.

Having identified themselves as steeplejacks in their own right, Joe, Ken and Dennis set about helping to shore up and dig through the debris to reach Bob and Paul. Very much aware that there could be another fall of masonry at any time if care was not taken.

As he worked Dennis recalled in detail the personal experiences he had had during the blitz when a bomb had hit their house. His mother, his two sisters and he had been standing at the top of the stairs when a Dornier bomber flew over dropping its deadly load. The shadow of the bomber had darkened the stair well and afterwards there had been a tremendous blast before the windows blew in and the ceiling fell down on them. The rescue work he was involved in seemed similar, but he was now one of the rescuers and not one being rescued.

Firemen formed a chain to move debris from the hole in the chimney to the yard outside. It was essential to keep the hole as clear as possible in case more bricks fell and the rescue team should want to get out quickly. As heaps of brick rubble were removed, the steel covering of the chute began to appear. Soon an arm of a jacket was seen among the remaining bricks. It was quickly recognised as that belonging to Paul.

Fortunately the heavier pieces of masonry had struck a glancing blow on the inside of the chimney before ricocheting onto Paul's lower body. His head, although bloodied, looked as though it may have escaped serious injury. He was breathing but unconscious. However the unnatural way he was lying looked very ominous.

An ambulance crew scrambled up the chute with their stretcher and first aid equipment to where Paul lay. It was going to be a tricky removal as the ambulancemen suspected Paul had suffered a fractured spine.

After ensuring Paul was breathing regularly and bandaging the wound to his head, the ambulancemen placed a stretcher on top of him and tied him to it with a rope lashing and triangular bandages. Paul was steadied and gently turned with the rotation of the stretcher so that he could be placed on it and taken to the ambulance without causing any aggravation to his already serious condition. The ambulance crew had done a marvellous job and Paul was soon on his way to hospital with an almost certain fractured skull, a fractured spine and internal injuries.

The firemen found Bob, unconscious, in a sitting position, near to the hole inside the chimney. He was covered in dust, bricks and mortar. A large swelling on his head indicated he had been hit by falling masonry.

To avoid any possibility of further injuries to Bob or to his rescuers, he was quickly moved to safety outside the chimney by two burley firemen. Bob regained consciousness just after being loaded into a second ambulance, but was unable to tell the police what had happened to cause the accident.

Bob had always been a survivor and so it would be on this day. He remained in hospital under observation for twenty-four hours before being sent home to rest for a few weeks.

Paul was not so lucky. He was confirmed as having a fractured spine as well as a fractured skull and internal bruising. He remained away from work for many months.

The investigation that followed the accident showed that someone had tampered with the steeplejacks' equipment. The hauling line and tackle had been moved from their original positions at the top of the ladders and coiled around loose brickwork at the top of the chimney where demolition work had been taking place. It was thought that the hauling line had been disturbed by gusts of wind that toppled the brickwork inside the chimney whilst Bob and Paul were clearing a blockage at the time. It was only by chance that the falling masonry had hit the fire lining of the chimney twenty feet from the bottom, shattering it into smaller fragments and losing some of its impetus, otherwise events could have been even more serious.

Work on the brewery's chimney continued without further incident until its completion a few weeks later. In the final week, after rebuilding work had been finished, the steel chimney liners were taken out and the flying scaffold and ladders taken down in very pleasant spring weather.

The unfortunate accident at the old generating station reminded everyone about the need not to take unnecessary risks. Complacency apart, there should not have been any reason for both Bob and Paul to be inside the chimney whilst it was being demolished.

CHAPTER 7

BOBBYBOY

Wire Rope Tensioner

Late one Sunday morning Bob Massey called at Joe's home to see him. Usually Sunday mornings were set aside for relaxation and for doing very little and most members of the family remained in bed until after ten thirty. It was only after Beatrice brought them a cup of tea that they would stir and sit up bleary-eyed to ask "What time is it?"

Bob had become restless following a number of sleepless nights recalling the fall of brickwork at the old generating station and had decided to take advantage of the morning's summer sunshine to walk the short distance to the Walkinshaw's home. He had left his wife Elsie at home with their two daughters, Maria and Teresa and son, Bobbyboy. They were in their beds when he left them and he felt sure they would still be there until quite late in the morning.

The two girls were still at secondary school, Teresa was doing particularly well and her parents hoped she would stay on to take up a career in teaching. Maria had a happy-go-lucky approach to life who had no intention of becoming brilliant at anything. Bobbyboy, the eldest of the three, had modelled himself on his father and had received his father's name to ensure its continued use by current and future generations.

Immediately after he left secondary school Bobbyboy had followed in his father's footsteps to become a steeplejack. He was a quiet, beanstalk of a lad who kept his inner thoughts very much to himself. Even after four years as a steeplejack, he was still 'Bobbyboy' to everyone who knew him.

Bob Massey was back at work and, except for a spate of nightmares, was physically feeling few ill effects from his experiences at the old generating station. He had a new mate, Bill Bennett. They had been taking down the remaining part of the chimney where the Bob and Paul had been injured, and were about to start a new job in south east London taking down and replacing a steel chimney at a carbon factory.

When Bob rang the front door bell at the Walkinshaw's home he was carrying a small sack. Dennis was in the kitchen with his mother and his sister, Pam, who was a year older than he. Pam was receiving cooking lessons from her mother and together they were preparing Sunday's dinner. Pam, always ready for a laugh, was a cashier at Dewhurst's, a large chain of butchers. She terrorised Sid's mother, their next door neighbour, by sending neatly packaged parcels of small parts of animals and received similar presents in return in the form of packaged earwigs and spiders. Pam was keen to learn as much as she could about cooking, for George, her boyfriend, looked forward to the meals she prepared when he visited at the weekend.

Joe showed Bob into the sitting room where he had been reading the News of the World. It was his favourite Sunday paper for he claimed it had the best sports pages of all the papers. Making room on the settee, he invited Bob to sit down so that they could exchange news about who was working where and what they had been doing. Beatrice remained in the kitchen, for she didn't like becoming involved in 'men's' conversations 'she had heard it all before and they could be crude'. Dennis was, therefore, to take the tea and rock cakes she had just taken out of the oven to Bob and Joe. Pam was to stay with her, in the kitchen.

Interrupting their conversation, Dennis entered the sitting room and handed out the teas and cakes.

"How are you feeling Bob?" Dennis enquired. "Got over the bump on your head?"

"I'm fine," Bob replied. "I was off work for a while getting over the wallop on my head. You know, I didn't get paid while I was off. Means I'm a bit short of the readies at the moment. A pound out of the till would help or you could give me ten bob for the chicken in this sack."

Joe looked towards the sack that was on the floor beside the sofa and agreed ten bob for a chicken was a bargain. He pulled a small wad of bank notes from his wallet, selected one of the small brown ones and handed it to Bob in full payment.

"I'll leave the chicken here, next to the sofa for Beatrice to collect when she comes in," suggested Bob as he tucked the note into his back pocket.

Joe turned to pick up his teacup and this gave Bob the chance to return to his accident and to continue, "Thanks to both of you and Ken, me and Paul got out of the chimney alive. Those bricks crashing down on us was something neither of us would want to experience again. The ambulance blokes did a good job on us. The staff in the hospital, well, they were bloody marvellous. Paul's doing ok. I went to see him in hospital last weekend. He's lucky to be alive you know."

Bob moved to the end of the sofa to give Dennis room to sit down. Dennis was in on the conversation.

"Think nothing of it," said Joe. "It was lucky we were close by. All three of us had a premonition that you and Paul had been hurt, that's why we shot along the road as quickly as we did."

"You know," said Bob, "I've been having serious thoughts about what happened. Neither Paul nor I can remember moving the tackle at the top of the chimney. We both mentioned this to the accident investigator, he thinks that there could be something fishy about the whole business."

The more Bob went into the details of the accident, the stranger it seemed.

"I'm convinced that Bert from the café knows more about what happened than he makes out," confided Bob. "I was so convinced of this, that I asked Bill Bennett to call into the café the other day, on the pretext of collecting our belongings, to find out the lay of the land there. Our kit wasn't there of course, Bert had chucked it away. But he seemed very interested to hear about me and Paul and where we were. Bill was wily enough to tell him only what he had to, and no more."

Unfortunately, Bill had, unwittingly told Bert where their next job was. Bob didn't know this at the time.

Bob was short of money. Just before it was time for him to leave, he mentioned being short again, probably in the hope that Joe would arrange a loan, but Dennis never saw any money passing between them.

"Elsie has taken in a lodger," Bob explained as he raised himself from the sofa. "He pays her a few quid a week. He's a bit thick but he's company for her when I'm away."

"That could lead to complications," replied Joe ruefully.

"I suppose so." Bob paused, thinking quickly. " You're right. Mind you, I know that a bit of hanky-panky is going on between them, but it's not as if he is putting it in bare-backed. I've told her I don't mind him shagging the inside of a French letter."

Dennis' horizons were being broadened with Bob's every word.

Beatrice came into the room at that moment, seemingly she had not heard Bob's revelations.

"Bob has brought us a chicken," Joe interrupted in an attempt at avoiding further embarrassment. "It's by the sofa in a sack."

"Thanks Bob," smiled Beatrice. "I'll take it in the kitchen. It'll come in handy for next week as I haven't been to the shops for a few days."

As she picked up the sack she shrieked with alarm.

"There's something moving in there. It's not a dead chicken. It's a live one."

"Your right," agreed Bob. "It's alive alright. Fresh from the chicken sheds along the road."

"What am I going to do with a live chicken?" Beatrice wanted to know. "I've never killed or cleaned a chicken before."

"I'll do it in for you while I'm here," said Bob full of bravado. "Have you got a carving knife handy for I'll need something like that after I've rung it's neck. Let me have the sack then clear the kitchen so that I can get on with the job."

Apprehensively Pam left the kitchen to hide behind her mother. Everyone, except Bob with the sack in his hand, piled into the hallway.

"Can Bob really ring a chicken's neck?" enquired Beatrice looking at Joe for some form of confirmation.

Joe didn't feel he was in a position to confirm or deny Bob's professed abilities.

It will never be fully known what went on in the kitchen after Bob closed the door behind him but there were sounds of breaking crockery and the flutter of wings against the kitchen door and windows that indicated Bob was not the master executioner he claimed to be. When finally the chaotic noises came to an end, Bob opened the kitchen door and joined the group in the hallway looking bewildered and blooded.

"It's a bit of a mess in there," he reported. The chicken flew all over the place after I cut its head off."

The mess in the kitchen was beyond belief. Red bloodstains were everywhere, including on the walls, windows and ceiling. Beatrice was beyond herself with indignation.

"That poor bird. Bob, have you ever killed a chicken before?" she wanted to know, her eyes flashing with rage.

"Not exactly," he confessed as he made his way out of the front door and into the street. "But a mate of mine told me how to do it. The bird never suffered. Honest."

Beatrice closed the door noisily behind him.

"You don't want to take too much notice of Bob," said an embarrassed Joe. "Most of what he says or claims to know is rubbish and is quite often untrue."

Beatrice and Pam, both calling loudly from the kitchen, interrupted his assurances.

"Are you two going to clear up this mess, because we're not! And we're not going to pluck or draw the chicken either!"

Joe and Dennis cleaned the kitchen as never before. They didn't feel qualified to pluck or draw the chicken after the panic was over, particularly after Bob had made such a hash of his part of the job.

"I'll give the chicken to Sid's mother," decided Pam after seeing the reluctance of the pair to prepare the bird for the table. "She'll know what to do with it and I won't tell her how we came by it."

In the week that followed Bob's visit, Bobbyboy, who was employed by the same company as his father as a steeplejack foreman, was engaged in demolishing a chimney at a derelict factory at Bromley in south London. He and his mate, John, were using the same demolition procedures as Bob and Paul had at the old generating station, taking the chimney down brick by brick and dropping the masonry inside.

The two men working high in the sky on a local landmark attracted a great deal of attention. People living in a tall block of flats close by had a grandstand view of the daily proceedings and saw the chimney getting lower and lower as the days went by. An old sailor, Tony Bates, lived in one of the top floor flats. Each morning he brought his high powered binoculars to bear on both men when they climbed up to start work and gave his wife a running commentary on what the steeplejacks were doing as she prepared the breakfast. He had great interest in reporting on the size of the blocks of masonry being levered inside the chimney and watched in anticipation for the bouncing bricks and clouds of dust to come rushing out of the hole in the bottom after the rubble hit the chute.

At around midday that Saturday, Bobbyboy and John were sitting astride the top of the chimney cutting away and levering aside large slabs of masonry. It was a chore they had been busy with since eight o'clock that morning when, without warning, a large masonry slab immediately in front of and slightly above Bobbyboy twisted and broke into two pieces. One piece, the heavier of the two, fell back into his lap, pinning him to the top of the chimney. The other fell outside the chimney and, in so doing, careered into the scaling ladders smashing a long section into shreds and ripped them away from the side of the chimney as it fell.

John stopped hammering and looked across to the other side of the chimney as he heard the frightning sounds of the ladders being broken into to pieces and falling to the ground. He could see Bobbyboy trying to free himself from the weight of a massive block that was trapping him and heard him screaming with pain. John had to find a way to help him and attempted to crawl towards Bobbyboy over the crumbling, uneven top of the chimney. It was soon clear to see that even though he might eventually get to his foreman there would be no way down the ladders for Bobbyboy or for him to raise the alarm.

Fortunately Tony Bates was watching from the block of flats and had seen everything as it happened. After first giving his wife a commentary on what he was seeing, he dialled 999 for the emergency services.

In the meantime John could do little to help Bobbyboy for he couldn't reach him without first cutting away and levelling the brickwork at the top of the chimney. Some of it was already cracked and loose but needed to be broken free and pushed over the side before he could move in his direction. Once this was done he should be able to crawl round the top of the chimney towards Bobbyboy, but this would take some time.

John began calling down to the ground for help, but builders who had heard the sound of falling debris assumed he wanted help because the ladders had broken and couldn't get down. They had no idea that Bobbyboy was trapped on the top of the chimney unable to move.

Bobbyboy was in a very precarious position. John, realising that his foreman could topple over the edge of the chimney at any time, cut desperately away at the blocks of obstructing brickwork then inched along the top of the chimney to get hold of him. How could he let people below know of the situation? They both needed help but it would be a long ordeal before it could arrive, as there seemed to be no way up or down the chimney at this time.

Over the telephone Tony Bates warned the Fire Brigade they faced a very difficult rescue indeed. From his commentary point he gave them minute by minute accounts of what was happening and how John was progressing in his bid to get to where Bobbyboy lay.

John had a good aerial view of the fire appliances, police cars and ambulances as they arrived at the gates to the factory. They were so near yet too far away. Even if the firemen could reach them he had grave doubts they had a turntable ladder long enough to get Bobbyboy down.

John, crouching on all fours, at last reached Bobbyboy and caught hold of him. He found he couldn't move the block away, it was far too heavy. He listened to Bobbyboy's cries and tried to think of all of the possible ways of any rescuer reaching them from the ground.

What about the iron rungs built into the inside of the chimney he wondered and shouted the idea out almost as soon as it came to mind.

"Someone climb up the iron rungs inside the chimney," he called down to the firemen. "You can get to them through the hole in the side of the chimney."

A fireman with a white band round his helmet waved his hand in acknowledgement, climbed over the rubble in the yard and disappeared into the hole in the chimney with a first aid kit and a two-way radio.

John looked down through a dusty haze into the innards of the remaining stump of the once proud chimney to get a view of their rescuer. "Look out for any bent or missing irons as you climb up and don't look up," shouted John. "Your helmet should protect your head if anything breaks loose."

After an exhausting climb the fireman joined John on the top of the chimney. There was not a lot he could do from there except radio back to the fire control vehicle in the yard below to let them know how things looked from where he was. There was hardly sufficient room for two on the broken top of the chimney where Bobbyboy lay and definitely not room for three. It looked an impossible situation. How could they move the slab off Bobbyboy without causing him further serious injury?

A successful rescue was looking impossible unless they called for another team of steeplejacks to refix the scaling ladders and put lifting equipment on the top of the chimney to raise the heavy weight off Bobbyboy.

"I suppose we could do with a bloody sky hook," John suggested to the fireman in absurd desperation. "It's the only way I know of getting out of this predicament."

"That's not such a daft idea," replied the fireman after some thought. "A sky hook is just the answer we've been looking for. Let's see if we can get a rescue helicopter here straight away."

He reached for his two-way radio and spoke with his control vehicle. The crackling on the radio suggested to John that the idea had received approval and matters were being put in hand without delay.

Within seconds the Fire Brigade Control made an emergency call to the Royal Air Force Co-ordination Centre to inform them of the incident and called for immediate helicopter rescue assistance. Good luck was on everyone's side that day for the RAF informed them that an air display was being held relatively close by at the Biggin Hill airfield in Kent and a Royal Navy air/sea rescue helicopter was in attendance there and was being scrambled to the factory at Bromley.

Squawking noises coming from the fireman's radio alerted John to the news of the dispatch of the helicopter. But for them, it would seem an eternity before they saw the small profile of the helicopter on the horizon beating its way steadily towards them.

The long wait, in reality only a few minutes, was rewarded by the unmistakable sound of helicopter rotor blades thwacking the air and the roar of its engine. As the helicopter approached it circled the chimney and then stood-off a short distance at chimney top height so that the pilot could assess what he was going to do to effect the rescue. John could see the helicopter's door open with the winchman sitting in its opening waving encouragingly and looking across to him. There was a second man, the helicopter's observer, crouched behind the winchman, also looking intently at John holding onto Bobbyboy. John assumed the man sitting in the doorway would be the man who would be joining them on the end of a wire rope within the next few minutes.

The turbulence and noise of the helicopter's engine and rotors made verbal communication impossible. Hand signals and gestures were the only way to pass on intentions. From the signs given by the winchman it seemed the helicopter was going to gain height then hover over the chimney. The winchman would then drop down on the wire rope above them as the pilot manoeuvred the helicopter into position.

The helicopter's engine roared louder and its rotors thwacked with ever increasing intensity as it rose further into the sky and crabbed sideways over the chimney. John saw the winchman strapped in his harness swing out on the helicopter's rescue boom to begin his descent towards them.

Small pieces of brick and dust lifted into the sky from the top of the chimney as the helicopter hovered above until the down draught from the rotors blew the top of the chimney clean. John covered Bobbyboy's face with his hands and kept his own eyes closed whilst the dust and grit flew about and noticed the fireman had taken similar precautions of his own.

Not a second too soon the helicopter's winchman was with them, dangling precariously from the end of the wire rope like a puppet on a string. He planned to use his rescue harness to remove the heavy slab off Bobbyboy before lifting him to safety.

Hovering slightly above John, the naval man on the wire indicated he wanted his rescue harness tied to the slab. He and the slab would then be lifted away by the helicopter. The helicopter would return once the slab was off-loaded elsewhere.

John set about doing as he was bid, slid the rescue harness around the slab, pulled it tight and, with a thumbs-up sign, signalled he was ready for the lift. They would need to be very careful for Bobbyboy was now unconscious and the weight of the slab was helping to hold him in position on the top of the chimney. Once the slab was removed John was concerned he might not be able to keep Bobbyboy from falling over the side.

The winchman's outstretched arm signalled to the pilot to lift him and the slab up and away from the gevely ingured steeplejack. Grasping the heavy burden in his arms he pulled it tight into his body.

John pointed emphatically towards the inside the chimney. "Drop it down there'" he shouted.

The helicopter's winch wire tightened further as it lifted the winchman and the slab upwards and moved them slowly towards the centre of the chimney before a point was reached when the slab could be safely released. The slab dropped free and disappeared silently into the depths of the chimney without adding to the noise of the helicopter on hitting the ramp below.

During the short time it took the winchman to release the slab from the harness the fireman had taken the opportunity to work his way round to get to the other side of the limp body of Bobbyboy who was by then slipping out of John's grasp. As best they could, they held Bobbyboy between them and applied first aid dressings to his abdomen to try to stop the bleeding. By the time the helicopter's winchman returned above them the fireman and John were almost ready for Bobbyboy to be strapped into the rescue harness and winched up into the helicopter.

They watched as the winchman and Bobbyboy, dangling on the wire rope, rose higher into the sky towards the open door of the helicopter. Everyone within viewable distance, on the ground and in the air, watched in awe at the short movements of the wire rope backwards and then forwards as rescued and rescuer neared the helicopter's doorway and then saw both men pulled safely inside.

It was a short flight down to the ground where an ambulance was waiting. Bobbyboy was rapidly placed in the ambulance where he received medical treatment and was then urgently taken to hospital. The helicopter made another flight to the top of the chimney to collect the fireman and John and, after lifting them to safety and into the helicopter, deposited them on the ground a short way from the Police Control Point and a throng of observers.

Regretfully, Bobbyboy's internal injuries were so severe that he could not be saved. He died a few days later in hospital without regaining consciousness.

CHAPTER 8

BILL BENNETT

Reef Knot

Following Bob Massey saying that Bill Bennett had been taken on as his new mate, Dennis had a feeling he had heard the name before. He mentioned this to Joe after Bob had been shooed out of the family home by his mother.

"Bill Bennett. There's a name to remember. He's a small time crook and not one to get too close to."

"Did he work for the Firm at some time?" Dennis enquired.

"That's right. About a year or so ago."

Dennis could now recall Bill Bennett. He was the man he had sportingly boxed and wrestled with as a boy at a boatyard on the River Thames during one of those occasions he had gone to work with Joe on a Saturday morning. Bennett had punched him about the head and then seized him around the neck until he had almost lost consciousness. With that realisation Dennis wondered when Bennett would get his come-uppance.

Weekly wages were paid, in cash, every Friday. Joe and Dennis received theirs at home in separate wage packets, although they were sent through the post in the same registered envelope. Other men preferred not to have their wages sent by post to avoid their wife finding out how much they earned. They also preferred to receive their wages in cash on Fridays, for it was doubtful if many of them, or their families, could have managed over a weekend without cash in hand to buy cigarettes, groceries and provisions.

It had become almost a ritual for many of the steeplejacks employed by the Firm to meet late on Friday afternoons at a café in the City, as the office was close by and they could draw their wages and receive instructions for the following week.

The owner of the café was known as 'Phil the Greek'. He had earned his 'handle' because of his uncanny likeness to the Duke of Edinburgh. He knew most of the steeplejacks by name, for they had been regular customers of his over many months.

When Joe visited the Firm's office, Dennis usually waited in the van until he returned. Dennis was not to accompany him on those occasions, even though Joe could be gone for up to two hours, in case Dennis was asked too many searching questions. "No need for them to know too much," was Joe's candyd opinion. On return to the van he would let Dennis know where they would be working for the next few weeks and the type of work they would be doing. But not a lot more was brought to his notice.

On one particular Friday afternoon, Dennis was sitting in the van, parked close to the office, when he saw a small group of steeplejacks walking along the road towards him. He put up his hand to them and two of the men came over.

"Don't see you up here very often Dennis," commented one of them. "Come and join us for a cup of tea in the café while you're waiting for your father."

"I'll tell your dad where you are," said the other as he turned to go into the office.

Dennis had been waiting in the van for almost an hour and was bored watching 'shiny arsed office wallers' walking from one office block to another with pieces of paper in their hands. When he entered the cafe he found the people there to be friendly with the conversation and banter centred on how they would spend their football pools winnings, the performances of east and north London football teams and how their teams were doing in the league.

There was a short silence and then a change in the course of the conversation when another man came into the café and joined the group. Light-hearted conversation became serious business, with particular emphasis on rates of pay and bonuses. Dennis was singled out to become an item of interest, for they had suspicions Joe's team was earning more than they were. If they could find out how much Dennis was getting then that might give a clue as to Joe's and also Ken Missen's earnings.

"How much an hour do you get Dennis?"

"Two and four pence," he replied.

"Blimey, don't spend it all at once," laughed the man who had been the last to come into the café and who Dennis immediately recognised as Bill Bennett.

"I suppose your dad earns four times that amount," suggested Bill, inviting further comment that did not follow.

Bill Bennett's interest, and that of others within the group who sat in awe of him, lay in learning as much as possible about Joe, Ken and Dennis in the short time available before Joe returned to the scene. Dennis recognised their motives and pleaded ignorance, giving as little away as possible. For it was clear by this time why he had been invited into the café. He was there to receive a grilling.

The first to leave was Bill Bennett. Dennis hadn't been the push-over he was expected to be and Joe would shortly join the group. Dennis had noticed Bill slyly watching Phil the Greek to see what he was doing and where he was likely to go next. At the first opportune moment, Bill got up from the table where he had been eating and dashed across to the door leading into the street.

Phil came from behind his counter faster than a greyhound out of a trap at Romford Stadium. However, he was not fast enough tp intercept the abscondee. He called after Bill as the doorbell clanged behind him but Bill did not hear or did not want to hear what was being said. He kept looking straight ahead and walked quickly away from the café towards Chancery Lane underground station.

"The bugger's left without paying," complained Phil on his Greek accent, raising his arms in disbelief.

"He must have forgotten. He's got a lot on his mind, " said one of the group. "No doubt he'll pay next time he sees you."

Dennis had thought the Firm employed trustworthy men. Bill must have made a genuine mistake. Even Bill wouldn't have done such an underhanded thing.

"How much does he owe you Phil?" Dennis enquired. It wasn't a large sum and he paid it there and then.

"What did you do that for?" a quiet spoken male voice enquired.

Dennis looked round to find Tom Aimhurst to be the enquirer.

"Well, Bill left without paying."

"That may be so Dennis, but you should never pay another man's debts. Let this be the first and only lesson for you in such matters. Let me know how much it is and I'll pay on this occasion. I'll catch up with Bill next week and get the money back. You've got a lot to learn."

Tom Aimhurst, was a keen West Ham football club supporter and this had become known during the lighter moments of their conversation when they had first come into the café. Tom thought Ernie Gregory, West Ham's goalkeeper, had 'ands as safe as 'ouses.

Joe came into the café as Tom was explaining the responsibility for each individual to keep his own house in order. He wound up the conversation as Joe went up to the counter to order a round of teas for all of the steeplejacks in the cafe.

It was well known that Bill Bennett owed money to many people, this being the result of a flamboyant life-style. Bill kept his social life completely separate from his work. With his thin moustache freshly pencilled, he loved to be seen in the evenings and at weekends in expensive clothes, in well known pubs and driving a large car. He had a strong need to flash a thick leather wallet, padded with pound notes, over the counter of saloon bars.

Bill's bravado was really a thin veneer over an inadequate personality. He had served in the Royal Air Force for three years until the RAF recognised he was unsuited to the discipline of service life. His mother had bought him out before serious charges caught up with him.

Some months after Dennis' meeting with Bill Bennett in the café, he was sent as a matter of urgency to a factory at Stratford, in east London, to help Tom Aimhurst complete work on a factory chimney. There had been a serious problem. Bill Bennett, who had been the foreman on site, was under arrest for stealing lead from the roof of a derelict factory.

"It's difficult to understand," said Tom when Dennis joined him at the Purrkins Cat Food factory that morning. "How he thought he could get away with it."

Dennis was all ears. It seemed Bennett had received his overdue come-uppance?

Stepping from the ladders onto the scaffold around the cast-iron cap of the chimney, they looked down through the greyness of the morning and over the factory complex.

"There's Stratford Broadway over there and over there are the railway marshalling yards," Tom pointed out. "Look the other way and you can see the sprawl of east London right through to the City." He leaned against one of the guard-rails before continuing.

"See those roofs over there belonging to the disused factory? I'm told that's where Bill was caught at two o'clock in the morning, two nights ago. He was using our climbing gear to get over the wall separating the two factories and was bringing the lead back over the wall when he was spotted by a night watchman. The cops swarmed over the place within minutes and Bill was taken away in a black Maria. Silly sod will end up in gaol, that's for sure."

It was to be one of the most difficult periods in Dennis' career. The manager of Purrkins had lost trust in the Firm. Even though Tom and Dennis were fresh faces and had been called in to finish the job after the theft, whatever they did and wherever they went it was clear they were under surveillance.

Tom was generally tight-lipped about passing opinions on others. "If you can't say good about a man, then don't say anything," was one of his favourite sayings. However, with Dennis and he on the receiving end of comments made by a hostile factory manager, Tom became less reticent about Bill Bennett who had been summarily sacked by the Firm and would later receive a term of imprisonment for the theft. Over cups of tea in the factory's canteen he told Dennis of some of Bennett's past history.

Bennett had been involved with an east end gang for a number of years. Their common interests lay in anything that made money without too much effort being required of them. Dennis knew Bennett was a small time thief who also fenced stolen goods for the gang. What he didn't know was that Bennett was in considerable debt to the gang of thugs, not having paid for some of the goods he had fenced on their behalf.

On an earlier occasion, when Bennett had been in a similar situation, two 'hard men' had been sent to 'do him over'. Bennett realised he was in danger as he walked along the Longbridge Road at Barking, but had managed to escape from a severe beating by running after and catching hold of the pole on the passenger platform of a number 87 bus heading for the railway station. He told Tom after the incident that although he had managed to keep hold of the pole as his feet left the ground, his arm had almost been pulled out of its socket.

Bill Bennett's first car had been a pre-war Morris 8 that was regularly used to take his mates around the east end and to travel to and from work. The car was also used to move stolen goods from one place to another.

After the War, a number of disused factories were being demolished in London to make way for new housing, usually blocks of flats. Bennett had set up his own demolition business to take advantage of the work available at that time. One of the demolition contracts involved him and a mate taking down and cutting up a large lead tank, although the disposal of the scrap lead was not included in his contract. It seemed shameful to Bill to leave the lead unattended in the factory overnight.

Bennett devised a plan that would beat the security guard at the factory's gate. He knew that the rear seat of a Morris 8 had two removable air cushions. If he cut up the lead into small enough pieces and took out the airbags he could hide the lead inside and under the leather covers. No one would be the wiser. Provided he could get the car into the factory, his plan must work.

Using the pretext he had a number of heavy tools to bring in to the factory, the security guard gave Bennett a vehicle pass that permitted him to park his car next to the building where he was working. This suited Bennett perfectly.

Late every afternoon, on finishing work, he made journeys from the factory direct to the local scrap metal merchant with the stolen lead packed tightly under and in the rear seat covers. The weighbridge at the scrap metal merchants showed that Bennett was bringing in just over half a ton of metal on each occasion.

The bonanza did not last long. For on one of the journeys to the scrap metal merchants the car's handbrake jammed on. If Bennett stopped, it would have been embarrassing if the police showed interest in his car. He decided to drive on to the scrap merchants with the car's engine labouring, clutch slipping and brakes overheating.

After the car was unloaded, the handbrake freed itself. Later, when he got home and crawled under the car to see what the problem might have been, he found the chassis had broken about mid way along its length due to the extra weight the car had been carrying. The Morris was a complete right-off. The cost of buying another car would have to be deducted from the proceeds of his scrap metal enterprise.

After Bill Bennett served his term in gaol, he managed to get another job as a steeplejack's mate with Bob Massey, working for a competing company. They would work together on a steel chimney at a carbon producing factory in south east London.

CHAPTER 9

THE FALL GUY

Wire Rope Grip

Bill Bennett's term of imprisonment changed his character beyond all recognition. He found prison to be a hard mistress and had no intention of returning there. Mary, his girlfriend of many years, had stood by him while he was locked away and had agreed to marry him shortly after he completed his sentence. The change in Bill's attitude was so noticeable that Bob Massey spoke up for him and successfully convinced his employers to give Bill a job with him as a steeplejack's mate.

Bob and Bill (Bed and Breakfast as they were to become known) had been working together for about a month and, after completing the demolition work at the old generating station in Kent, were engaged in renewing a steel chimney at the carbon factory in south east London.

The ninety-foot chimney at the carbon factory was built in sections with steel ladders permanently attached to its side. The flanges at the end of each section of chimney joined one section to another and provided fixing points for the ladders and six evenly spaced guy ropes that looped out at two levels to anchorage points on the ground.

The bottom one third of the rusty chimney was under cover of the asbestos boiler house roof whilst the other two thirds jutted out through the roof like a long, black cigar.

Immediately after lunch, Bob and Bill arrived on site in an open, flat-bedded lorry. Bob being in the cab with the driver and Bill sitting among the gear at the back.

"My arse is pleased we've arrived," said Bill as he jumped stiffly from the deck of the lorry rubbing his rear parts to bring them back to life again. "This looks a god forsaken hole if ever I saw one. I could imagine myself working here for a day or two and never wanting to come back."

After reporting their presence to the factory's gatekeeper, Bob dropped the lorry's sideboards whilst continuing to listen to Bill complaining about the journey. Both men looked towards the driver to give them a hand for there was a lot of gear to move and they would have their work cut out to get all of it off the lorry before five o'clock.

"Going to give us a hand mate?" enquired Bob.

"Not me comrade. Can't do that. I'm paid to drive the lorry, not to load or unload it," was the reply from the driver who remained seated in his cab with a flask of tea on the engine cowl and his sandwich box open at the ready.

Bill wanted to join in the conversation with his own words of criticism but changed his mind.

"Shows you how far we've advanced with the nationalised industries," Bob commented to Bill who was within easy earshot of the driver.

"You hire a lorry and a driver from them and that's just what you get. No more and no less."

His less than complimentary words fell on deaf ears for the driver couldn't hear anything that was said through the newsprint of that day's Daily Mirror.

Fired up with indignation, both men set about the task of off-loading the gear from the lorry and began carrying it into the boiler house where it was to be stored.

The steel derrick sections still on the lorry were newly designed and this would be the first time Bob and Bill had had the opportunity to use them. A strong man could carry one of the four feet triangular sections, but it was more comfortable if two men worked together. Each of the lattice work sections had a flange at both ends that could to be bolted to another section to form a slim, climbable tower.

"May as well leave these derrick sections and the winch close to where we'll need them tomorrow," suggested Bob. "No need to pick them up twice when once will do."

Bob and Bill got stuck in to move all of the sections of derrick and equipment close to the bottom of the old chimney and finished ten minutes before their time to knock-off from work. Each time they returned to the lorry for another load they looked towards where the driver still sitting reading his paper hoping he would have a change of mind and give them a hand. But it was not to be. Bolshy Barry, the driver, stuck to his principles and refused to leave his cab until he saw the manual work was finished.

"If you knew you needed three men to off-load the lorry you should have brought another man along," he suggested to them after his thick skin was at last penetrated by dagger-like glances. "That would have given someone else a job instead of them being on the dole unable to feed their family. It's as well you're finished now because it's time for me to get back to my depot. If you had been any longer I would have had to take any remaining load on the lorry back with me. I don't work overtime as it deprives my brothers of work."

"We would like a lift to the railway station brother," said Bob opening the door of the cab forcefully after the lorry had been unloaded. It's on your way back to the depot and it can be either with you or without you personally driving the lorry, if you get my drift."

With Bob's intentions fully understood Bolshy Barry got off his bottom, secured the side boards of the lorry and returned to his driving seat in the cab. Being without too many options, he drove the lorry out of the carbon factory with his passengers and dropped them off at the railway station on the way back to his depot.

"I've made a note of your names," he told Bob as he got out of the cab. "At the right time you'll be hearing further from me and my brothers about this."

"Come the revolution, I suppose so," replied Bob. "But make sure brother that you live long enough to see it happen."

The next morning Bob and Bill positioned the first section of derrick on the concrete floor alongside the old chimney inside the boiler house. One section after another was bolted onto the one below it and guy ropes were attached until the top section of derrick reached the inside of the asbestos roof. Bob, who had taken on the responsibility for erecting the new tool, paused at this point to remove a section of asbestos sheeting from the roof to allow the derrick to pass through the opening. Having removed the asbestos sheet, he continued with the erection of the derrick until it stood two sections higher than the top of the steel chimney.

At the top of the last section he fitted the lifting tackle in place and set up his boson's chair.

Bob tied a wire hawser to the top section of the chimney and shackled the free end of the winch wire to it. He called down to Bill to 'take the weight' of the chimney section with the winch wire while he undid the rusty bolts holding the top two sections together. The ring spanners in his haversack were usually more than capable of moving the heavy-duty nuts but in this instance, because the chimney had been out of use for some time, the nuts had rusted onto the bolts and resisted all of Bob's efforts to move them.

"You'll have to use a hammer and chisel to crack those sods," shouted Bill from the ground. "I'll get them and tie them to the end of your riding line and you can pull them up."

Resorting to heavy-handed methods proved to be successful and the resisting nuts were cut in halves with the hammer and chisel and the bolts hammered through the drilled holes in the flange. As the last bolt was driven out, the top chimney section suspended from the winch wire, drifted away from the derrick and then swung back again to its original position with a resounding 'clang'. The section rotated a quarter of a turn and then swung from side to side for a while until its momentum eddied away after which Bill lowered it to the ground with the hand winch.

In all, Bob and Bill took down and replaced nine chimney sections and their steadying guy ropes in two days. But they had three other jobs to do before their work at the carbon factory was finished. These involved greasing the guy ropes, painting the new chimney and taking down the derrick.

"I suppose you're going to ask me to grease the guy ropes," winged Bill as Bob collected a large tin of tallow from the carbon works storeman.

"Seeing that I took down the old chimney and then put the new one up again it seems only fair you should do the greasing," insisted Bob. "Besides you're a younger and fitter man than I am. It'll take both of us to do the job. You shackle your boson's chair to the guy rope and I'll lower you down as you grease it. Now that must be a good compromise."

"That may be a good compromise from your point of view," worried Bill. " But the wind's getting up and I'm going to have a rough ride hanging from the guy rope. None of your tricks and don't let me down too fast!" he insisted. "I'll let you know every time I'm ready to be lowered."

Bob knew how it felt to be the grease monkey. He'd done the job many times before and had never looked forward to it.

"Have no fear. Bob is here," he joked as he held onto the end of Bill's riding line. "I'll be very gentle with you."

Bill dangled, greased and glided down all of the six guy ropes in turn. Bob, recognised Bill's concern at taking on the job and kept to his word until Bill was half way down the last guy rope. He couldn't resist the temptation. With a sack protecting his hands, Bob let the riding line slip free for about six feet. Furious language from a swaying, bobbing Bill confirmed the desired effect had been achieved. After roaring with laughter at the Bill's reactions, Bob pulled him up again to where he had been on the guy rope before his sinking feeling had begun.

The day after Bob and Bill finished greasing the guy ropes they returned to the carbon factory to paint the chimney. Their riding tackles, with boson's chairs attached, were already in place hanging over the top chimney flange on *chimney hangers* (long steel hooks with rings forged onto one end of them). They were to apply two coats of bitumastic paint to the chimney over the next two days and after that they planned to take the derrick down and then have a 'freeby' day off without letting the company know. Bill could then take his new wife shopping to buy curtains for the front room window, something she had been pressing him to get for some time.

Suspended in their boson's chairs they toshed on the first coat of paint, dropping down their riding lines a yard at a time in competition with one-another, keeping below the wet paint line. Reaching the bottom of the chimney they neatly finished off the painted surface where it connected to the boiler and left the paint to dry overnight. Bill pulled the riding lines away from the side of the chimney and tied them to a stanchion to stop the ropes rubbing on the fresh paint before knocking-off for the day.

The following morning the factory's storeman met up with Bob when they arrived on site.

"Got a moment?" he enquired.

"You go on Bill," Bob suggested to his mate. "I'll join you in a few minutes after I've finished here."

Bob joined the storeman in conversation as Bill continued on towards the chimney to release the riding lines and get the paint and brushes.

"One of your mates called in last night after you left," reported the storeman. "Said he had been sent to bring you some new fittings for the steel derrick. There's been a modification to the lifting arm and he's fitted it for you."

"That must have been Battey Butler," said Bob. "He's the only one I know who would take the trouble to bring a modification out to the job without letting us know. Thanks for telling me."

Bob left the storeman and went inside the boiler house and along to the chimney in time to see Bill start up the ladders.

"Seems Battey Butler came out last evening to fit some modifications to the derrick," he shouted upwards in Bill's direction. "We'll check on what he's done when we take it down."

Bill looked down on hearing Bob's shouting and waved in acknowledgement. Another few steps up the ladder and he would be within reach of a boson's chair.

Once Bill was seated, Bob was to send up two buckets of bitumastic paint on the hauling line and then join him with the intention of toshing on the final coat of paint by late afternoon.

Reaching the top of the ladder, Bill was seen to pause before lowering himself into the boson's chair. Bob noted Bill had chosen the boson's chair he had been working from the previous day.

"Crafty bugger," he shouted up to him. "You've chosen the sunny side of the chimney this morning. I'll pull the paint up when you're ready."

Bill waved an arm, then shouted something inaudible as he untied the chair from the ladder. He stepped through the ropes holding the boson's chair to the riding line ready to slide down onto his seat. What he said will never be known, for the swan-necked block, chimney hanger and riding line, with Bill half in the boson's chair, came hurtling down towards the roof of the boiler house.

Bill desperately reached for the ladder as he fell. He managed to thrust a leg between two of the ladder rungs. This action broke his fall for a split second as his leg became entangled in the rungs of the ladder and his body slammed into the side of the chimney. The force of Bill's descent was so great that the weight of his body tore off his lower leg and he continued to fall towards the roof, entwined in his riding line.

Bill died immediately his head burst through the asbestos roof and hit a roof girder. His body somersaulted and, with a sickening thump, it fell behind the boiler onto the factory floor below. The only remaining record Bob could see of the fatal fall was the swan-necked block swinging from a length of rope and knocking metalically on a roof girder.

Bob was a shaken man. It would be left to him to break the news of Bill's death to Mary, Bill's wife of a few weeks.

Bob Massey made a point of calling on Joe a day or two after Bill Bennett's death. After settling into an armchair in the sitting room, he relaxed a little. Beatrice brought in cups of tea and ginger biscuits on a plate.

"I haven't got a chicken with me today Beatrice. I apologise for what happened the last time I was here."

"No apologies necessary Bob," she said. "I'm so sorry to hear about Bobbyboy and now, of course about Bill. As you know we knew Bobbyboy very well throughout his short life. It's a great tragedy."

It appeared Beatrice had less concern about the loss for Bill Bennett when later Dennis spoke with her in the kitchen. "He was a villain who got involved in all kinds of dreadful things," she said. "Not a nice man at all. I know that you shouldn't speak ill of the dead, but I can't think of much to say about him that's good. He brought, what he called 'stuff' over here some time ago for us to keep until he could find a buyer for it. The 'stuff' turned out to be office equipment, typewriters, adding machines and an electric fan he had stolen after breaking into an office. When we saw what it was, we told him to take it away." She left the subject of the conversation at that.

Dennis joined Joe and Bob in the sitting room. Bob was in the middle of explaining how Bill Bennett had met his end.

Sipping at his tea, Bob continued. "First it was Paul and me, then Bobbyboy. I thought I would never get over losing him. His mother still cries every night when he doesn't come home. Now Bill Bennett's bought it. It should have been me. I used the chair he was sitting in the day before. I'm bloody sure someone changed the chimney hanger to a larger one than should have been there. And I think I know who it was!"

Bob looked a man who was set on revenge when he left the house later that day.

CHAPTER 10

SNAKES AND LADDERS

Sheet Bend

The Press is always interested in taking photographs and reporting on repairs to tall buildings, particularly in London where these structures may have been historical landmarks for many years. This was the case when work started on a very tall brick chimney in a factory that made sheet lead on the north bank of the Thames on the Isle of Dogs.

The chimney was notorious for being one of the worst to climb in the country for its brickwork had been permeated by fumes from the lead manufacturing process. Dennis had had first hand experience of the chimney some ten months earlier when Joe and he refixed the lightning conductor that had come loose at its very top. It was clear then that the lightning conductor should be replaced in its entirety but they had not received the order to carry out the work in full. Joe had reported the condition of the chimney to the Firm and pointed out the state of structural deterioration he had found. The crumbling brickwork had reached a point where it became necessary to double-up on the number of dogs (steel hooks) driven into the brickwork to secure the scaling ladders.

The chimney moved alarmingly as it was climbed, swaying with the force of the wind that blew off the River Thames as a poplar tree might do in a stiff breeze.

Some steeplejacks had tested the flexing of the stack to almost its full potential, although they reserved this experience for novice steeplejacks when they climbed the chimney for the first time. Standing inside the cast iron cap at the top, they deliberately increased its backwards and forwards motion by moving the weight of their body in time with its natural rocking movements. When Joe had demonstrated the movement to Dennis he found it to be a very alarming experience to say the least.

Bob Massey had joined the Firm as a foreman steeplejack following the death of Bill Bennett. He felt that a change of employer would be for the better after taking recent events into account. He and his new mate, Reg Brundell, had been given the job of inspecting the lead works chimney for repairs and to renew the lightning conductor that had deteriorated even further over recent months.

Bob was determined to attract the attention of the national Press to the work he and Reg were about to undertake on the Thameside chimney, albeit that they would be on site for only a few days. He had received approval for the Press to enter the factory to take photographs of Reg and himself at work for it could enhance the public image of the Firm and also that of the lead factory.

Bob was looking forward to being photographed climbing up the outside of the chimney and to the close-up photographs of him looking over the Thames from the top. Reg Brundell, an ex-paratrooper who claimed to have the inclination to jump off the top of chimneys if only he had a parachute with him, agreed to take the photographs because the Press photographer was not suited to working at such heights.

As arranged, the men and women of the Press arrived at the lead works at nine o'clock that Tuesday morning with their cameras and recording equipment. Bob, freshly shaven, in a new boiler suit and smart cloth cap, was taken to one side to be photographed and interviewed before beginning his climb to fame. His attempt at personal publicity seemed to be paying off and he hoped he might become a national celebrity.

During the interview Bob referred to the other locations he had recently worked at and the three incidents involving Paul, himself, Bobbyboy and Bill Bennett. He placed particular emphasis on the short length of time it would take to inspect the chimney and for them to renew the lightning conductor. If the weather remained good they would be finished within the next two days.

The Press reporters agreed with Bob that it would be in everyone's interest if the interview material could be published that night, or the next day at the latest, for the most effective publicity, otherwise the Press reports would appear after work had finished on the chimney.

The interview over, Bob walked across the yard to the foot of the chimney to begin his climb to the top. Reg Brundell had already made his way up and was concealed with a pressman's camera in the cast iron capping, away from the smoke and heat. The photographers on the ground clicked away as Bob waved cheerfully from the ladders that snaked their way to the top. Bravado made him make the climb without pausing for rest and by the time he reached the final ladder he was almost exhausted by the effort.

Reg, seeing Bob's cloth cap appear over the top of the last ladder, pointed the camera at him and snapped off six photo frames in rapid succession.

"I've got you on film now," he said. "These pictures could be worth a fortune in a day or two."

Bob stepped from the ladder, sat down and swung his legs over the cap of the chimney to join Reg.

"That went very well," he gasped. "But I feel knackered. I must be getting old as I used to make it up here with some breath left. Not so today!"

The view was spectacular in the morning sunlight. The Isle of Dogs lay beneath and behind them. Buildings within the square mile of the City of London could be seen on the horizon to the west of a shining River Thames. Up-river, flotillas of barges rode at peace on their moorings among companies of nodding cranes on their riverside jetties. But the panorama disguised the real purpose why Bob and Reg were there.

"Do you think we'll get the publicity we're after?" wondered Reg.

Bob felt this would be the case and went on to mock the Bard. "As Shakespeare once said, 'tis one thing to set up the props on the stage, but tis not certain that all the players will be there on the first night."

Bob and Reg had told their families how essential it was for them to complete the work at the lead works within two days, even if this meant working at night as well as during the day. The boilers feeding into the chimney shaft would be closed down during the two days to allow them to fix lightning conductors around the top of the shaft. With this white lie they had completed a plan of entrapment. No one else was to be taken into their confidence about the plan in case any part of it leaked out and their meticulous planning came to nothing.

Almost everyone interested in the steeplejacking business had got to know that Bob and Reg were to be mentioned in the national Press the following day. However, not many people were aware that they would also be included that evening in a Home Service documentary programme on the radio covering air pollution. Bob and Reg knew and listened intently to hear their names mentioned and were delighted with the result.

The next morning, on the way to the lead works, they bought a newspaper at a kiosk outside Barking Railway Station to find a photograph of Bob on the inside page. The caption above it read, 'Bob is Head and Shoulders Above London'. There for the world to see were Bob's features pictured as broad as daylight with the City of London in the background. Bob felt he would now be classified among the major celebrities of the day and Reg was beginning to wonder whether he should personally change his job and become a newspaper's cameraman.

Even after the publicity neither Bob nor Reg were completely sure their intended prey had heard or read of their presence on the Isle of Dogs, but they were hopeful this would be the case. During the next forty-eight hours they worked twelve hour shifts during the day and at other times one of them always stayed close to the chimney whilst the other relaxed or slept in the boiler house. They didn't want to miss an expected visitor.

Except for a small disturbance at the main gate to the factory at a late hour during the first evening, when a drunk sang loudly and rattled the gates next to the security guard's hut, the night passed peacefully. The next morning they were both subdued with doubts as to whether the bait was going to be taken up.

"We must give the bastard another night," said Reg in a positive way. "These things don't always happen when you expect them to. We have to stay vigilant as he's bound to turn up very soon, then we'll have him for sure. I'm looking forward to collecting my bounty!"

"You'll have to earn it first," said Bob. "No half measures Reg, it's shit or bust for both of us. Don't forget to loosen off the ladder ties half way up the stack before we finish this evening."

"No problem," assured Reg. "There'll be a positive outcome to this, that's for sure. The Paras aren't known for taking half measures when full measures are deserved."

Around eleven o'clock that night, Reg was on watch in the yard when he thought he heard the sound of soft footsteps making their way towards him. He was not completely sure, because a gentle breeze had been blowing through the yard and this had turned into short gusts of wind that now blew pieces of loose cardboard skidding over the ground. Reg hid alongside a pile of rusty steam pipes that lay in the yard just outside the boiler house door to observe who might be approaching. Looking through one of the pipes he was sure he could see the outline of a man. The man was keeping close to the wall of the machine shop, his faint shadow thrown to the side by the light from the lamp that lit the doorway to the fitters' tool room.

"Here he comes," Reg murmured to himself. "Let's see what this bastard plans to get up to."

The shadowy figure went across to a steel gantry where the riding line had been tied away from the side of the chimney. He undid the rope lashing holding the riding line in place, picked up the boson's chair and loose coils of rope and stole across the yard to place them against the chimney.

Gusts of wind soon caught hold of the long lengths of riding line hanging from the top of the chimney. It moved the ropes away from the side of the chimney and then let them go again. As the rope fell back it tapped gently on the ladders as though to alert Bob, who was inside the boiler house, that something unusual had begun to happen.

Bob had made himself comfortable for the night hours in the boiler house. He was lying in the middle of a coil of rope placed over a wheelbarrow. The handles and legs of the barrow being the legs of his bed; his head rested on an old pullover he had brought from home.

Bob became fully alert when he heard the tapping of the rope. Pebbles of steam coal rolled under his feet and crumbled as he trod on them after he got up from his makeshift bed. He crept towards the door of the boiler house, switching off the lights as he went. He knew that Reg would be out there on his own, but the plan was for him to stay by the boiler house door until Reg called for him to come out into the yard.

He couldn't resist opening the door a little to look out into the night and, hopefully to see what was happening. Glancing round the corner of the doorway, he could see someone at the bottom of the ladders preparing to climb up. It wasn't possible to see who it was in the darkness, but he guessed he knew. A little to the left of the doorway he could make out the prone figure of Reg concealed behind the steam pipes.

The night visitor climbed the ladders until he reached about half-way up the chimney. He might have continued to the very top if he had not found that the riding line was tied very securely to the ladders at that point. He paused, slid his leg over a rung of the ladder and sat back in true steeplejack fashion in preparation to untie the offending rope.

Before the climber had time to untie the riding line from the ladder, Reg yelled to Bob "Go man. Go!" as he raced from his hiding place to grasp the riding line and boson's chair. He and Bob reached their objective at about the same time. Both men heaved and jerked on the rope as they ran back with it into the centre of the yard. The tension they applied to the rope pulled at the ladders and the dogs holding them to the face of the chimney. Reg had done his preparatory work to perfection, the dogs popped out of the brickwork like champagne corks out of a bottle. A long section of ladders moved lazily away from the face of the chimney and the silhouette of a man could be seen clinging onto one of them in the darkness.

The long section of ladders hung in the air for a while. Then gracefully the lower ones broke away from those above them and fell to the ground breaking into pieces as they hit the concrete. This process continued until only one ladder was left below the point where the riding line was tied to it. The two men holding onto the rope on the ground seemed unconcerned about the cries for help coming from the man clinging to this ladder.

"Give him a twirl Reg," shouted Bob in a voice loud enough for everyone in the factory to hear.

They heaved on the rope and spun the unhappy climber round in a circle high above their heads. The side of the chimney loomed so close to the circling ladder that the man clinging to it came within an ace of being scraped off like a piece of cheese going through a cheese scraper.

"Now we'll put him out to dry for an hour or two," decided Bob as they kept tight hold of the rope and ran towards the steel gantry. "We'll tie the ends of the riding line here and leave the bastard hanging where he is until it gets light."

The cries from overhead got louder as the climber realised what was about to happen to him. There was only one way down. He could have chosen to slide down the riding line, but a hostile reception party was waiting for him at the bottom. The climber decided to wait and take his chances with others, should they arrive.

The terrified cries of the climber, the shouts of jubilation from Bob and the noise of falling ladders as they crashed to the ground were heard by security staff at the main gate. Within minutes a posse of police cars with flashing blue lights and bleating two-way radios appeared on the scene followed a few minutes later by an ambulance and the Fire Brigade with a turntable ladder.

They found more than they could possibly have expected when the Brigade's floodlights were trained on the chimney. Puzzled policemen tried hard to find out what had happened but Bob and Reg were reticent about their knowledge of events that led to a man being suspended on a ladder half way up an industrial chimney in the middle of the night. They were also unsure how to get him down, at least until daylight, as the Fire Brigade's turntable ladder was far too short to reach him.

A police sergeant attempted to speak with the man on the ladder by shouting up to him, but this had little effect on someone who's brain had been numbed by earlier traumatic experiences. The firemen felt obliged to attempt a rescue by some means and, rather than see anyone put themselves in danger, Bob and Reg agreed to work from the turntable ladder with the aid of the floodlights to reinstall the scaling ladders up to the suspended climber.

Reg would not let Bob take on the work of reladdering the chimney. He knew there was the likelihood of an ugly scene if Bob reached the climber before anyone else. Reg would do it, albeit in his own time and after a proper assessment of situation.

It took Reg an hour to fix a new set of ladders to the face of the chimney from where the turntable ladder ended. Bob released the riding line from the steel gantry and eased the suspended ladder back to the side of the chimney with its clinging human cargo. In the full glare of the floodlights Reg coaxed the unhappy climber to scramble from the swinging ladder onto the safety of the newly erected ones. Step by step they made their way down the scaling ladders and onto the turntable ladder where a fireman lead them down to the comparative safety of the ground.

With trepidation the climber turned to look for refuge among a group of policemen, Bob caught sight of the climber's face outlined by the headlights of a police car. He immediately recognised the face to be that belonging to Bert, the café owner from Medway. Thrusting forward, Bob chinned him with a cracking right uppercut with the sole purpose of putting his lights out for the night.

Two police constables wrestled an incensed Bob Massey to the ground, placed his arms behind his back, attached handcuffs to his wrists and sat on him to avoid any further chance of violence.

"Ask the bastard what he was doing here!" demanded Bob from beneath the bulk of the restraining officers. "Ask him what he knows about the murder of Bill Bennett and the attempted murder of Paul and me at Medway! Go on. Ask the bastard!"

Bob was helped to his feet. He stood there exhausted by emotion and the restraining measures the policemen had taken. He told the police sergeant that he and Reg had suspected there would be an attempt on his life sometime that week by the same person who had killed Bill Bennett. There was no doubt in Bob's mind that Bert was on his way to the top of the chimney to sabotage their riding tackle.

Bert was lying on the ground concussed and receiving attention from two ambulancemen. He was loaded into an ambulance and a policeman was detailed to travel with him to hospital. A statement would be required when he had recovered sufficiently to do so.

Bob and Reg began to realise they could be in a difficult position and would need to clarify the reasons they had taken the measures they had. But it could be said they had only made a citizen's arrest of a suspect who was certainly up to no good.

They volunteered to make their own statements at the local police station and after completing the formalities and eating a hearty breakfast in the police canteen, they were told they could leave and go about their lawful business. No charges were ever brought against them.

It would take some months for the whole truth to be revealed at the Old Bailey where Bert was successfully charged with the murder of Bill Bennett and the attempted murder of Bob and Paul. His murderous actions had been prompted by jealousy and lust for June at the café and the damage that Bob and Paul had done to his treasured car. The separation of Bert and his wife following his discovery of her in compromising circumstances was a key factor used by his defence lawyers, but she was never present during the trial.

Bob dined on the story for many years. He paid Reg a bounty for his co-operation in the entrapment of "Bert the Bastard", as the café owner became known. What the sum of the bounty was, he would never reveal, but Reg was a frequent visitor to Bob's home thereafter, particularly when Bob was working away from home.

CHAPTER 11

A BURNING SENSATION

Back Splice

Graham Potts joined the Firm just before his sixteenth birthday. He was a very big lad for his age, six feet four tall, well built and good looking. Graham had his downside too. He was loud-spoken and self-opinionated and eventually became ridiculed by the many people he upset.

At school, Graham had earned the nickname of 'Potty', but at work he was better known as 'Enos' after the fruit salts and his 'know-all' attitude. Enos could be strung along without knowing he was the butt of someone's joke.

Dennis worked with Graham on just the one occasion, at the newly built Malvern crematorium in Surrey where a lightning conductor and a cast iron edifice was to be installed on the crematorium's chimney.

Joe had been given instructions to complete the job without interrupting the operation of the crematorium as the crematorium's superintendent was in a panic. A flu epidemic was rampant and had taken its toll of many elderly and frail people in the area. The superintendent was unsure where he was to store the bodies awaiting cremation. Even with the burners working at full capacity he had difficulty clearing the backlog. Joe's original request to have the burners turned off while work on the chimney was in progress had raised the superintendent's blood pressure to danger point.

Joe and Dennis met Graham at seven o'clock one frosty morning on the A13 Trunk road at Dagenham. Graham was waiting by the Chequers public house looking blue with cold, shoulders hunched, hands in his pockets and haversack over his shoulder. He looked relieved when the Ford van drew up beside him just before the traffic lights and reached for the door handle on the passenger's side of the van.

Dennis, seated in the passenger's seat, could vaguely see what was about to happen. He shouted through the frosted window,

"Graham, don't touch the handle!"

Graham couldn't see Dennis through the iced up side window and didn't hear the warning because of the noise of passing traffic. As he grasped the handle and pulled the door towards him the door came away from its top hinge and hung at a crazy angle over the pavement.

Dennis had got into the van from the driver's side earlier that morning as the rusted frame around the passenger's door had been threatening to break up for the past few days. Joe had decided not to use the passenger door again until it could be repaired.

Graham, still holding the door handle in his hand, looked bewildered. "Sorry Joe" he apologised. "Didn't know my own strength. What do you want me to do with it now?"

"Not to worry Graham." Joe reassured him. "Keep hold of the door until I get out and take it from you. We've been expecting that to happen. Get into the back of the van when you're ready and make yourself comfortable."

Once Joe had hold of the door, Graham squeezed his bulk past Dennis and clambered in.

"Where do I sit?" he asked.

Joe lifted the door into a nearly closed position, then opened it again to tell Graham to sit in the middle of a coil of rope on the floor of the van. He slammed the door hard to until the lock clicked into place and returned to the driver's side of the van.

Joe stood in the road pressed up to the van ready to open the driver's door once a gap in the traffic permitted. He proved to be a past master at ignoring the beeps and shouts from irritated car and lorry drivers queuing up behind the van waiting to pass.

A car managed to get by, its wing mirror almost clipping Joe's arm. Someone shouted from within it, "You with the 'f***ing froze up windows. Get that f***ing tin can off the road."

"I've upset at least one person this morning," said Joe as he corkscrewed himself into the driver's seat then wound the window down to scrape the frost off the door mirror before driving off. "Everyone's in a bugger's rush this time of the morning."

Graham soon found the benefits a coil of rope could bring to a weary traveller, or to a traveller who hadn't previously had a full night's sleep. Within ten minutes he was asleep, his head nodding in time with the bumping of the van as it drove over the cobbled streets of the east end of London.

The journey along the A13 to the Blackwall Tunnel proved uneventful. Immaculately turned out Tate and Lyle liveried Scammel trucks, powered by their Gardner diesel engines, steadily maintained their position beside the van as they passed by the tall walls of the dock and eventually turned into the entrance to the tunnel.

The white tiled walls of the tunnel were as dirty as ever from the exhausts of ten thousand engines. The lorry driver in front of the van stopped regularly at each of the bends in the tunnel to allow other large oncoming vehicles to manoeuvre round the tight turns ahead of him. He waited until a flash of headlights signalled there was sufficient room for him to drive forward once again round the next tight turn in the tunnel.

After a while, daylight could seen filtering round the last bend in the tunnel and heard the gearbox grinding the van up the slope into the morning sunshine. The sun rose more fully in the sky as they drove south. Ice on the side windows turned into a slushy mass before slipping down and being flipped away in the slipstream. The van's engine churned on and the miles past by until they reached the outskirts of Malvern and could see the newly laid out crematorium at the end of the road.

The crematorium had only recently been finished and the builders' scaffolding was still in place around the tower. Being curious and not having worked on such a building before, Dennis peered in through an open doorway next to the tower. Backing onto the wall in front of him looked to be a very tall, old fashioned kitchen range with a bank of four square doors.

Taking a second look Dennis noted all of its doors were closed but its clean, white enamel finish suggested it couldn't be so old after all.

"You're interested in seeing what we do in here son?" enquired a gravely voice that seemed to come from nowhere. "Come in. Don't stand out there in the cold."

Dennis was taken aback by the depth of the voice and looked into the room once again, not sure whether to go forward and accept the invitation or step back and make out he hadn't heard anyone speak. He now realised he was looking into the place where bodies were burned and all of the cremators were in use.

Dennis, Joe and Graham filed into the room, one pushing the other in front of him, trying to give the impression that it was all in a day's work.

"Come on, don't be shy. Come over here. I'm just sorting out the ash list for today. I have to make sure the right ashes go into the right urns." The speaker was a tall, bony man with dark, deep-set eyes topped by eyebrows long overdue for attention by a barber. He certainly looked the part for the job.

"I'm Cyril. The crematorium's a bit crowded this week." He spoke with the air of a man who knew and enjoyed his work. "Never had so many visitors stay for so long. They normally come in through the hatch and, within the day, leave by the chimney."

Dennis hoped Cyril was talking of the dead and not about them.

A number of coffins could be seen stacked around the walls of the room. Cyril peered at Dennis as he viewed the scene through disbelieving eyes.

"Oh, they're all full," he said. "We don't take empties in here. Some of them talk to you if you listen carefully, but they're all very friendly. Never hear a cross word from any of them although their manners can leave something to be desired when I move them around on the trolley."

This was a new experience for Dennis and he could see from Graham's face, it was new to him as well.

"These are the cremators," Cyril continued. "It takes about four hours to do the job. You can take a look through this inspection hole if you like. This one here is about to sit up. It always happens after the coffin burns away, just before the body disintegrates."

Graham joined in the conversation after a long unnatural silence on his behalf. "I'll take your word for it," he agreed and drew back from the inspection hole.

"I see you have an intruder alarm fitted to the windows and doors," commented Dennis after he spotted the wires leading to the sensors. "I wouldn't have thought you had anything in here that anyone in their right mind would want to steal."

"Now that's an interesting observation," replied Cyril. "It's not what might be taken out of here that concerns us you see. It's what might be brought in whilst we're not around. Somebody might want to bump off their mother-in-law and there can't be many better places to get rid of her remains than in a crematorium."

"I hadn't thought of that," said Dennis thoughtfully. "Do you know if anyone has ever tried to burn a body in a crematorium to conceal a murder?"

"Not that I am aware of," answered Cyril. "But Sod's Law being what it is, there will come a time when it's tried by someone if it hasn't already been attempted."

No one knew where Joe had gone, but he certainly wasn't there to join in the conversation.

"We would like to close the burners down this afternoon for maintenance, but we're so busy it won't be possible. Hope that's alright and fits in with your schedule," apologised Cyril.

"I'll let Joe know," Dennis replied, taking the opportunity to leave the room to find him. He sensed Graham was close behind as he went through the doorway and out into the yard.

They found Joe close to the tower, that in reality was the chimney leading from the cremators, preparing the lightning conductor materials.

"So you've met Cyril," he said. "Unusual character, isn't he? I met him on my first visit here a month or two ago. He frightens the life out of me."

Joe preferred to ignore Cyril's operational problems and to concentrate on the business he knew best.

"I think we should run the lightning conductor tape this morning and this afternoon we can place the ornament on top of the chimney. They should be a fairly straightforward jobs," he suggested.

Graham was given the job of running the lightning conductor tape down the wall of the tower from the builders' scaffold whilst Dennis drilled holes on the top of each corner of the tower for the base plates of the lightning conductor finials.

"Keep out of the smoke," Dennis had been told before starting to drill the holes. He tried hard to follow this advice, but after a while he would have given anything to be in Graham's shoes running the copper tape down the wall of the tower.

The squally wind blew black and then yellowish coloured smoke here and there from the innards of the chimney. Dennis tried working from the scaffold on one corner of the chimney and then from another until the stench drove him away. Wherever he worked the smoke followed him.

His mother had burned a joint in her oven on one occasion and he remembered the smell of burned flesh for weeks afterwards. Here, the same odour pervaded everywhere. There was no escape. He choked and almost vomited. It was in the back of his mind that those bodies burning below died of something. The smoke he was breathing in could contain a deadly virus. Sickened, he thought he might be dead himself by the end of the day.

"Dennis. Are you finished yet?" called Joe from the ground.

If it had been anyone else, Dennis would have been tempted to reply with a more appropriate comment.

"Almost. This smoke's a bit strong though."

"A bit of smoke never hurt anyone," came back a derisory shout from Graham who was sitting on the scaffold some way below.

Dennis was pleased and very relieved when he could confirm his job done and the finials were ready for connection to the lightning conductor tape. He was even more pleased when Joe decided to make the connections himself. He couldn't have put up with the smoke for much longer.

The smell remained in Dennis' hair and in the back of his nose for days afterwards, even though he bathed and washed thoroughly that evening and daily thereafter. It was a smell that never left his sub-conscious memory, a smell that can only be associated with burned flesh and nothing else.

After work on the lightning conductor was finished, Joe set up the tackle to lift the cast iron edifice to the top of the scaffold. It was extremely heavy and its shape made handling difficult. Two of them would lift the structure in place whilst the third placed eight bolts into their respective holes to fix it to a frame positioned just inside the rim of the chimney. Dennis chose to help Joe with the lifting. Graham, he thought, could insert the bolts and tighten the nuts, as he didn't fancy ending up looking like a Lowestoft kipper.

Knowing which direction the smoke was blowing; Joe positioned himself up-wind of it. From here on, Graham would be amongst most of the upwellings from the chimney as he reached over to insert the bolts. Joe held his breath for as long as possible and ducked and turned his head whenever the wind blew in his direction to avoid the worst of the smoke. Even with the banter he received to hurry up, Graham took much too long to put the nuts in place and tighten them. The longer he took to tighten the nuts, the longer they had to endure the smoke.

Extreme relief was sighed by all when Graham tightened the last nut and the lightning conductor tape was bolted to the frame. It was two o'clock and they could withdraw from the fires of Hades. They had not eaten since breakfast although they had brewed up in the van at around nine o'clock before beginning the unpleasant work. Stomachs were empty and complaining that it was time to eat.

Graham was first down the ladders. He went across to the van to retrieve his sandwich box from his haversack. Dennis, designated tea boy for the day, following close on his heels, ran to the small kitchen attached to the crematorium to fill the kettle.

"No need to stay out there me boy. You know you can all come into our rest room to make your tea and eat your lunch." Cyril's invitation was not refused. Dennis called to Graham and Joe to join him.

"I suppose you'd like to wash your hands and face and get changed before lunch," said Cyril as busy as ever. Without hesitation Dennis agreed, as did Joe who had come into the kitchen. Graham had gone to find the toilet. He returned a few minutes later, got out his sandwiches and sat down at the table.

Graham was a pig when it came to food and was taking a bite out of the second of his four sandwiches when Cyril, seeing Graham eating like a man who had been starved for a month, enquired, "So, what have you got on them sandwiches mate?"

In between bread crumbs bursting out of his mouth, Graham told him they contained cheese and pickle and were very good.

"No mate, I didn't ask you what was *in* them. I asked you what was *on* them. Looking at the colour of your hands and knowing where you've been, I'm still not sure."

Graham stared down his nose and looked at his hands holding the sandwich to his mouth. They were partly grey and partly black and caked with dust and sweat. Even his overalls were covered in flaky-grey dust. He spat out the remaining contents of his mouth and rushed to the toilet to clean up amid shouts and laughter from everyone.

"We really shouldn't take the Mickey out of him," said Joe. "But I know he invites it. Ken Missen had trouble with Graham the other day. Graham tends to give the impression he knows everything from time to time, and Ken sent him back to the yard for a long stand. Graham was not sure what length of stand was wanted, but Ken assured him, before he left, that there were only two sizes, long and short. Graham had to make sure Fred didn't give him a short one.

To make sure there were no hitches Fred had been forewarned that Graham was on his way. When Graham arrived at the stores, he told Fred that he had been sent for a long stand, definitely not a short one. Graham stood in the stores for a full hour before he became fidgety and demanded to be served. Fred reminded Graham he had come for a long stand but if he felt he had stood long enough he could now sit down!"

Graham returned to the kitchen as the laughter died away looking a little cleaner to find his lunch box. He wasn't going to be put off from eating his sandwiches by anyone.

CHAPTER 12

THE CONVENTION

Snatch Block

The successful prosecution of Bert the Bastard at the Old Bailey gave Bob Massey hero status in the tabloid press. He received an undisclosed sum of money for his story from one of the newspapers and felt he should share some of it with his mates whom he had known for a number of years. Those mates included Joe and Dennis' grandfather, who lived in Forest Gate in east London.

Bob drew up his list of 'delegates' then consulted Dennis' grandfather to make sure no one of merit had been left out. Grandfather's house was fairly central to where most of the delegates lived and he sought agreement from him to use the house for a 'convention of senior steeplejacks'. The convention would really be a gathering of close friends to chew over old times, play cards and plan activities for the future, but it would be nice to give the meeting a grand title to confuse the 'governors' who would, no doubt, become aware of the meeting.

Grandfather had retired from steeplejacking some five years earlier after many years in the business. He now led a lonely life sitting exhausted in his armchair in the dining room with one foot over the brass fender in the fire hearth, rolling matchstick thin cigarettes from Rizzla cigarette papers and Old Holborn tobacco. Chronic emphysema and the Old Holborn tobacco had laid him low.

On a bright Sunday afternoon, Joe, Butch the dog, and Dennis drove to grandfather's house in the Ford van. Dennis hadn't seen his grandfather or his grandmother for some time and was concerned when he met them, after seeing the poor state of health his grandfather was in. Grandfather was bent almost double and had difficulty standing for any length of time. He spoke in laboured whispers, halting from time to time to draw whatever breath he could. Grandmother, on the other hand, was still as bright as a button. As well as being fully in charge of the household, she worked part-time at the local hospital as a cleaner.

Dennis sat in the dingy dining room with his grandfather and tried to imagine the eleven children his grandparents had brought up in this house, Joe had been the eldest of them. It must have been extremely difficult to have fed and clothed all of them on a steeplejack's wage. Beatrice, Dennis' mother, on the few occasions she spoke of Joe's family, told him that the first child out of bed in the morning was always the best dressed. When she visited Joe's home as a young woman, children seemed to appear from everywhere.

A red tablecloth with tassels hanging from its edges covered the dining room table that was pushed back against a wall under a net curtained sash window. Dennis stared in its direction wondering how long it had been there. He imagined a small child coming from underneath the table, the child's fair hair brushing the tassels aside as he might have looked up at him. A child that could easily have been Leonard, one of his father's brothers who had died at a very young age when he was badly scalded after pulling a jug of hot milk over his face and chest from that very table. Dennis' aunt had told him about Leonard. He had been a very pretty boy with locks of golden hair. She said that the angels must have wanted him, for he was too pretty for this world. His grandmother had nursed Leonard at home, tending his painful, badly blistered body without realising the final outcome.

Dennis jerked his thoughts back into reality and tried to remember the more humorous sides to life that had gone on in that house. More probably the tablecloth was the one Joe had cut a tassel from to roll into a cigarette. That 'cigarette' had nearly choked him when he tried to smoke it!

Grandfather's house was at the end of a terrace of houses built in the late nineteenth century. It was typical of many houses in the east end of London at that time. Narrow frontaged with a small, brick-walled front garden mainly overlaid with concrete.

Next to grandfather's house was a vacant building plot, temporarily occupied by a prefab, the previous houses on the site having been flattened by a doodlebug.

Once inside the house, a long narrow corridor, lit only by feeble daylight entering through the glass in the front door, led through to the back. The door to the sitting room where the convention was to be held was on the right hand side of the corridor at the front of the house. Further along, propped against the wall and just before the start of the stairs to the first floor, stood a man's 'oh sod it' drop-handlebar bicycle. That bicycle had been there for years to the bane of all visitors who, in attempting to pass it in the gloom, cracked their shins against its outstretched pedals and cursed, "Oh sod it!"

Dennis was called to help set up the chairs in the sitting room for his grandfather, Joe and their visitors. Two armchairs and a settee were already in the room facing towards a smokey coal fire. The sitting room faced north and was always in need of some heat to bring it up to a comfortable temperature. Whilst Dennis busied himself bringing more chairs from the dining room, he heard the Ford van's engine start up and saw the van head towards the end of the road and the off licence. Within twenty minutes it was back again. It had hardly stopped when out tumbled Bob Massey and another man from the back carrying two crates of brown ale between them. They brought the crates into the sitting room, set them down, then returned to the van for more.

The toing and froing between the van and the house went on for some time, among cheerful backchat, until all the supplies had been brought in. There were bags of potato crisps, peanuts, bottles of lemonade, crates of Taylor Walker's light and brown ales, bottles of Guinness and a tall cardboard box containing numerous pint glasses. A long table was placed in the middle of the room and Bob produced two new packs of playing cards from a jacket pocket. He stood, back to the fire, hands in trousers pockets jingling his loose change. This was going to be some convention.

Grandfather had become as excited as the others by the preparations. It was unusual for him to get out of his chair, except when nature called, and wander about the dining room. He was eager to become involved in the card game, drink brown ale and smoke fags among friends. He rummaged around for grandmother's handbag for he knew she would have some small change in there. Not being able to find it, he fumbled his way into the kitchen to look for her, holding onto the dining room table and then to the doorframe with his knobbly fingers as he shuffled between the dining room and the kitchen.

Grandmother knew the convention was planned for today and was well prepared.

"I suppose you're after some small change Dad. It's lucky for you I've been saving my threepenny bits. They're in my purse in the drawer of the dresser."

Grandfather waved a hand in thanks and returned to his chair, open mouthed, stifled of breath.

From time to time the doorbell rang to let everyone know another guest had arrived. Butch barked loudly each time until told to keep quiet. The arrival of guests at the door were followed by roars of welcome as old friends came in and were ushered into the sitting room with the others.

"I think they're all here now," said Grandmother as she looked along the corridor from the kitchen. "Are you ready to join them Dad?"

Grandfather was already grasping the sides of his chair to get to his feet. Dennis gave him a helping hand as he rose unsteadily into an almost upright position. Grandmother handed him her purse with the threepenny bits and left him to take them out and put them into a pocket in his trousers. He shuffled in his slippers along the passageway to join the rest of the men in the sitting room, his braces holding up creased, baggy trousers at half-mast, with Dennis following behind.

With grandfather settled in the armchair closest the fire, Dennis noted there were eleven other card players sitting around the long table. Tails of cigarette smoke rose from the ashtrays placed on the beer crates that now acted as side tables. Half-filled glasses of beer, froth clinging onto their inner surfaces, wobbled as they were put down by excited hands, ready to be picked up again at the whim of their owners.

Dennis recognised four of the men, Joe, Grandfather, Bob Massey and Reg Brundel, but the others were strangers to him. Their interest was fully taken up by the card game and exchanging wise cracks among themselves. They were in no mood to take time out to pass the time of day with non-players like Dennis.

It had been many years since Dennis had been in this room. His Uncle Stan and Stan's new wife, Margaret, had lived in that room after they married until they had saved enough money for a deposit on a home of their own.

Dennis, not feeling part of the scene, looked out of the window facing onto the road and recollected that a few years before a huge bonfire had been built there for a Guy Fawkes' night celebration. Neighbours had collected all kinds of combustible material over the preceding days and the bonfire grew daily to be over eight feet tall. It was so large delivery vans and cars had had difficulty passing by it. He had watched from this room as the bonfire was lit, the flames reached high into the night sky, lighting up the fronts of the houses on both sides of the road with a red glow, threatening to burn down the telephone cables trailing overhead.

The next morning, of course, the remaining ash had to be removed in wheelbarrows, but the circle of burned road remained in that state for many months before it was repaired by the Council.

He looked round to view the men behind him. They were a close knit group with whom he had no common interest, except steeplejacking. He decided to rejoin Butch the dog and his grandmother in the kitchen where she was preparing cheese sandwiches and pickled onions.

Butch was getting under grandmother's feet, watching her every move intently and making sure no tit bit was left unattended if it fell on the floor. Grandmother set aside a plate of freshly made sandwiches for Dennis and herself whilst Dennis made the tea.

From time to time one of the men came through the kitchen to visit the outside toilet. As the afternoon wore on, their visits became more and more frequent and they became less and less steady on their feet, as they passed by in a happy frame of mind.

The supply of brown ale ran out around mid-afternoon. Dennis was summoned to the sitting room, given a five-pound note, and asked if he would mind going along to the off licence to get another four quart size bottles. It was an errand that gave Dennis the opportunity to exercise the dog and return some of the empties.

Returning to the house with the brown ale in two carrier bags and Butch pulling at his lead, Dennis saw the bedroom window over the sitting room was open. He recalled he had slept in that room as a child when his grandparents gave house parties for their children and their grandchildren. The parties always seemed to go on into the early hours after he had been put to bed. At one of those parties, when Dennis was about eight years old, he had to sleep in his grey school shirt as he hadn't packed his pyjamas. It was quite a surprise to find two of his aunts sleeping in the same bed with him the next morning. They were highly amused when he found himself on the side of the bed against the wall and wanting to get out. He had to climb over them, bare bummed, with his shirt riding high and them laughing like drains.

"I don't suppose they'd do that now!" He laughed to himself as he went through the gateway and into the front garden. "More's the pity. Especially Lillian, the red headed one."

The card school finished at around six o'clock. The men had had their fill of beer, food and cigarettes, had either lost money or gained it, and were ready to make their way home. Grandfather was delivered back to his chair in the dining room, where everyone knew he would soon fall into a deep sleep. A slow procession of men left through the front door to calls of "thanks for a nice afternoon" and, "hope to see you soon". Joe and Dennis tidied the sitting room, opened the windows to let the cigarette smoke and smell of stale ale out and placed the empty beer bottles back in their crates. They said their fond farewells to grandfather and grandmother and got into the van with the dog, as Dennis thought, to drive home. It was clear that the convention had been a success.

It was not long before Dennis noticed Joe was driving erratically and they were not taking their usual route home.

"Where are we off to?" he enquired looking at the road signs pointing towards the North Circular Road.

"I've been asked to visit an old friend, Gron Williams, in Edmonton" explained Joe.

The name, Gron Williams, didn't mean anything to Dennis. "I don't think I've met him."

"No, you haven't. He hangs around a billiard hall in Edmonton when he's not at home. We'll go to his house first to see if he's in."

From snippets of alcohol derived conversation on the way to Edmonton, it became clear that Gron Williams had been a steeplejack until quite recently. That was until his younger brother had been accepted to play a child's part in a theatrical production. Gron was now looking after his brother and had grown to like 'easy street' where he could mix with the stars and starlets of the day on equal terms. His problem was, of course, he enjoyed a champagne lifestyle on a beer income.

Joe and Dennis arrived in the road where Gron's house was to be found and parked a discreet distance away. After Joe rang the doorbell Gron's wife answered the door with a baby in her arms. She was a pretty woman in her late twenties, heavily made up to hide the signs of bruising to her face. She recognised Joe and appeared to be concerned to find out why he and Dennis had called on her.

"Hello Sheila. We were just passing by and we thought it would be nice to call on Gron and yourself to see how you are," explained Joe in a matter of fact way. "Do you know where he is?"

"He should be in the billiard hall," she replied suspiciously. "But I don't know for sure."

"OK, we'll walk down there to see if we can find him," replied Joe. "It's been nice to meet you again."

Dennis felt uneasy. There had been no pleasantness, only mistrust in their meeting. It seemed he was being drawn into something that could end up having a nasty smell attached to it. Joe and Dennis walked along the road in the opposite direction to the billiard hall to where they had parked the van. Joe indicated for Dennis to stop when they were a short distance from it.

"We'll wait here and see where she goes."

Sheila, baby in her arms, closed the door to her terraced house behind her and walked across the road to a neighbour's house. After a while the neighbour's front door opened and, following a short conversation, the baby was handed to her and taken inside. Sheila turned, looked along the road to where Joe's van was parked and then ran along the road towards the billiard hall.

"That means she's gone to warn him. Better step it out so we can catch up with him before he buggers off."

They got to the door of the billiard hall just as Sheila came out.

"He's not in there," she said. "I've just looked."

"Wait there!" ordered Joe, as he ran unsteadily towards the back of the hall. "If he comes out the front, stop him!"

Dennis was in the mire, right up to his neck. He stood in the doorway hoping no one would come out of the billiard hall. He hadn't got a clue what Gron Williams looked like. Luckily Sheila stayed with him and he looked to her to recognise her husband if he came their way.

Joe came back to the main entrance of the billiard hall after a while. He must have run quite a distance for he was staggering and breathing heavily.

"Lost him over the wire fence at the back," he gasped, looking at Sheila. "He must have known we were at the front door because he came out the back. Never mind every dog has its day. We'll be back for him some other time."

When Joe and Dennis got back to the van Butch was pleased to see them again. Dennis tackled Joe about their involvement in what looked like a gangland feud.

"Gron owes us a lot of money," Joe told him. "And we're going to get it back."

"We!" Dennis complained. "Where do 'we' fit in? I don't know the first thing about what's going on and I don't want to." Dennis realised how easy it must be for any young man to be drawn into old men's feuds that had probably been ongoing for years.

"You don't understand yet," explained Joe as he drove unsteadily towards Ilford. "These things are bigger than any one of us. If we don't get what's owed to us, we're seen to be a soft touch. It's as simple as that."

Dennis knew that he didn't belong to this culture that had its roots back in the nineteen twenties when policemen walked in two's wherever they went in the east end of London. He had heard the stories of houses being attacked by gangs of thugs. His aunt, on his mother's side, had told him how she and her husband had waited up all night with a cauldron of boiling water at the ready at the top of their stairs in case of attack by hoodlums. And they were kindly people.

"It's time to get out of this mess," Dennis told Joe, for the first time in his life taking the initiative. "Make yourself a new life. I'll not get involved in this sort of business again." The remainder of the journey home was covered in total silence. The friendly nuzzling of the Butch' nose against their hands gradually bringing father and son to a state of truce.

CHAPTER 13

A NOT SO EARLY RETIREMENT

Hand Winch

As part of his 'on the job training' training, Dennis was sent to the Firm's South London Stores for a week to help Fred make up new ropes, lashings and wire hawsers and also to repair equipment after it had been returned to the stores from building sites. The damage to some of the equipment whilst it was used on site was quite extensive and Dennis began to understand the reasons for concern expressed by directors of the company.

The Firm's stores were located under a railway line inside two arches of a brick viaduct leased from the British Railways Board. The open sides to the railway arches were infilled with green painted wooden boarding and two wide doors in one of the arches provided access to the stores.

Inside, Fred had made use of his scaffolding expertise to make up racks for ladders, scaffold poles, scaffold boards and the heavy timbers used for the old fashioned wooden flying scaffolds. Coils of hemp rope hung over the horizontal poles at the end of the racks, each rope labelled to identify its length and the date when it was last inspected. Rope blocks and large ring spanners hung vertically from the same poles like bats in a cave, whilst on the floor, against a wall, stood two hand winches and numerous sections of steel derrick.

In the gloom of the store, set back from the cold draught that came from under the doors, the red glow from a small coke stove shone out. On top of it, singing softly, sat a kettle of boiling water, seemingly always ready to make tea. By the side of the kettle a wire toasting fork hung from a hook screwed into the wall. This was where Fred spent his time cutting ropes and lashings to length and whipping their ends. Close to the metal flue of the chimney, hanging from the side of a makeshift wooden shelf, was a marline spike, a wicked looking tool kept there by Fred for splicing wire ropes and for 'keeping thieving hands off his precious charges.

All in all, Fred had made the most of his surroundings and, in a practical way, had become well organised. Being slightly deaf was an advantage to him, for he couldn't hear the continual grind and rumble of slow trains passing overhead or the less frequent thundering rush of express trains as they travelled between London and the south coast.

Joe called into the stores a couple of days after Dennis reported there. He briefed Fred and Dennis about the need to introduce an inventory of equipment for the stores and, as importantly, a record keeping system for equipment issued to steeplejack teams travelling the country. They were also to introduce a new method of stock control to help overcome some of the losses the Firm was incurring when equipment was not returned to stores after jobs were completed.

Fred and Dennis got on extremely well and complemented one another. Fred was a practical man with a wealth of knowledge but was not adept at completing paperwork. On the other hand, the training Dennis had received at grammar school would now become useful in setting up the new stock control system. Fred knew what equipment he should have in the store and where he had despatched it, but there were few paper records. However, once they had the new system in place Joe felt sure Fred would maintain it, as Fred was a conscientious man who liked to keep a tidy ship.

It was clear from the comments made by Fred as he and Dennis worked their way through the inventory, that Brian Wardle had been a busy man following the upset at the builder's yard at Mile End. No doubt Brian felt that his position within the Firm had been threatened by Fred's knowledge of his adulterous relationship with the buxom secretary, for Brian had a wife in the south west of the country unaware of his 'goings on' in London. Although Fred had been given a few almost worthless handouts to keep him sweet, he knew he was vulnerable. Brian had suggested to Fred that he should consider retiring to enjoy the remaining years of his life doing the things that he had always wanted to do but had never found the time to do them. This suggestion had not impressed Fred for he knew how Brian's mind worked and he had known little else but steeplejack's work from twelve years of age after he had left school.

In turn, Brian was not impressed by Fred's reaction to his suggestion of retirement and resolved that 'old Fred' would have to go. But first of all Brian must be sure that Fred did not have too many friends in high places in the company who might speak up for him if he was found to be in troubled waters.

Brian began keeping a diary. Every time he visited the stores or called at sites where men were working, he made notes of the deficiencies he came across. When he found Fred absent from the store, even if this was due to him taking his lunch break, he would record this in his diary ready to use it as evidence at some later date. It was when Brian started asking possibly incriminating questions about Fred that he aroused suspicion among Fred's mates and began to meet with stony silences.

It was recognised by the Firm that the rural location of most of the churches under repair created travel difficulties for the men and, within reason, a blind eye was turned on prompt start and finish times. Provided the men didn't exceed the maximum number of hours quoted for the work, there were few complaints from the directors.

Dennis was beginning to realise that a certain type of person found pleasure in reporting unfavourably about his comrades with the intention of gaining personal advantage. This easy, underhanded means to an end became more important to Brian than the work he had been employed to do. He began to spend less time travelling the country to seek new contracts and more time calling unannounced on sites where steeplejacks were working to see whether they arrived on time and whether they stayed until the end of the working day.

There had been a number of occasions when Brian arrived at sites only to find the men were not there. The main reasons given by them for their absence was 'we had to go into town to collect building supplies' or 'we had to call in at the stores'. In reality, on most occasions, the reason for them not being there was due to them taking the day off with pay, without letting anyone know.

Brian, after all, was a poacher turned gamekeeper and knew most of the dodges employed by the men. He decided it was time to introduce a recognised sign to indicate whether the men had reported for work. Every morning the foreman steeplejack on site was to tie a piece of white cloth to the bottom ladder and remove it at the end of the day. When Brian called he could then determine whether the men had been on site that day. The introduction of a 'flag of surrender' as the men called it, was not popular and there were many that took umbrage at it and did not comply with the instruction. 'After all, those confounded village kids would steal anything left unguarded around the churchyard.'

Fred was not surprised when one afternoon he received a telephone call from a mate telling him of Brian's early morning visit to the site he was working at. He and his colleague had arrived late for work and had subsequently received a warning about this. He also told Fred of Brian's intentions to have him removed from the stores, one way or the other. After all it was Fred who had put the finger on Brian at Mile End and he reminded himself once again that he would have to mind his back from hereon. Besides, he had been giving the matter of retirement more thought, particularly now he had reached his seventy-fifth birthday. But before he left, he and a mate would have a surprise or two up their sleeves for 'that git Brian'.

Brian was still seeing the young secretary who worked at Coles the Builders. They regularly met after she finished work when Brian picked her up in his car and they would go to her rented flat in Bethnal Green. Brian stayed overnight when work took him into London the next day, for it was easier to get into the City from Bethnal Green than travel up from Dorchester where he lived.

On the fourth day of Dennis' secondment to the stores, Fred received an urgent request from Ken Missen to send Dennis with two very large ring spanners to Waterloo Railway Station. Joe would be waiting at the station to take Dennis to a church

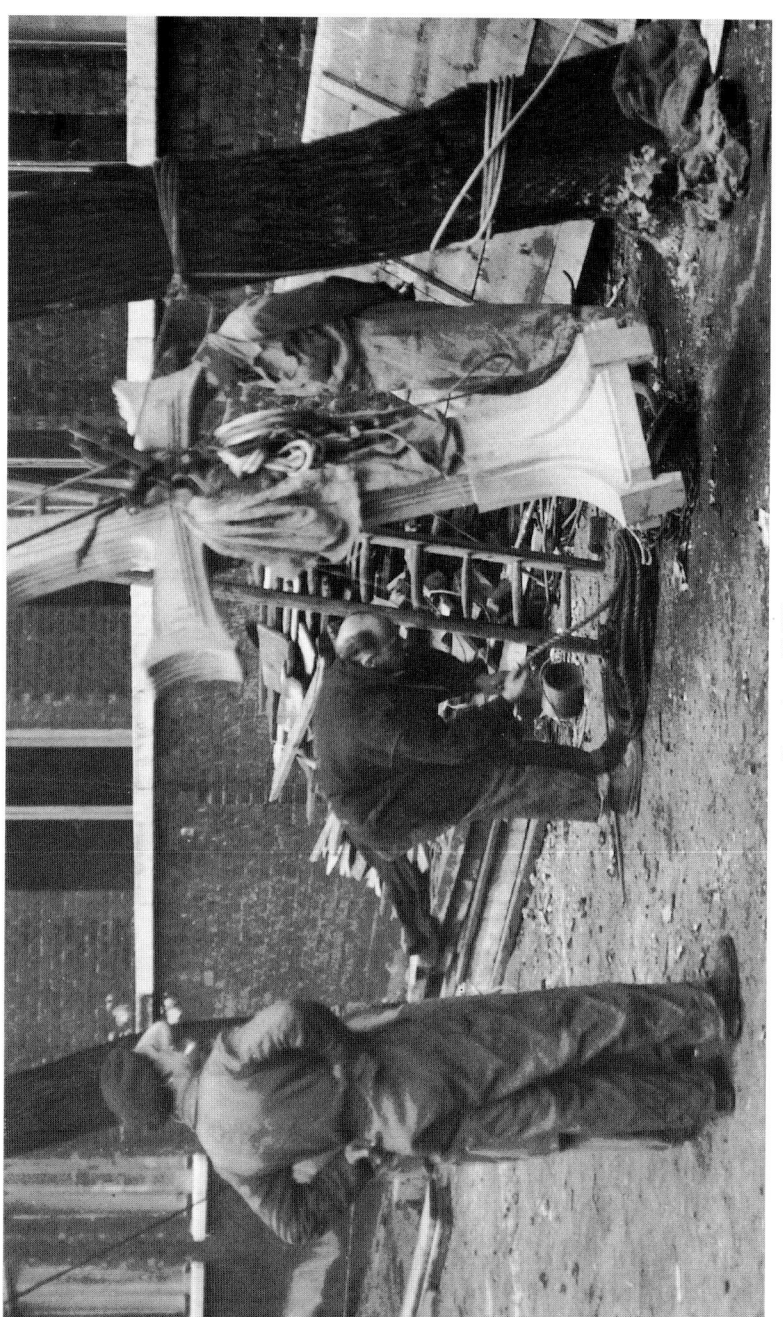

Preparing a "Lift"

The cross on the way up at St. Pancras, London

in central London where they were working. The ring spanners were needed to tighten the bolts holding a cross to the top of a church tower.

Norwood railway station was a short walk from the stores and Dennis was soon striding out carrying the spanners in a sack. As arranged, Joe was waiting for him under the clock at Waterloo station when he arrived. There hadn't been mention of the hundred or so other people who might be milling around the same spot, but the sight of Joe's black beret above the heads of the crowd drew Dennis' attention to where he was standing.

The Ford van was parked nearby on a bombsite that had once been gardens to a row of houses. Lakes of ruined cellars once belonging to the houses lay half-filled with rainwater and open to the sky. Where walls to the houses remained standing, lonely fire hearths framed by still peeling wallpaper faced out depressingly with blinded eyes from their niches one or two storeys up.

Waterloo railway station was not the best of places to be if you had no pressing reason to be there and Joe and Dennis had another destination in mind. The journey to the central London church didn't take long and they soon met up with Ken Missen in the churchyard, cigarette in the corner of his mouth, tying a line to the cross in readiness to haul it to the top of the scaffolding around the tower.

"You're just in time Dennis," jested Ken when he saw him. "Just in time to give us a hand to haul this cross up there." He gestured upwards with his head, a motion that left the long length of ash drooping from his cigarette hanging in mid air.

Realisation rapidly caught on. This was why Dennis had been called so urgently to the site. The urgent call for the ring spanners was a cover to get him there quickly so that he could help them.

"So you didn't need the spanners then?"

"Well they may come in handy at some stage," said Ken with a grin as Dennis walked away to do something useful.

Raising the cross directly from the ground was easier than taking two bites at the job as had been the case at the Medway brewery where the chimney liners were first lifted onto a flat roof using shearlegs as a derrick. Here, a long wire rope was already in position, one end tied to the trunk of a tree in the churchyard and the other to the top of the scaffolding. The wire rope would act as a guide for the cross as it made its way up the tower.

Joe was seen talking to a bald-headed man who was wearing a donkey jacket. Dennis heard Joe tell the man not to get in the way as they had important work to do, but the man didn't seem to take any notice of the warning and went rummaging among the coils of rope lying on the ground.

"So, let's go to it then," suggested an exasperated Joe making his way towards the free end of the hauling line. "It'll take three of us to pull the cross up most of the way. When it reaches the bottom of the scaffold, I'll go up and ease it past the overhang and land it on the boards at the top. When I've done that, I'll call for you both to join me so that we can manhandle it into position. If Max Wall over there gets in the way, let me know and I'll kick his arse out of the churchyard."

Together, the three of them heaved on the line; all watching the cross climb steadily up the guide wire, a foot at a time. It was clear that two men would have had difficulty managing the weight of the cross on their own, particularly when it had to be landed on the scaffold above. Foot by foot, the cross slowly made its way up the guide wire until it reached the boards on the scaffold.

Joe left Ken and Dennis holding firmly onto the hauling line before starting to climb the ladders. Reaching the point where the cross was suspended on the rope, he signalled for them to heave upwards again and then pulled the cross onto the scaffold after untying it from the guide wire.

When Ken and Dennis joined Joe on the scaffold they found he already had company. Unnoticed, the bald-headed man had climbed the ladders ahead of them and was walking about the scaffold reaching out and touching or tapping on everything within hand's reach for no apparent reason.

"What the bloody hell are you doing up here mate?" asked Ken in an almost aggressive tone.

There was no reply from the bald-headed man.

"I can't get through to him," said Joe. "He's not in the way at the moment, but just by being here he's bleeding annoying."

Hearing these disparaging remarks the bald-headed man looked blankly in their direction before seizing hold of the guide wire with both hands. He swung out from the scaffold gripping

Cross and "Sheerlegs" at the top of the tower St. Pancras, London

the wire between his legs and lowered himself, hand over hand, down to the ground. All three men watched him jump over the church wall and walk off in the direction of the shopping centre without looking back.

"We must have upset him, but that bald bugger was lucky," said Joe in amazement. "If just one steel splinter had jagged into his hand on the way down the silly sod would never have held onto the wire. He'd have joined the rest of the poor souls buried in the churchyard."

The unexpected entertainment over, the trio set about lifting the cross onto a bronze dowel they had set in its stone plinth. The orientation of the cross would have to be perfect for the architect would definitely check and then recheck with a compass which way it faced. If the positioning of the cross ended up being only one or two degrees out from true, this would become the talking point in the local community for years to come.

It was almost dark by the time the cross was finally bedded into position. Dennis looked across London before climbing down the ladders and he could see the traffic moving slowly along the streets, headlamps shimmering in the beginning of a thick London mist that tends to creep up on the city during early evenings in calm November weather. When he reached the bottom of the tower the tombstones in the graveyard looked strangely unreal among the grey shadows cast by the streetlights and he hurriedly made his way to where the van was parked.

On the way home in the van Joe mentioned to Dennis he would be needed for a couple of hours the next morning to run a new lightning conductor down the wall of the tower and to drive four earth rods into the ground. After he had finished this work he should return to the stores to complete his training with Fred. Dennis was pleased to hear this for he liked to be working in the open air again away from the half-light of the stores, although he missed old Fred's stories and his peculiar ways.

The following morning father and son arrived on site and, as usual, Ken had arrived ahead of them. Tea was ready, as was a special treat on this occasion, two pieces of buttered toast each. Ken, an ex matelot, was well used to looking after himself and had toasted the bread from the flame of a blow lamp he had lit to warm the bell ringers' chamber.

Dennis brought the four copper rods from the van whilst Joe unravelled the roll of copper lightning conductor tape. After making their way to the bottom of the tower they paced out four yards from its wall into the churchyard.

"This is where you drive the rods into the ground," explained Joe. "Make sure you don't drive the rods through a root of a tree because if you do, you'll never pull them out again."

The first copper rod began to bend with each hammer blow after being driven into the ground a foot or so. Dennis found the rod could neither be driven down nor pulled up. He called Joe over to get a second opinion.

"It's probably gone through a root of a tree. You can't always tell where you'll find them. Let me see if I can move it."

Joe took the hammer and tried to free the rod by driving it from side to side. The rod didn't budge at first but then succumbed to the mistreatment it was receiving by loosening in the ground and then, without warning, disappearing from view.

"Oh bugger, I bet I know where that's gone, " said Joe.

"Where's that?" enquired an incredulous Dennis.

"Into the bleeding crypt. I was told the outer walls of the crypt were close to where I intended to drive the rods but they must extend even further out than anyone thought. The rod must have gone through a joint in the stone roof below the ground. We'll have to get it back."

"Crypt! What's in a crypt?" Dennis wanted to know for that moment and that moment only.

"Not a lot goes on in a crypt," said Joe. "You'll find out when we get in there."

Count Dracula and the monsters he created in crypts began to fantasise in Dennis' mind. He had also read that the crypts in Paris were filled with millions of bones of previous generations of that city's inhabitants, all neatly stacked so as not to take up too much space. Somewhere between his two mind sets would be found the truth. It was comforting to know that Joe would be with him when they entered the 'place of the dead' for he didn't relish the thought of being close to the remains of those who had left this life. His experiences at the crematorium had been more than enough to last a lifetime.

Joe walked across the churchyard to where Ken was coiling a rope on the ground to let him know of the dilemma they were in and suggested he should find the churchwarden to get the keys of the crypt. Dennis thought he had detected something cunningly devious by this and came to the conclusion that Ken would also end up in the party entering the crypt in search of the copper rod.

Ken returned with the key after a quarter of an hour or so accompanied by the churchwarden who wanted them to remember they were entering an area of the church that had not been used for some time. "Anything could have happened down there," was how he put it.

As Ken had the key it was only right for him to unlock the door and go down the steps first with a storm lantern. The churchwarden followed with Joe and Dennis in the rear. The crypt was a gloomy, eerie place to be in. Their footsteps and low voices echoed through the vaults as they made their way towards where, they hoped, the earth rod had gone through the roof. On both sides of the dark passageway they walked along were rows of single iron gates that led into even darker recesses where wooden coffins lay silently with their contents at rest. Dennis was so taken up with looking around in the gloom that he found himself detached from the main body of explorers who were now a short distance ahead of him. The light from Ken's lantern disappeared as the group rounded a corner and he was left alone in the darkness.

Nervously he hurried along the passageway to catch up with them. He had lost the sound of their footsteps and their voices when falling behind the party but the sound of his own footsteps and that of his heart beating made up for the loss. He rounded the corner expecting to find them waiting for him to catch up, but he was disappointed. The way ahead was in complete darkness and there was no sign of any living person.

Dennis froze where he stood. Should he go back in the direction he had come from or should he go forward to meet up with the group? They must be somewhere up ahead.

As he pondered he heard sounds of scratching and then a short hissing noise coming from somewhere to his right. The sounds must have come from inside one of the chambers where a coffin lay. He looked in the direction from where he thought the noises came from to see a small light flickering. It partially illuminated a black figure propped up against an open iron gate. A hand gestured him to approach.

Dennis was about to make a momentous decision. Should he accept the invitation to approach the figure or should he take up his preference to run for it for as long as his cowardly legs would allow?

The light continued to flicker and then moved up and then down before going out. About the same time Dennis heard a cry of pain coming from within the now blackened chamber and then the sounds of scratching and hissing again. A light began to flicker once more and the hand again gestured for him to come towards it. The light moved upwards as Dennis captively approached it to illuminate a weather beaten face surrounded by darkness. The face looked familiar, very familiar. Joe stood there with a lighted match in his fingers that had been burnt by his first attempt at scaring the living daylights out of Dennis. In the shadows Ken and the churchwarden stood behind him shielding the light from the storm lantern and silently shaking with laughter. Here was where they had found the missing copper rod.

The party's thin veneer of courage quickly evaporated when the iron gate to the chamber they were gathered in clanged shut. An unholy scramble to get out followed as four men battled in the darkness to be the first out of the crypt. Ken's storm lantern overturned in the melee and its light went out. The churchwarden, who was holding onto the back of Dennis' boilersuit and second in line to be the first out into the daylight, cried out for salvation as he fell over a body lying in the passageway that hadn't been there when the came in. Joe and Ken, having fallen over the churchwarden in their panic, joined in the fracas on the floor.

Dennis had made it up the stairs and to the outer door of the crypt. From there he witnessed the shadowy events taking place inside. Three figures rose from the stone floor. One figure held what appeared to be a spear in one hand and with the other was dragging a body behind him. The two other figures overtook the first and ran in Dennis' direction shouting wildly. Dennis didn't wait to be caught. He ran out into the churchyard and hid behind a tree. As the figures bundled into the daylight it became clear who they were.

The churchwarden had come out of the doorway ahead of the

pack followed by Ken and then Joe dragging 'Max Wall' behind him. Max had followed them into the crypt and had been up to his old mischief of touching things. He must have pushed on the gate to the chamber and closed it on them.

In Dennis' panic to get out, he had knocked Max over and the churchwarden had fallen over Max lying on the ground. Ken and Joe bringing up the rear had then fallen over the two men on the floor and all hell had been set loose. Joe, who was carrying the copper rod, had seized hold of Max when they tumbled together on the floor. In his annoyance at becoming an unwilling part of a wild stampede, Joe would not let go of the kicking and punching body until he had the culprit in a position where he could see who he had hold of. Joe didn't voice the opinion at the time, but later he confided he could have had hold of the devil himself.

Whilst Dennis was away from the store Brian Wardle called to see Fred. It was close to five o'clock and Fred was due to finish about that time. Brian wanted to check that an order for materials and equipment was being processed for he didn't want 'any mistakes to be made this time'.

Fred took Brian to one end of the store to show him where the order was being made up. Part of the consignment, of ropes and lashings, hung neatly from a frame of scaffold poles used a storage rack.

"Where's the hand winch?" demanded Brian. "Have you got it ready!"

"There it is," said Fred pointing to one of two winches standing against the wall. "I've bin checking the wire rope on its drum. The rope's bin pulled through that there block on top of the storage rack. I'm gonna put a weight on it ter straighten the kinks out. Stand 'ere by the winch an yer kin see it fer yerself."

Brian moved across to the winch to see more clearly what Fred had meant. Fred climbed up a short ladder to get high enough to reach the heavy weight on the storage rack. He attached it to the wire rope, glanced quickly across to make sure Brian was standing where he would like him to be and pushed the heavy weight off the scaffold board.

The wire rope tightened as the weight fell towards the ground and set the unchecked drum of the winch in motion. The winch handles spun wildly out of control, one of them hitting Brian continuously on his legs until he had the presence of mind to move out of its way.

"You sod," shouted Brian in pain. "What did you do that for?"

"Me, I never did nuffink," pleaded Fred. "You should've known not ter git in the way!"

Brian reeled about the store clutching at his bruised upper and lower leg where the winch handle had caught him.

"That'll teach the bastard," muttered Fred under his breath before he raised his voice once again. "Wan't a cup of tea?"

Dennis reported back to the store the following morning. Fred had arrived much earlier and was in an extremely good mood.

"Allo mate," he said in a welcoming voice. "Teas made. Brian called in last night. Won't see 'im fer a while I guess. E's got sore legs."

Fred went on to tell Dennis what had happened. The telephone rang as he finished his tale and he walked across the store to answer it.

The number of "Ohs and Ahs" as the conversation progressed indicated something was amiss and Fred's final "Serves 'im bloody well right. 'E ad it coming to 'im," was enough to suggest there had been a successful outcome from his point of view.

Brian had failed to understand that the men would not put up with his underhanded behaviour. That very morning he had paid an early visit to a church where steeplejacks from the Firm were working alongside builders. At around ten to eight a scaffold clip fell from the scaffold immediately above him as he waited for them to report for work. It hit him on the forearm, breaking his arm in two places.

Strange as it may seem, no one had reported their presence on site before Brian arrived and all of the steeplejacks and builders reported to the clerk of works office at eight o'clock not knowing what had happened before their arrival. Brian's injury must surely have been caused by an Act of God!

Brian was a physical and mental mess. His legs had not been in the best of condition since the operation on his knees and the injuries inflicted by the winch handle in Fred's store hadn't helped. Now he had a broken arm and would be out of action for some time.

Brian's wife was brought up from Dorchester to collect him from the hospital. A month's recuperation at home was just what the doctor ordered.

News of Brian's injuries circulated throughout the Firm like a fragrance from Yardley's perfume factory at Stratford. At least one steeplejack would take advantage of Brian's absence and Fred decided to stay on as the Firm's storeman until his next birthday.

CHAPTER 14

WHEN THE CAT'S AWAY

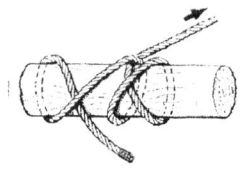

Rolling Hitch

Bob Massey, as with the other men employed by the Firm, soon got to hear about Brian Wardle's predicament. He telephoned Brian's home to find out if he was feeling better and made arrangements with Brian's wife to visit him the following Sunday afternoon.

When Bob called to see Brian he found him in a very depressed state of mind. Brian felt very restricted and cut off from events at work and also from Lorna, the buxom secretary who lived in Bethnal Green. Brian felt sure he could speak in confidence to Bob and chose a moment when his wife was out of the room to ask him to call at Lorna's address to pick up some of his clothes he had left there and also some business papers.

"You're a man like myself Bob," he said in a hushed tone. "Worldly wise, if you know what I mean. Not like the other dipsticks employed by the Firm. When you call there, if Lorna's not in, use my duplicate key that I'll let you have. I've got another just in case I lose this one. I'll telephone her in the meantime at Coles to let her know you'll be calling and I'll ask her to parcel my things up for you to collect. Her flat is on the top floor almost opposite York Hall. I plan to go to London myself within the next couple of weeks, but the directors urgently need my papers. If you can drop them off at the office by next Friday that will be of great help to me."

Fully briefed and in possession of crucial information, Bob agreed to call on Lorna. He thought about his planned visit very carefully and decided it would not be in his best interests to call on her on the way home from work as he knew he always looked scruffy on those occasions. He would make the visit in the evening dressed in his best suit with a box of dairy milk chocolates as a present for her. After all, the girl must be getting lonely without Brian around.

On Bob's first visit to the flat he found no one at home, but he had the key to the front door in his pocket and thought he may as well use it to see whether Brian's parcel had been left out for him. Lorna must have received Brian's message for the parcel was there on a chair in the hallway. Bob could have tucked the parcel under his arm and left without further ado, but that meant he would have no reason to return at another time. Not only was he a fanciful man, he was also an inquisitive one and chose to look about the flat.

For a young lady living on a secretary's money the flat was well furnished. The hall and sitting room had wall to wall carpeting and the three-piece suite was brightly coloured and comfortable. In the tidy kitchen he found a washing machine and modern fitted cupboard units. On entering the girl's bedroom he realised he was seeing things that were very new to his eyes.

Snow-white bedroom furniture with a white satin quilted cover pulled over the bed stood on fluffy-white carpeting. Gilt-framed mirrors decorated the walls, there was also a large oval mirror fixed to the ceiling immediately above the bed.

Bob gazed in awe at this den of intrigue and imagined the kind of debauchery that probably went on here from time to time. "I'd like a piece of the action," he voiced whilst talking to himself.

It was when he was looking up into the mirror on the ceiling that he saw the reflection of a long-haired white cat asleep on the bed. Bob gave the cat a poke to see if it was real and it awoke and looked at him lazily but it wasn't inclined to move from its comfortable position for anyone. Bob had met 'Fluffy Balls' for the first time.

Bob had seen enough in the short time he had been in the flat to make him want to return when the flat's owner was at home. Leaving Brian's parcel of belongings untouched on the chair in the hallway, he left the flat with the intention of making a telephone call the next day to Coles the Builders to make arrangements to meet up with Lorna.

Fatguts, the quantity surveyor, answered the telephone when

Bob called. After passing the time of the day with him, Bob asked to be put through to Lorna's office as he had a message from Brian. Obligingly Fatguts transferred the call but sneakily remained on the line listening to the conversation. He heard Bob ask Lorna if he could call on her later in the day to collect Brian's parcel as he hadn't been able to make it earlier in the week. Bob went on to explain he had seen Brian who had sent his love and best wishes to her. There was also a present he had to deliver personally.

Lorna agreed that sharp at eight thirty that evening would be a suitable time for Bob to call as she would be home by then after a hairdresser's appointment. Bob was excited by the arrangements and had great difficulty in passing the time between making the telephone call and when he was due at the flat. He finished work early that afternoon on the pretext of having a doctor's appointment, spruced himself up and took an underground train to Bethnal Green station.

Bob arrived at the block of flats sharp to time, a box of chocolates in one hand and a spray of red and white carnations wrapped in white tissue paper held close to his chest. He didn't want his intentions to look too obvious.

"You going to number twenty free mister?" enquired a skinny boy sitting on a beaten up bike by the entrance to the flats.

"Yes. How did you know?" enquired Bob.

"Don't know nuffink," shouted the lad over his shoulder as he rode off down the road in a well rehearsed fashion.

Bob tapped sheepishly on the front door. That boy knew something and had almost put him off his stroke. The door opened and Bob was once more overcome by what he saw. He had been used to the rough and tumble of life in the east end of London where refined life-styles were almost totally unknown, but here in Bethnal Green he had discovered an oasis of high-class sensual pleasure. Provided he played his cards right he knew he was on to a winner.

Lorna stood there in a welcoming pose, arms outstretched dressed in a loose fitting green satin kimono, "It was so nice of him to call to collect Brian's things."

Bob was embarrassed by the welcome and looked for a way to avoid becoming embraced on the front doorstep. A little later would be fine, but this was all so sudden.

"Aren't you going to give me a kiss Bob," Lorna enquired as she drew him inside the flat.

"Ahem. Well, now we're old friends," he replied. "Why not."

The embrace was short but sweet. Lorna's perfume smelled pleasantly unusual and got up his nose a bit. He had difficulty avoiding a giant sneeze.

Bob looked about the hall, pretending it was the first time he had been in the flat and commented how lovely everything looked. His eyes glanced at the chair where Brian's parcel still lay undisturbed since his last visit. Lorna noticed his glance and instinctively reached for the parcel to hand it to him.

"Lorna," Bob quickly interjected to avoid being dismissed from the flat in short time with the parcel and none of the other delights he had come for. "I've brought you presents that I hope you will accept. The carnations are from me and the chocolates are from Brian. It's been a long day and I'm pleased to be with a friend of a friend."

The ploy seemed to work. Lorna couldn't throw him out now. She must at least make him a cup of tea after being offered the gifts.

Lorna thanked Bob whilst accepting the presents and invited him into the kitchen where she filled the kettle to make two cups of Earl Grey tea. While the kettle was boiling they discussed Brian's unfortunate accidents and how he was getting along at home with so little to do.

"I'll take the tea into the sitting room," said Lorna. "You can bring the chocolates. I'll place the carnations in a vase of water in a minute or two, we can't let them get droopy. It was nice of you and Brian to think of me. Thank you very much," she drooled.

Bob, seated in a comfortable armchair began to relax. So apparently relaxed, that the house cat chose to jump onto his lap for comfort.

"I see you've met my cat. He seems to like you and treats you like an old friend," laughed Lorna. "Brian calls him Fluffy Balls because of his hairy genitalia."

"I don't know much about cats," replied Bob. "I've never met your cat before and I don't ever remember seeing Brian's private parts!"

His quick response seemed to go down well with his hostess.

Lorna paused for a moment and then continued, "He won't have them for much longer for I'm going to have him neutered. I mean Fluffy Balls, not Brian."

Bob moved onto a fresh subject as every time he entered into a conversation with Lorna Brian's name came up and took the gloss off his own attempts at winning her over.

Fluffy Balls began to take advantage of his position on Bob's lap and continually dug his sharp claws into Bob's leg. When Lorna went to refill the teacups in the kitchen Bob gave the cat a cuff with his hand that resulted in the cat falling to the floor in a heap.

"You won't have to wait for the vet to take your balls off if you keep doing that to my leg," he muttered. "I've got just what's needed in my pocket my lad if you try that on again."

"Are you two getting on alright in there," enquired Lorna from the kitchen. "I thought I heard a thump."

"It's ok," replied Bob. "Fluffy has decided to get off my lap and has gone into the bedroom."

"I think he loves it in there," suggested a sensually voiced Lorna. "He takes after me in that respect. I spend a lot of my free time in there, it's so relaxing. You haven't seen my bedroom, have you Bob?"

Bob was lost for words. "No, I haven't seen your bedroom yet. But I should certainly like to. With you of course."

"After we have had our second cup of tea I'll show you everything in the bedroom," she promised. "But you mustn't take unfair advantage of a defenceless girl while Brian's away."

"Bugger Brian," thought Bob. "This is going to be my night."

The conversation between Lorna and Bob continued in light hearted fashion with many innuendoes being thrown in to sweeten Bob's thoughts of a pending promiscuous relationship.

"Let's share the wonders of your beautiful fluffy-white boudoir that lays waiting to be explored only a few footsteps away," he heard himself saying in an affected way not dissimilar to that of Lorna's.

"I didn't think you'd seen by boudoir," chirped Lorna.

Thinking quickly once again and gesturing with his hand Bob replied "Oh, I saw heaven through the slightly open door as I came in this evening." Then gently holding Lorna round the waist he steered her out of the sitting room towards whitefluffiness and a night of passion.

Lorna escaped from Bob's clutches, told him she needed to make herself comfortable and disappeared into the bathroom. "I'll see you in a minute Bob dear," she laughingly told him.

"Relax on the bed for a while and I'll join you very, very shortly."

Bob didn't need any further encouragement and began to loosen his tie. His eyes caught sight of a photograph on the dressing table. Brian Wardle's face beamed at him from its silver frame. Bob bent down and squinted to read an endearing note written on the bottom right hand corner. It read 'To my own Fluffy Fanny. For the wonderful times we've had together. Love Brian.'

Bob was not impressed and placed the photograph face down under the lace dressing table cover. "Don't want him looking up my arse," he thought as he continued to undress.

Bob was pent-up with excitement as he took the last of his clothes off and he threw himself face up on the bed. His expectations had overcome his usual cautious nature and he had not seen Fluffy Balls lying on top of the bed camouflaged by the white bed linen. The cat reacted immediately to the intrusion, leapt high in the air between Bob's legs and, descending in a growling fury, seized hold of Bob's unrestrained appendage with his sharp teeth.

Bob howled with indignation and then pain as he swiped at the cat for the second time that evening. He was out to kill the fluffy bastard. In Bob's efforts to free himself from the cat's attentions, Fluffy Balls dug his claws into the most tender of parts of Bob's anatomy before being booted out of the bedroom.

Lorna, on hearing the noise, rushed from the bathroom in her dressing gown as the cat ran from the bedroom. She found Bob crouched over the bed, his hands covering his bleeding private parts.

"That bloody tom cat got me," he explained in an obviously insulted voice. "I need to patch myself up."

Lorna, with concern and concealed amusement, helped him to the bathroom and, at the same time exchanged her clothes for his on the hook behind the bathroom door, for it was certain Bob would no longer be in the mood for frivolous pursuits.

"Give me a call love when you've sorted yourself out," I'll close the door to save you any further embarrassment. That cat has spoiled many a cooked dinner in its time."

Bob had just closed the bathroom door when he heard the sound of a key being put into the lock of the front door.

"Anyone at home?" enquired a voice that sounded very much like that belonging to Brian Wardle.

Bob decided his best course of action was to remain quietly where he was, like a mouse in a hole being patrolled by a fluffy-white tom cat.

"What's wrong with Fluffy Balls, Lorna?" enquired Brian. "When I opened the front door he streaked out of the flat and down the stairs as if a demon was after him."

"Not to worry dear. He's been in all day and probably has an urgent appointment." Lorna placed her arms around Brian's shoulders smothering his chest with her bosoms. "I had an idea you might find a way to come to see me, even with a broken arm. I've stayed in tonight with that in mind and started to wash my hair just before you came in. How is your arm and your legs?"

"I wondered why you were in your dressing gown," remarked Brian. "I'm getting better by the day and came up to London by train to be with you. By the way, has Bob Massey been in touch?"

"That's kind of you darling," said Lorna in her most passionate voice. "You may ask about Bob Massey, for he was due to call this evening, but I haven't had the pleasure of his company yet. He'll probably call later on." Changing the subject she went on, "You'll have to wait a while for I've left the bathroom in a mess. Don't go in there until I've tidied up. Settle yourself in a comfortable chair in the sitting room to rest your legs. I'll pour you a drink then straighten myself out. I'll be with you, and you alone, very shortly."

Bob had heard every word of the conversation between Lorna and Brian. He had not been wasting time for he had placed toilet paper around his damaged parts and was now fully dressed. He thought how cool and casual Lorna had been in dealing with the situation. He saw her in a different light now. She would definitely be his nominee for actress of the year.

A light tap on the bathroom door and a slight movement of the door handle suggested to Bob that it was time for him to fly the nest. Lorna opened the front door as wide as it would go and went out to the top of the stairway. "Fluffy Balls. Fluffy Balls," she called.

There being no sign of the cat, Lorna returned to the sitting room leaving the front door open. "He'll soon come back now his dinner is ready," she told Brian. "I'll leave the front door open for a while so that he can come in when he's ready."

Bob, looking through the gap between the bathroom door and its frame saw Lorna close the sitting room door. It was now or never. Light footed, he stole like a thief in the night, out of the flat. Blooded and bruised but still in possession of his gift-wrapped manhood.

It had been a hard lesson for Bob to swallow. "Some women," he thought ruefully as he made his way down the stairs, "are not always what they appear to be. I wonder why Brian calls her Fluffy Fanny?"

The skinny boy on the beaten up bicycle was waiting for him as he joined the public footpath outside the flats.

"Double booked was she mister?"

Bob kept his head low and didn't reply but couldn't help but smile at the cheek of the lad as he walked towards Bethnal Green underground station.

The short walk did him good and gave him time to analyse the events that had certainly brought Brian post haste to London that evening. He remembered speaking with Lorna on the telephone at Coles that morning, but only after he had spoken with Fatguts. Fatguts must have listened in on their conversation and then phoned Brian. He could imagine Fatguts telling Brian to be careful because of Bob's own known reputation with the ladies. No doubt that fat slob had derived some pleasure at getting even with Lorna.

"You can't trust any bastard," said Bob as he passed the ticket collector at the railway station.

"That's right mate. So where's your ticket then?" the collector wanted to know while holding out his hand.

Bob went across to the ticket office to pay for the journey that would take him home to reality and the council estate in Dagenham.

CHAPTER 15

THE GAS WORKS

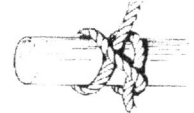

Clove Hitch

For three years running the Firm chose Joe and Dennis to spend two weeks at the West London Gas Works. Each year their annual selection came up in June when the weather was at its warmest. The work was dirty but routine and involved cleaning and replacing broken gutters and down-pipes, and painting them with bitumastic paint. After reporting for work each morning Joe and Dennis put on old boilersuits and respirators, very much as they had at the Medway brewery. The respirators were essential to avoid breathing in the fine coal dust and gave some degree of protection from the coke fumes.

To get to the gutters they climbed over moving conveyor belts with ropes and tackle slung over their shoulders, then up into the latticed cast iron roof supports sheltering the retort house from the elements before dropping down again to reach the down-pipes from boson's chairs.

Each day huge amounts of coal were delivered to the gas works by railway wagons. The coal was emptied onto a conveyor belt and taken to a small coal mountain in the middle of a storage area. Bulldozers levelled the mountain throughout the day so that more coal could be fed onto its peak before it was taken by smaller conveyor belts into the retort houses. The movement of coal puffed light clouds of fine dust into the air, that settled one or two inches deep in the gutters over the twelve months between maintenance intervals. Whenever it rained, the dust was washed into the down-pipes from the gutters as soggy lumps and in many instances blocked them up.

When it came to painting, the dust mixed with the paint and coagulated into a warm sticky mass. It stuck to overalls, hands and face alike and if it was allowed to remain on one's skin for too long in the sunlight, it left red burn marks.

Unlike other work locations Dennis had experienced in the past, the gas works had excellent cloakroom facilities and a first class canteen. Joe and he were allocated personal lockers in the immaculately kept locker room, use of the changing area and use of the showers.

Reporting for work on one particular morning when they had almost completed the maintenance contract, the site engineer asked Joe to inspect a steel chimney that stood alongside the engineering workshop. One of the chimney's guy ropes had been broken by a reversing dump truck. Joe agreed to do this and, as the Firm was undertaking the contract on day work, there should be no complications with payment.

Joe and Dennis had very similar thoughts when they looked up at the dangling guy rope from the yard outside the engineering workshop. It would be a welcome change to get away from the soot and grime of the retort house and work in the open again. But this feeling of relief was only second to that Dennis had enjoyed after they had finished the disgusting work at the crematorium. There was not much that could possibly be worse than that.

Shading his eyes from the early morning sun, Dennis could see white, cotton wool clouds skimming slowly over the top of the steel chimney. He noticed that when the clouds floated towards him, there was an illusion that the chimney was falling down on him. He squinted and adjusted his gaze to concentrate on the steel ladder running down its side and followed its path to the ground. The point where the broken guy rope was fixed seemed only a short distance to the right of the ladder and he was sure they could get to it from a boson's chair without too much difficulty.

"We're not using chimney hangers on this job and I've never done so," were Joe's determined words. "We'll tie the rope blocks for the boson's chair to two of the drilled holes in the top flange of the chimney with a wire bond. We don't want any more Bill Bennetts. Do we?"

It was then that a lipstick smart, well-manicured woman dressed in a pressed nurse's uniform closed in on Joe. He caught sight of her out of the corner of an eye.

"Hello Mr. Walkinshaw. Do you remember me? I'm Ruby. We got to know one another about four years ago when you and Ken were here."

Dennis' eyebrows almost met up with his hairline. What was all this about?

"Ahem. Hello Ruby. It's been a long time."

"Helen is three years old now you know. I've just returned to work in the medical centre now that she can be left with her granny. Have you seen Ken recently?"

Joe suggested that Dennis should go to the engineer's stores to collect the new guy rope. He would meet up with him there in a few minutes time.

Wondering what his father's relationship had been with Ruby, Dennis made his way to the speak with the storeman..

"Dad told me to report to the stores to collect a new guy rope for the chimney," said Dennis when the storeman eventually came out of his office to find out what Dennis wanted. Immediately he had said this he realised he had invited a derogatory comment.

"Did Dad! And what else did Dad tell you to do sonny?"

"Oh forget it," Dennis implored. "Just force of habit. But I would like the new guy rope."

Dennis was dragging the rope into the yard from the stores when Joe caught up with him. Smiling to himself, Dennis wondered what tale Joe would have tell to get out of the embarrassing situation he seemed to be in.

"Been busy then," Joe acknowledged as he grasped an end of the rope to help pull it to the side of the chimney."

Dennis kept a respectful silence as he and Joe struggled to pull the long, weighty rope across the concrete.

"I was speaking with Ruby earlier on. She became friendly with Ken Missen when he and I were working here about four years ago. I never knew what happened between them, but they split up after Helen was born." The explanation ended at that point.

Dennis didn't press for any further knowledge of events but began forming his own ideas. Joe collected a marlin spike from the van and showed Dennis how to make a thimble eye in the end of the guy rope by splicing it in place.

"Once we know the final length of the guy rope after it's in place, we'll use wire rope grips to clamp an eye into its end at ground level," he explained. "We can then use a bottle-tensioner to tighten up the guy rope to keep the chimney from moving."

Joe picked up a rope block and hauling line, placed them over his shoulder and began to climb the ladder to where he would fix the rope block to the top rung. Once in position he was to send the short end of the hauling line down to Dennis for him to tie the riding equipment onto it and Dennis would pull it up.

Being minus one of its guy ropes, the chimney swayed with every step Joe took. Dennis shouted to him to let him know that things were not looking too good, the chimney looked as though it was swaying too far one way and then the other to his liking. Joe shouted back that it was no more than he expected and Dennis shouldn't take too much notice. The clouds passing overhead tended to make matters look much worse than they really were.

"Remember the round chimney at the Albert Hall" Joe tormented. "It's still standing, even though you thought that swayed like a pendulum when we climbed it. This chimney is no worse than that one."

Dennis said no more. He had voiced his opinion, but his father usually knew best under such circumstances.

On reaching the top of the ladder Joe hooked the rope block over the top rung and sent the free end of the hauling line down to Dennis. When it arrived within arms reach Dennis siezed it, tied the riding tackle to the rope and pulled it up to where Joe was waiting.

"I'm ready now," Joe yelled as a bulldozer roared by. "Send up the end with the thimble set in it. I want about three feet of slack wire so that I can manoeuvre the end into position."

Dennis, with added help from Joe sitting in his boson's chair, pulled the end of the guy rope up to where it was wanted.

"Tie the hauling line off and come up and join me with the tools," Joe yelled again against the clamour of more heavy machinery moving about the yard.

Haversack slung over his shoulder Dennis looked forward to climbing the ladders into the blue sky, even if the effort of pulling the end of the guy rope up to the top of the chimney was still evident from his shortness of breath. Reaching the top Dennis, breathing even more heavily, placed his leg in between two ladder rungs and squatted there to recover from the effort. He looked across to where Joe sat swinging effortlessly from his riding line and handed him the haversack.

"Dennis. When you've had your blow, reach across from the top of the ladder and insert the bolt of the shackle through the drilled hole in the chimney flange where I've cut the old shackle away."

Dennis moved further up the ladder and reached across to attach the shackle to the flange, conscious that the sides of the chimney were very hot. He had noticed Joe was working on tiptoes from his chair to avoid getting his knees burnt.

The smoke from the chimney was being gently wafted away by the breeze. But its gentleness was deceptive for the upper part of Dennis' body, being just above the rim of the chimney, created a miniature vacuum that attracted the smoke back towards him. Before he realised, he had inhaled a poisonous concoction of smoke, heat and coke fumes that were flowing out of the mouth of the chimney.

Dennis' chest became rigid, making it impossible to breathe in or out. He felt his lungs were about to burst at any second and realised he was in serious trouble. Joe was only an arm's length away in the boson's chair but Dennis was convinced Joe would not be able to help him before he used up whatever oxygen he had left in his body. It would take Joe a couple of minutes or more to get out of the chair and onto the ladder below him. He probably had two or three minutes of consciousness ahead of him if he stayed where he was and after that he would fall to the ground.

Dennis was experiencing a severe attack of asthma. Something he had occasionally experienced as a child and had thought he had grown out of. His only chance was to make an immediate and rapid descent down the ladders to the ground.

Dennis glanced fleetingly across to Joe, unable to speak or let him know what was happening to him then, without further thought, started down the ladders in a race against time. Although each downward step brought him closer to the ground and, if he was to lose consciousness he should have that less far to fall, each step took more oxygen from his body than he could afford.

The pain in his chest became worse, much worse, and his lungs reached a point where they must surely explode. It was when his racing feet slipped off the rungs of the ladder five feet from to the ground that he knew once again what it was like to suffocate. Dennis had not drawn breath at any time coming down the ladder and he was sure he was about to die. He didn't care, as it would be such a relief to be free of the pain.

The ground came up to meet him. A sudden sickly jolt and he knew no more until he felt a rubber mask being placed over his face. It hissed continuously as it shared its life supporting oxygen with him. Dennis could feel a cold metal container at his side when he reached out to try to get up from the concrete.

"Stay where you are for a few minutes Dennis," instructed a female voice. He became aware of the smell of perfume and the soft touch of a hand under his head. The muscles of his chest were beginning to relax and move again as the coke fumes began to have less affect on his lungs. His chest still ached, but little by little he was able to take in the soothing air that kept him alive.

The asthma attack lasted about ten minutes before Dennis began feeling well enough to talk about his experiences and raise himself off the ground. Ruby was beside him in her nurses uniform and Joe was close by.

"I saw you making your way down the ladders in a bit of a hurry but didn't realise anything was wrong until you jumped the last few feet and ended up on the ground in a heap. I came down in the chair in the shortest time I could and called Ruby in the medical centre."

Joe was interrupted by Ruby who was making arrangements for Dennis to be taken to the medical centre to recover. There, during his recovery, Dennis would learn the full details of Joe's meetings with Ruby four years earlier.

Dennis lay on the couch in the medical centre with a pounding headache for almost an hour attended by Ruby who was making a bit of a fuss about everything. She had a real patient needing nursing care, not the usual run of the mill one who walked into her surgery with a small cut, was patched up by her and sent away within a few minutes.

"Joe has gone to finish off the work on the chimney," she explained. "He says he can manage the rest of the work without you helping him, so everything is alright. You must rest for a while."

Dennis was feeling brighter and bursting to ask a number of

questions about Joe's past relationship with Ruby. He didn't have to put those questions to her for in conversation she explained how she had got to know him and Ken Missen.

"You know Ken Missen I suppose," she said as she rearranged the pillows on the medical couch. Ken and I met some time ago when he and Joe came to work here about four years ago. They were working during the night hours taking down the last section of the old steel chimney near the engineering workshop when I received a call in the medical centre that told me a steeplejack had been burned on his back by hot metal. Joe brought Ken into the medical room a short time afterwards. They had been burning a rusted bolt off with a welding torch when it blew-back and a piece of red-hot metal lodged down the collar of Ken's boilersuit. Joe got it out but Ken was left with a nasty burn between his shoulder blades. I treated Ken here and we got to know one another very well when he came in for dressings."

Ruby hesitated before continuing and replaced a thermometer into its holder above the couch.

"Within six months Ken and I got married, but our marriage only lasted a year. Joe was Ken's best man. But Ken couldn't settle. He had been used to his freedom as a merchant seaman and I didn't like him being away from home for all the weeks he seemed to be. One thing led to another and I wasn't at home when he came back from working on the airshafts of the Severn Tunnel. I went to live with my mother and Ken and I haven't seen each other since then."

Dennis could see where Joe's embarrassment had originated. He must have felt caught between two stools working as he did with Ken and now having met up with Ruby again.

"Anyway, those things happened some time ago and life has moved on since then," said Ruby. "We may wish certain things had never happened, but they have and we live with them. Now, let's talk about you Dennis. From what I can see you shouldn't be climbing industrial chimneys..........."

It was on completion of the work at the gasworks that Joe decided Dennis would never work on the industrial side of steeplejacking again. It would be too risky to tempt fate again.

CHAPTER 16

MAID OF SHENSTONE

Sheepshank

Dennis was approaching his eighteenth birthday when Joe and he got to know they were due to go to Shenstone in Essex to repair the red brick tower at St. Margaret's church. Joe had been forced to decide it was time to sell the Ford van and buy a replacement after a very nasty confrontation on the road between Bow and Stratford late one Friday afternoon.

Joe and Dennis were in the van driving at a steady twenty-five miles an hour, which was almost at its limit by that time, when a three-ton platform lorry loaded with scaffolding drove into the back of the van, apparently intending to hurry it along the road. The next set of traffic lights along the road were on red and Joe brought the van to a stop. He got out to enquire whether the lorry driver realised what he had done, but for his trouble he received a lot of verbal abuse and no apology.

Hearing raised voices Dennis scrambled out of the van to see what was happening and was in time to see the lorry being driven into the back of the van once again.

"If you bastards want a fight then we'll sort you out in one of the back streets over there," promised the stocky, unshaven lorry driver. "That or get that f***ing heap of rubbish off the road."

Two other scruffy men in the lorry's cab leered forward to support the driver's sentiments.

Dennis was all for sorting them out there and then. He wasn't going to have his father spoken to in that way.

"There's no need for that sort of language or threat," said Joe in a conciliatory tone. "My van earns me my living and I don't want you denting it. If you want a fight you'll have to look elsewhere."

Traffic steadily built up in both directions as drivers and their passengers rubber-necked to see what was happening to cause such a commotion.

"You in trouble mate?" shouted a passenger from a passing

minibus loaded with building site workers.

"It's ok," said Dennis. "These blokes feel we shouldn't be on the road and want to punch our heads in."

"And you lot can f**k off too," shouted the driver of the lorry. "Or we'll sort you out at the same time."

"Will yer bejesus?" Came a loud bellow from inside the minibus originating from a broad speaking Irishman. "You and who's flaming army?"

Joe pointed for Dennis to get into the van as he hastened to get into the driving seat. He drove forward to allow the minibus to pull in behind them and in front of the lorry. The Irish Cavalry had arrived in the nick of time!

"They deserve one another," said Joe as he changed from first gear into second leaving a trail of oily blue smoke in the van's wake. "We'll not wait to pick up the pieces."

The decision having been made to part with the Ford van, the next day, a Saturday morning in March, they travelled to Pride and Clarke's second-hand car emporium at Stockwell in south London to view what was on offer.

Joe parked the van fifty yards or so from the entrance to the sales office, Dennis lifted the nearside door open on it's sagging hinges and slammed it shut before walking the short distance to view the seemingly acres of vans for sale on the derelict land fronting the roadway.

It was surprising to see how many reasonably new vehicles were for sale. Joe and he were looking for a second-hand motor and having difficulty finding the money for a deposit, but other people had bought these vehicles from new. Here was an indication that other people were working smarter than they were and able to afford new vehicles.

A dark blue Morris Oxford van was parked at the back of the rows of commercial vehicles. Joe and Dennis threaded their way past other models towards it.

"I'd like to look inside this one Dennis. See whether you can get the keys for it from the salesman whilst I look at the tyres and for any body damage."

Dennis needn't have bothered for the van salesman was already on his way towards them from his wooden office with a set of keys in his hand.

"Like to take a test drive mate?" enquired the salesman. "I can see you've got a Ford van parked just down the road. I assume you'll be scrapping it!"

Joe was taken aback by such a suggestion as he had been hoping to put the Ford van in part-exchange.

"Yes, we would like to test drive the Morris and no the Ford is not to be scrapped. I'd like to exchange it as part of a deal."

The salesman drew a deep breath through thin lips and condescendingly handed Joe the keys to the Morris.

"How much were you hoping to get for the Ford?"

"One third of the cost of the Morris," replied Joe. "I don't have any spare cash and the Ford will have to be taken as my full deposit if I'm going to replace it."

"That's a tall order," replied the salesman. "I'll see what my manager has to say about an arrangement while you're taking the motor around the block. There's not a lot of petrol in the tank so don't go too far."

It was obviously clear that the salesman was not too impressed by the part exchange value Joe placed on the Ford van.

They set off in the two year old Morris van for a short drive along the cobbled streets of Stockwell. The Morris van's brakes worked wonderfully well as was proven when Joe mistakenly trod on the brake pedal when he intended to use the accelerator. The steering column gear change was a novelty, the bench seat was luxurious and the suspension something that they had only read about in motoring magazines. The Ford's cart springs had given the old van a tendency to leap from one pothole into another but the Morris cruised over the uneven surface of the cobbled road like a dream. If they bought this van they would certainly be making progress up the social scale.

Returning to Pride and Clarke's sales office in limousine silence Dennis found the controls for the heater under the dashboard. Blow lamps and Primus stoves in the back of the van would be out of the question if they bought this British Leyland, state of the art means of transport. Everything was now subject to any 'arrangement' the salesman might have in mind.

Joe enjoyed haggling. Dennis was sure there must be Arab blood in their family and to prove the point it was not long before Joe had struck a deal that involved the taking out of a hire purchase agreement. The hire purchase company required a one-third deposit and this was overcome by agreeing an artificially high buying-in price for the Ford van and Joe paying the full asking price, plus a little more, for the Morris. The needs of both parties satisfied, Dennis moved all of their equipment, including the blow lamp and the Primus stove, from inside the rickety old Ford van into the Morris Oxford. Equipment transferred they drove off in the direction of home like two lords on the way to the Ascot races.

Leaving the Ford behind seemed unkind at first after all of the miles they had covered in her, but the comfortable bench seat and warm air from the heater blowing up their trouser legs soon dispelled any sentimentality they had in her direction.

Once home, Joe took Beatrice for a short drive along the Longbridge Road to convince her of the reasonableness of the part-exchange. The family, Sid and his mother were waiting outside the house when they returned and drew up to the kerb. Sid opened the passenger door as a footman might on a State occasion for the Queen and welcomed them back in mock salutation adding, "I can now rest in my bed in the morning without having to listen out for the starter motor to spin. When I broke my leg I didn't expect to have physiotherapy quite so early in the morning."

Beatrice had enjoyed the drive along the Longbridge Road. She told Joe the new van was alright but would only repeat, "Providing it takes me from 'A' to 'B' and back again, I don't mind what sort of vehicle it is. You men see it differently. You have to have the best money can afford."

The more Joe and Dennis used the Morris for journeys to and from work the more they realised how basic and uncomfortable the Ford had been. Journeys that had taken them hours to complete were now taking two-thirds of the time and they both felt fresher at the end of each journey, not having to endure the noise and fumes from the Ford's worn out engine.

Shenstone Church.

The reason for Joe and Dennis' first visit to Shenstone church was to plan the layout of the scaffolding for the work to be done there. It was decided to hang a flying scaffold from a large square frame of scaffold tubes that would sit on the brick parapet wall of the tower. Boson's chairs could be hung from the scaffold and bricks and other building materials could be stored on the scaffold boards. Every nook and cranny of the outside of the tower had to be accessible from the chairs so that the crumbling soft red bricks could be cut out and replaced where necessary.

The architect overseeing the work was keen to keep the tower looking as original as possible. But there were problems because many years before builders had repaired the tower with bricks and cement mortar that had not been available at the time the church was first built. These modern aberrations, as the architect put it, were to be cut out where possible.

To meet with the architect's building material specifications Dennis dug out a lime pit about six feet square and two feet deep in the churchyard. The pit was to be used to 'slake' lumps of dry lime that were delivered in sacks from time to time. He was shown how to drench the unslaked lime with water and how to be sure it had fully 'worked'. After soaking with water, the lumps of lime self-heated and dried into a powder. The slaked lime was then left in the pit for a few days before it could be used with sand and a small amount of cement to make lime mortar.

The Gravediggers.

As with all jobs in country villages, regular contacts were made between steeplejacks and local folk, usually in the churchyard. At Shenstone, two gravediggers regularly looked in on Joe and Dennis to see how work was progressing. The gravediggers had personalities that were poles apart. Albert was a slow but kindly man and his partner, Les, deceitful and cunning. Joe often received complaints from Les about pieces of broken brick that had fallen onto the grass for they damaged the cutters on his lawnmower. Although everything was done to avoid the problem, it was not possible to stop every piece of brick from falling onto the grassed area and Joe gave him ten bob from time to time to meet the cost of setting up his cutters again.

Albert, the gravedigger, knew he was to dig a six-foot hole, a yard and a half square and three yards from the side of the tower. He was unsure why the hole should be that size as he had, over the years, been used to digging holes about two yards long and somewhat narrower. A yard and a half seemed a bit short for any of the purposes he had in mind.

Joe explained to him that a lightning conductor earth plate

was to be placed in the bottom of the hole. Once it was in position he would rivet and solder the lightning conductor tape to it.

At about eight o'clock the next morning Albert arrived in the churchyard with a short ladder, a fork and a spade. Joe pointed to where he would like the hole to be and left Albert to carefully remove the turf and begin digging down the required six feet.

It was about half past eleven when Dennis heard Albert calling from the churchyard below to let them know he had finished and was about to take an early lunch break. He would see them in an hour or so, on his return. Dennis, looking down from the scaffolding, acknowledged Albert's plans and saw him amble cheerfully off to his cottage a short way along the road.

Albert returned to the churchyard after his lunch with a parcel under his arm. It was about the size of a shoebox and covered with brown wrapping paper. Joe and Dennis met him at the side of the freshly dug hole in readiness to lower the earth plate into it. Albert hung his cap on the top of his short ladder, handed Dennis the box and climbed down into the hole.

"I've already connected the earth plate to the lightning conductor tape Albert," explained Joe. "When you're ready I'll hand it down to you."

The square copper plate was lowered and Albert laid it horizontally in the bottom of the hole. He reached up to receive the parcel from Dennis and placed it on top of the earth plate. Albert stood silently in deep thought for a moment or two then climbed up the ladder and out of the hole.

"I suppose you think I'm acting strangely," he said as he reached for his spade to begin filling in the hole. "Well, I'll tell you this, and only this. A local girl recently gave birth to a stillborn baby. She comes from a family that I know very well and they have asked me to bury the baby's body in consecrated ground in the churchyard. I've agreed to do this, but I shouldn't really because the baby never drew breath."

Albert seemed touched by his own remarks for he avoided Joe and Dennis' eyes and kept shovelling the earth into the hole.

There would be no record to show that the stillborn infant had been buried in the churchyard, for the church authorities at Shenstone did not permit the burying of stillborn infants in consecrated ground. Dennis felt it must be hard for a mother and father to bear the consequences of a stillbirth and for this not to be properly recognised by their faith. No religious service accompanied the burial and no one, except the child's grandfather and two steeplejacks were present to witness the shabby interment.

It is not always obvious to people on the ground who may be trying to cross a busy road or struggling with their shopping that eagle-eyed steeplejacks could be watching them from above. From such heights many things may be seen that others would prefer to keep to themselves. Such was the case one morning, when Joe and Dennis were repositioning their riding tackle on the scaffold before the beginning of a funeral service.

The day before they had seen Les, the second of the two gravediggers, open up an old grave immediately below them for a new interment. Dennis had dropped small pieces of brick onto him as he bent over to cut into the ground with his spade. Whenever Les looked up after being hit by a missile Dennis was nowhere to be seen, having hidden behind the brick parapet wall after taking aim. Dennis' game had gone on for some time until Les roared with rage and threatened to put him in the hole and cover him up.

At about ten thirty a funeral cortege arrived at the gates of the church. Many people had come to pass their last respects to an old, well known resident of the village who had passed on a few days earlier. Les had placed wooden boards and a green tarpaulin over the disturbed ground around the grave for the rector and mourners to stand on during the interment that would follow the funeral service in the church.

Joe and Dennis stopped work on the scaffold to avoid making any noise that might interfere with the service and retired behind the parapet wall. Their plan was to spend the next half an hour quietly filling in their time sheets and looking over the surrounding fields and winding lanes that threaded through the village. Taking stock of their surroundings had not been something they had had the opportunity to do before.

The sound of organ music welled up from time to time from within the church as they waited. Joe rolled a cigarette as Dennis looked down on the main street to watch a young lady walk by. He liked the way she moved and was disappointed when she stopped at a lady's hairdressers and went in.

A protracted silence from within the church would signal that the church service was over and they could expect the mourners to start making their way to the graveside. On cue, the door into the churchyard opened and the rector, followed by the pallbearers with the coffin on their shoulders and the mourners walking behind them, trickled out into the daylight to make their way along the gravel path to the graveside. The pallbearers lowered the coffin on top of the two boards and coffin straps that Les had laid across the grave and each took a step back. When all present were gathered at the graveside, as is customary, two of the best wreaths were placed on top of the coffin just before it was lowered to its final resting place.

The rector completed the graveside service and afterwards mingled with relatives and friends of the departed before discretely moving away to return to his church. After a while most of the mourners began to walk slowly in two's and three's towards the churchyard gates to go their respective ways but a few remained behind at the graveside, gathered in one or two small groups. It was not long, however, before they too left the cemetery.

Les hovered in the background ready to collect his tools from under an old tarpaulin sheet he had neatly placed nearby. He appeared slightly agitated. It was as if he wanted everyone to leave so that he could get on with filling in the grave and tidying the disturbed ground.

"Just a minute," said Joe as he tapped Dennis on his arm to stop him reaching for his hammer and chisel lying on the scaffold. "Watch what he gets up to now. I bet we see a repeat performance of what happened after yesterday's funeral."

Les looked carefully around him, seemingly in need of reassurance that everyone had gone. Satisfied he was alone, he collected his tools from under the tarpaulin and went across to the grave. With the agility of a man half his age he jumped down the hole and onto the coffin. A moment or two later his two hands appeared from over the side of the grave holding two very expensive looking wreaths. He pushed them to one side then heaved himself out of the grave like a jack-in-the-box. Placing the wreaths in a large sack, he walked towards the compost heap near to the water tap and hid them under a pile of rotting foliage before returning to the graveside to begin shovelling a ton of earth on top of the coffin.

By one o'clock Les had made a very neat job of filling in the hole and finished off by covering the grave with the remaining floral tributes. He placed his spade in another sack and returned to the compost heap.

Les hand-rolled a cigarette, lit it and, after putting both sacks over his shoulders, walked confidently across the cemetery with the cigarette in the corner of his mouth. His bicycle, as usual, was conveniently propped up against the churchyard railings. He tied the sack with his spade in it to the crossbar, comfortably placed the second and bulkier of the two sacks over his left shoulder, mounted his bike and rode unsteadily towards the village.

"I wonder what he does with the wreaths?" enquired Dennis. "We'll have to find out."

An hour or so later saw Joe and Dennis in the café just across the road from the church. They had ordered their lunch and Joe was trying to win a fortune on the penny slot-machines while Dennis looked out of the window into the market square to see if anyone he recognised came out of the ladies hairdressers that was only a few yards along the road.

"Don't tilt the machine Joe," ordered Keith the owner of the café. "I can't count the number of times I have to call out the engineers to repair the blessed thing because some people will lift it off the floor and bash it."

Joe was not impressed. He was winning a few bob from the slot-machine with the technique he had developed and he knew Keith was on to him.

"I've won enough anyway," said Joe as he pocketed his paltry winnings and went across to join Dennis at a table by the window.

"Did you go to the funeral this morning?" enquired Dennis as Keith brought their meals to them on a light brown enamelled tray.

"With regrets, no," replied Keith. We've been so busy in here we didn't get the time."

"We watched the funeral from the top of the tower," Dennis continued. "And saw something unusual. The best of the wreaths that were to accompany the coffin into the underworld were spirited away by the gravedigger. He later rode off with them in a sack towards the centre of the village.

"Oh yes," Keith replied in a matter of fact way. "We know all about old Les and his enterprising ways. We call it his *eleven o'clock run*. He makes a pound or two returning the frames of the wreaths to the local florist. They use them again and again for other funerals as it saves them the trouble of making new ones. Les calls it 'recycling' as he uses his bike to return the wreaths to the florist!"

The Mushroom Farmer

Dennis was on the grassed area of the churchyard sweeping pieces of broken brick into a shovel when Ted Taylor, wearing his one and only pair of brown corduroy trousers and green pullover, paid them a visit. Ted wanted to know if Joe could find time to paint the overhang of his corn store, for it was too high for him to reach from his extension ladder. Ted was an upright, elderly man with a good head of hair who had been a captain in an infantry regiment in the First World War and had served on a number of battlefronts in Belgium. He now ran a mushroom farm from an old mill house a half a mile or so from the church.

Joe was not one to miss out on earning a few extra pounds over a weekend if an opportunity presented itself and this looked like a golden opportunity to earn that little extra. After a short visit to the farm a price for the job was agreed and spare scaffolding and ladders were soon moved onto site to help them out with their 'moonlighting'.

"This will have to be an 'in and out' job so that not too many people know we're doing it," explained Joe. "I'll get in touch with Ken Missen so that all three of us can knock the job on the head over a long weekend."

Ken met them at the mushroom farm late that Friday afternoon. Since all three had last worked together Ken had learned to drive. He had parked his small grey Austin A30 van in the farmyard next to the corn store and was waiting to show Joe and Dennis what a wonderful little runner it was.

"It's a nice van," commented Dennis. "Ideal for carrying your tools about and you don't have to rely upon public transport. I suppose that means you won't have to stay away from home so often now." Dennis went on to mention how he had met up with Ruby at the West London gas works.

"She seems a very nice woman," said Dennis. "She certainly helped me in a moment of crises and she told me about you when your back was burned. Ever thought about meeting up with her again?"

"I've been thinking about it," replied Ken. "But haven't got round to it yet. Besides, she's probably made a new life for herself by now. She wouldn't want to live with me again after the problems I made for her."

Dennis wondered whether that would really be the case and parked the subject in the back of his mind for more consideration at some other time.

Once Ted Taylor realised Dennis was about to be called up for National Service duties he took him into his confidence and told him about some of the experiences he had had during his time in the army. Some of those experiences, along with those of his regiment, had been tough and he had vowed on return to civilian life that he would never again fear death or any man again. This was almost certainly due to him being the only man to remain alive after a particularly horrendous attack on a German position. All of his comrades had been killed by machine-gun fire after they reached the German trenches, leaving him alone in a shell hole dreadfully wounded for two days before medical help reached him.

"I received the Military Cross for that action," he confided. "Not something you easily forget when all of your mates died fighting what was then a common enemy. I can remember the faces of all of the men who served with me in my Company as if I had only met them last week. I gained a lot from living so close to them in those terrible conditions for it built qualities in me that I hope I have retained for the rest of the years of my life."

Dennis felt he was being groomed for the two years of army life ahead of him.

The mushroom farm employed a half a dozen people who maintained the buildings, tended the mushrooms in darkened barns and packaged them for market. The Saturday afternoon Joe, Ken and Dennis were working on the corn store Ted stopped by to talk with them. Rolling up the arms of his green pullover above his elbows it seemed he needed to get a problem off his chest.

Joe came down the ladder he was working from after reaching under a gutter to clear away an old bird's nest and stood beside Ted to pass the time of the day with him. A visit by a Ministry of Agriculture official had upset Ted and he had to confide in someone.

"The bugger had the cheek to come onto my farm to check on what we were doing with my mushrooms," he exploded. "I asked him whether he really understood farming and he told me he did as he had been a farmer. I told him he couldn't have been a very good one otherwise he would still be running his farm, not travelling round telling others how they should go about it. The audacity of the man was proven when he admitted he was no longer farming because his own business had gone bust! What gives him the right to tell me how to conduct my business?"

Ted continued to release his pent-up feelings about the Ministry of Agriculture. "I don't suppose I'll be pestered by those buggers again for another year. They've probably placed a tick in their records to show they've been on my farm and that's probably all the local man has to show his done."

Ted's head of steam had been released. He seemed satisfied with the work being carried out on the corn store and left 'his boys' to carry on whilst he drove into the village to get his weekly supply of 'groceries', parting with the quip, "But then I don't suppose you fellows drink. Do you?"

Within the half hour Ted was back at the corn store with two bottles of whisky and four glasses.

"Time for a break," he called out. "Come and join me for a drink, it's my birthday and Dennis is joining the army."

The four men crowded into a small partitioned area of the store that served as an office, treble measures of whisky were poured and stories of the valiant and true exchanged. There was a general consensus that no further work should be done that afternoon.

Ted proved to be a generous man with his serving of drinks and the first bottle of whisky was soon emptied. The level in the second was down by a half when Joe decided it was time for Ted to be returned to his quarters to recover from his slurring speech. None of them were too steady on their feet as they stumbled their way along the farm track to Ted's house where his wife was waiting to find out what had happened to her husband.

"She won't be amushed when she shees all of us turning up in the shtate you lot are in," he slurred. "Better be prepared for hoshtile shtares, if nothing else!" Ted gurgled cheerfully.

"Use the back door man, we never use the front of the house unless the vicar calls, and he doesn't come that often," Ted instructed as he was helped along the track, propped up on either side by Ken and Dennis.

Three men, helped by a fourth pushing from the rear, trying to get through a doorway in a befuddled state cannot be viewed by anyone as tidy. Ted's wife had been expecting him to return home for the past two hours and to see him in the merry state he was in with those muddy boots on, in her kitchen, was almost too much to bear.

"Sit him on one of those chairs round the table and take his boots off. And that goes for the three of you as well. Hot, black coffee is all you'll be wanting for the next hour or two."

Cold stares from Ted's wife had been in the proportions expected but there was still warmth in her attitude to all of them.

"It's Ted's birthday today," she reminded them kindly as they sat round the table. Ted had sunk his head into his arms on the tabletop and was fast asleep by this time. "He lost most of the men in his Company on his birthday in the First World War. He's never forgotten it. You can stay for as long as it takes you to clear your heads. I don't want any of you driving on the road until you're fit to do so."

Two hours later Ted awoke from his slumbers with a thick head. He was surprised to find three other men in the kitchen still sleeping off the effects of the 'groceries' he had brought from the village. His clearing of his throat awakened the remaining sleepers who were slumped over the table as he had been.

"Time to return to your homes gents," he suggested. "But have one last drink with me before you go."

"Oh no you don't old man," declared his embarrassed wife. "These men have had enough, and so have you."

Ted saw his new found friends to the door and bade them farewell. He would meet with them again the next day.

"That was some drinking session," voiced Dennis as Joe and he drove home in the darkness of the evening. "My head is banging like a drum and I don't feel too good either."

Beatrice was not pleased to see them when they arrived home at such a late hour. She could smell booze on their breath and wondered where they had been.

The Maid of Shenstone

The need for Dennis to find his own identity was reinforced by a conversation he overheard between one of his aunts and Joe when she asked him whether Dennis was 'all right' and if he had any girl friends. Joe told her Dennis was quite happy being with Butch his dog and didn't feel that Dennis had any of those kinds of interests. Dennis didn't like what he heard and was, of course, very fond of his dog but the alarm bells began to ring.

Dennis was now a young man with all of the interests of male youth, including a healthy interest in young ladies. This interest was about to become more widely known after he met Valerie and her friend Janet one lunchtime in the recreation ground next to the church at Shenstone.

Regularly at twelve o'clock each day Joe and Dennis left the church for lunch and made for the café across the road in the market square. After lunch and on return to the church with Joe, Dennis found reason to walk round to where the bricks were stored. It was just good luck that the recreation ground was on the other side of the railings and he could see where the young hairdressers were sitting.

It was time to take courage in both hands. Dennis walked over to them trying to think of something to say. It was then that he noticed a group of cows grazing some distance away and chose this subject as an introduction.

"Hello. Any idea who owns those cows?" he asked.

Dennis never heard the reply for his mind was racing ahead for they must have thought he was a strange one asking such a daft question.

From then on he would visit them on sunny days when they were out in the recreation ground eating their lunch. The taller of the two girls was Valerie and the smaller Janet. A week or so passed before Dennis built up sufficient confidence to ask Valerie if she would like to go to the pictures with him one evening. The answer being, "Yes, I suppose so," came as a great surprise and changed his life completely.

On the way home that evening Dennis mentioned to Joe his meetings with Valerie and her friend Janet and told him he was taking Valerie out that evening.

"You had better learn to drive then," replied Joe. "Particularly since you'll be called up shortly and may be stationed anywhere."

Dennis began receiving driving lessons from Joe and learned quickly. Within a few weeks he had successfully taken his driving test at the Test Centre at Brentwood.

Party Time

Dennis' call-up papers arrived in the post early one morning in July. He was to report for his medical at Woodford a week later. Within two months he would start his training as a National Serviceman, his previous training as a steeplejack having no bearing whatsoever on the duties he was initially to be recruited to. Dennis Walkinshaw was to join the Royal Army Service Corps as a driver.

Beatrice and Joe decided to arrange a party for Dennis, it would probably be the last opportunity for sometime for everyone in the family to be together. Dennis couldn't see what all the fuss was about. He was only being called-up to do National Service. It wasn't as if the Second World War was still being fought. What he didn't understand was that memories of only thirteen years before, those of the Korean War and recently of the Suez business were still fresh in the minds of most thinking people.

"I think we should invite all the family and a few friends," suggested Beatrice.

Dennis was beginning to warm to the idea, for he could introduce his new girl friend to everyone.

"I'd like to include Valerie, Ruby and Ken Missen," said Dennis when the invitation list was discussed.

"I haven't met Valerie yet," said his mother. "And who is Ruby? Is she another one of your girlfriends I haven't had the chance to meet?"

"I've been meaning to bring Valerie home for a few weeks now," explained Dennis. "And the party will be a good time to make the introduction. Ruby is the nurse I met at the West London power station. She married Ken Missen some time ago.

They parted after a while and the party might bring them together again."

"So you think you're a budding matchmaker, do you? We will see," said Beatrice wistfully.

The invitations were sent out and the responses were encouraging. There would be over sixty people and at least one child at the party to be held at the family home. It would be a good send-off for the young recruit and a wonderful opportunity for him to introduce his fiancée to all of the members of his family. There was also an opportunity for the rekindling of Ruby and Ken Missen's marriage.

Dennis was embarking on a new chapter in his life. His experiences over the next two years would open up new horizons for him and lead him into a new and even more interesting career and a marriage that would last for many years. But then that is another story.